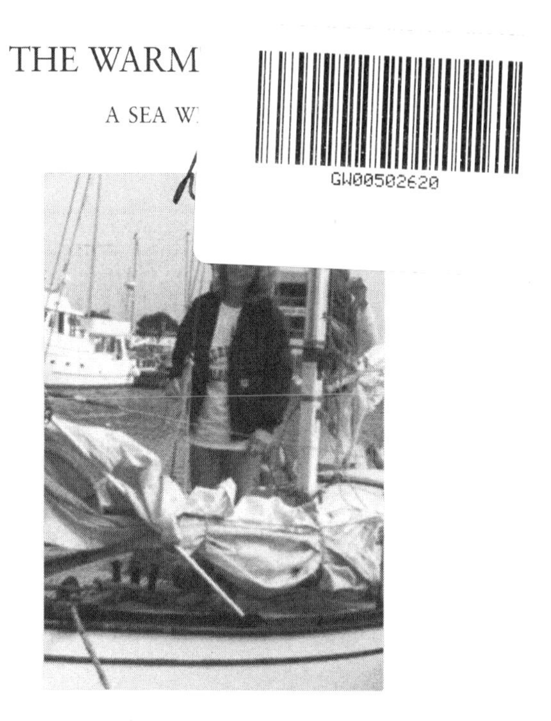

Born in Hampshire and educated at Godolphin School in Salisbury, Lynette spent the first twenty years of her adult life pursuing a successful culinary career on the ocean. With at least five Atlantic crossings under her belt, she still has a passion for old, wooden boats having owned and restored three, before finally succumbing to bricks and mortar, in 1991.

After the birth of her son, Lynette opened her patisserie, Le Vieux Four, in Dorset where she has been trading for 25 years.

Lynette has recently published two cook books, the first, *Recipes from le Vieux Four, The Secret Culinary Adventures of a Dorset Pastry Chef* follows her journeys with recipes collected along the way. The second, *Special Cakes from the Old Oven* is (as the name suggests) all about the cakes found at Le Vieux Four, with the individuality of Lynette's own recipes and photographs.

The Warmth of Waves, A Sea Witch's Tale is her first novel loosely based on her time at sea.

THE WARMTH OF WAVES

A SEA WITCH'S TALE

LYNETTE FISHER

Le Vieux Four Publishing, Dorset

ISBN 978-0-9927400-2-3

Typeset by Moira Read, Border Typesetting, Beaminster, Dorset
Printed and bound in Great Britain

cover image
Heatwave, Mike Jackson www.mikejacksonartist.com

drawings on pages iii & 274
Galuette (a small gull), Marion Taylor www.dorsetpaintings.co.uk

Shell image by Gosc from Clipart.org

For Julien and Janetta

With thanks and acknowledgement of the real canine characters long since passed away; Wanker (a Morrocan mongrel), V.I.P. (a canny French cocker) and Dammit (an aristocratic, truly British Dalmation).

"...the momentous fall of the waves on the beach which for the most part beat a measured and soothing tattoo to her thoughts and seemed consolingly to repeat over and over again the words of some old cradle song, murmured by nature, 'I am guarding you – I am your support,' but at other times suddenly and unexpectedly ... had no such kindly meaning, but like a ghostly roll of drums remorselessly beat the measure of life, made me think of the destruction of the island and its engulfment in the sea."

Virginia Woolf, *To the Lighthouse*

PART ONE

Gibraltar
1976

1

Janie...

"Elle began to write to us from Majorca, goodness knows how she came by our address, she simply said she had seen a picture of our boat, *Talisman*, and was desperate to spend the summer helping us on charter in Spain. She never said in her correspondence at the time exactly how old she was, but we guessed about twenty, and we were right. She had been crewing yachts in the Balearics, that was all we knew, and we also gathered that she had a genuine passion for old, wooden boats such as ours. We did explain her duties would include scraping, scrubbing and varnishing as well as sailing, in fact we tried to make the job sound as unattractive as possible, but she still persevered, begging in the end, until Don sent her a ticket to Malaga and we picked her up in José Banus.

She was a pretty girl no doubt about that, with her long blonde hair and a smile that illuminated her rather melancholy features. The agility of her slight frame made me feel rather ungainly, and I watched her with envy, always flitting about the deck, or walking our dalmatian around the port. They made a striking couple, the large spotted dog with his petite handler. Somehow this rather unusual girl fitted in with our lives as part of the family, enjoying my cooking with gusto and downing all our favourite Spanish tipples with equal enthusiasm. Don had bought her a case of sweet Martini because she said it was her favourite, but then she announced she didn't like the cloying taste at all, so we gave eleven and a half bottles away. That was typical of Elle, always changing her mind. She turned out to be brilliant crew, an expert hand both with the varnish brush and with the sails. She coped with Don's merciless teasing and nicknames, the one that stuck was 'Stupid Girl' from our avid listening of the World Service including *Dad's Army*, which was broadcast twice a day and we would listen to each and every repeat.

We knew she had minimal contact with her family and after leaving college she had fallen into a relationship that had ended badly, but we couldn't really pry or find out any details. It had nothing to do with us, unless of course, she had wanted to confide, in which case we would have listened.

Elle had huge admiration for my cooking, but the truth is I simply cooked whatever I found in the brimming baskets that Don brought back from the market. He worked the deck and I sorted everything below, with Elle helping both us equally, endlessly polishing the saloon and varnishing the woodwork outside. When we reached the end of the summer she said she would go back to England and learn to cook like me, which true to her word she did.

She came back some eighteen months later, to holiday with us for a couple of weeks and to help Don with varnishing the masts. She was much thinner than I remembered and had hatched a wild plan to go to the West Indies to find her grandfather whom she had never met. She flew to Mallorca to join us and then disappeared for a few days to stay with the same boyfriend who had caused her so much heart-wrenching sadness. We saw him once when he came to say goodbye to her on the day we left, but Elle continued to maintain her silence about whatever had happened between them.

We made a plan that we would take her to Gibraltar on *Talisman*. As there was no access at that time by road the only way was to sail there and drop her off on the quayside. The border between the Rock and Spain was still firmly closed. She had tremendous optimism that she would find a yacht willing to take her on as crew to the West Indies, and if she failed we would pick her up again two weeks later and take her back to Spain to look for a winter job. She had brought suitcases full of cook-books, knives, and utensils, a rather heavily laden prospective crew member for any skipper, but she was not inclined to listen to our advice. She seemed obsessed to follow in the footsteps of her grandfather who had sailed away, abandoning his family, some forty years previous and I think her determination attributed in part to the certainty of her success. So we left her on a grey, autumn day in the old stone-walled pens, which used to be home to the naval destroyers protecting the entrance to the Mediterranean, but had since become a place for transient, visiting yachts. She looked bereft as we motored back out to sea, but there had been no dissuading her so we checked through her emergency finances and left her seated on a bollard, watching for new arrivals."

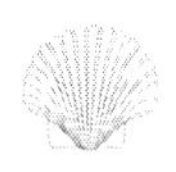 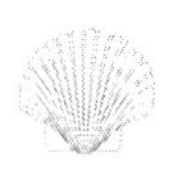 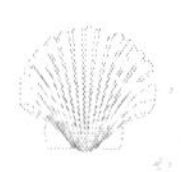

Elle thought for a moment about walking the long, straight road into the town, but this was not a sensible idea with all her baggage, especially as it had begun to rain. Sunny Spain maybe, but Gibraltar had a private black cloud positioned exclusively over the rock. She scrambled out of a taxi outside the open door of *The Star*, a dark, dingy bar in Irish town that Don and Janie had lovingly christened "Head Office". She could see Ben's familiar shape with a coffee inside and her heart lifted at the thought of a face she knew. If she had no success in finding a passage, it would take Don and Janie a day to sail back and fetch her and as she sat in the rain in a dirty-old back street, palm trees and islands had faded to a dream. The confidence she had when she arrived began to wane.

Elle had first set eyes on Ben in this scruffy pub nearly two years ago, and had discovered that he worked for the biggest supplier of all duty-free provisions, just up the road. It was hardly surprising that he should frequent such a place, being so conveniently close to his office. She had been sitting with Janie waiting for Don when he had first walked in and his air was so familiar, she recognised every gesture, and each smile drew her to him in the most uncanny way. She had not seen him again since that morning of simple greetings but she had treasured his image in her mind and now here he was again, in the flesh with his funny brown mongrel at his feet, grinning at her and tapping the stool beside him.

'The dog's called Wanker,' he remarked and Elle, stunned into silence by this introduction, bent to greet the shaggy thing at her feet.

'Where are your mates?' he asked looking around, as if he had seen them there but yesterday.

'They've dropped me here to try to find my way to across to the Caribbean,' she stuttered, looking for some courage as suddenly her idea seemed foolhardy, outrageous and probably a little embarrassing. She felt her colour rise.

'... and to look for my grandfather John', she mumbled addressing this last comment more to the dog as she was now overcome with the futility of her ambition and was unable to look Ben in the eye.

'You can stay at ours tonight and leave your stuff safe when you go to the pens tomorrow then.' She was all smiles and nods, this seemed a very good idea at last.

'Come on then,' he said and started to gather some of her luggage, slinging her knapsack around his own neck. At the door he paused, took a deep breath, and yelled, 'WANKER', his voice echoing off the walls in the narrow street. The poor creature had sloped off somewhere having grown tired of waiting for his master, but now he reappeared, bundling down through Irish Town, and off they set. They wended their way through gloomy backstreets … a strange threesome. People nodded and greeted Ben and then followed this up with backward, curious glances at the blond waif trailing behind him. Elle imagined Gibraltar would become an exceedingly small place when you lived there, like being on an island, everyone knowing everyone else and, unfortunately, their business.

Two more streets and they arrived at a front door with several bells and names, obviously flats, which were quite shabby from the outside. Elle had been thinking about Ben's use of 'ours' instead of 'mine' that she would rather have heard. Her worries were not unfounded for, as they went inside, there was Marianne, heavily pregnant, standing at the ironing board and the day to day domesticity of Elle's new knight-in-shining-armour became perfectly clear. Of course it was normal that this young man, whom she hardly knew, had a life going on that she knew nothing about, but she was irrationally disappointed at his status even though she was hopefully about to sail to the other side of the Atlantic Ocean. She was strangely comfortable with Ben and selfishly wanted to have him to herself for a few hours.

Doesn't everyone dream of that life-changing meeting with a special friend, where hours spent together can isolate one from the rest of the dreary struggle of life and all the day to day problems and boring routines?

Bravely she faced Ben's introductions. 'Marianne, Elle, Elle Marianne.' The latter nodded and carried on her ironing showing very little interest in the refugee that Ben had brought home.

'Feed Wanker will you?' she said, '… and there's only beans

on toast for tea as I haven't had time to fix anything else – and here is your shirt for work,' she added, and the shirt flew in his general direction.

'Fix up the floor mattress for Elle in here and I will bring her down to the club later,' and with that she took full command of the whole situation. Flashing Elle a winning smile, she added 'You can see Ben with his other hat on later, he's a DJ on Friday nights'.

That was the life of Ben and Marianne, it all seemed a bit haphazard to Elle and she allowed herself the cruel thought that he might be living with her because he had made her pregnant. It all seemed so mundane, unromantic and horribly dull. She had had only one experience of living with someone and the relationship had failed so miserably it was still too painful to think about but the precious time she spent with him had never, ever been dull.

Later in the club she shouted to Ben over the deafening music, 'I am not a fan of having my eardrums damaged so I am going to go back to yours.' Together, Marianne and Elle, their new careful friendship hanging between them like a thread, made their way back to the flat, the latter realising that Marianne knew that with her blooming motherhood she held every card over her predatory visitor. Falling onto her makeshift bed, still in her blue-layered dress, Elle was vaguely aware of a gentle kiss on the top of her head from Ben on his return. The gesture stirred no passion only a deep sense of loneliness and wanting to belong, haunting her descending dreams as she fell asleep.

Dreams of Peter, restlessly waking and then slipping back to try and feel him around her again, the tickle of his moustache the first time he had kissed her, the smell of cigarettes, previously loathed, had become a comfort now. Ben and Peter were two of a kind, physically similar, but also she had this strange feeling of compatibility and familiarity as though she knew Ben well which was of course absurd. Had she felt the same when she had first met Peter when he came to crew for her stepfather? She had been sixteen years old, flaky and vulnerable from her parent's divorce and their subsequent forming of new families. Her father with his four new little girls, no room for Elle there, and her mother quickly married to a bruised man who had suffered greatly with the loss of his previous family unit. Who knows, but she fell heavily and unconditionally for Peter's dear whiskered face and his voice with a coveted feint Australian twang, caught from a year of backpacking, but with his being eleven years her senior this infatuation failed to please anyone but herself.

They had sailed to St Malo in her sixteenth summer and he made her a woman there on the rocky beach. She had drunk a little beer, the cold pression slipping down deliciously and dulling her reason.

'Do I have to take all my clothes off?' she had asked, not understanding his request, or his need for consummation. She had to obey in order to become his proper girlfriend. Nothing could have prepared her for the ruthless violation of her innermost self. Laying her down, holding her hands gripped tightly in his above her head, fingers interlaced, the sharp rock beneath scored deeply into her back. This pain went unnoticed masked by the other, more powerful, agonizing intrusion upon her person. He had persevered relentlessly until she sensed he was spent, rolling away from her then, into the forgiving sand. She had sat in the road, covering her face so he would not see her sadness, or catch her fear of the possible consequences of the act performed. Transformed one hot French summer night into a woman, but still such a child.

In the days that followed, he became the Peter she understood again and in the cramped confines of her stepfather's catamaran their intimacy grew daily. He delighted in her and her sexual naivety charmed him all the more. She knew she would love him forever. Yet, as they sailed on grey waves back to his island home, he told her he was spoken for there and so all that had passed between them must be a secret and was best forgotten. Her heart quietly breaking, she tried to reach for his hand, but he pushed her firmly away.

This was not to be the end of it though, there was much more to follow but she could not reflect on the past without so much shame and regret that it threatened to destroy her or send her mad. Her recent two days with Peter before she rejoined Don and Janie were a tonic to both of them and she had slept in his arms, but they were set on separate courses, their lives briefly touching and then spinning apart again as if deflected by a strong force, just as a magnet sets a compass reeling.

There was another too, there always was with Elle, they had been close before she went away that summer. He knew someone would come and take her, he foretold it often enough. That she should so quickly surrender herself to a pirate on the sea almost destroyed the solid friendship they had cherished as teenagers. Maybe it is better to stay where we are loved than to follow passion and the unknown. To be content with a life that does not always offer such excitement but provides safety and emotional security.

Too late for such sensible thoughts, regret was a pointless emotion. She had to calm her anxieties and rest, all dreams and memories set aside.

2

"I can imagine nothing more terrifying than an Eternity filled with men who were all the same. The only thing which has made life bearable ... has been the diversity of creatures on the surface of the globe."

T.H. White, *The Book of Merlyn*

Elle awoke and with sleep still her master, she saw Ben placing a key beside her with a cup of tea. 'We are off to work,' he said. Marianne waved as she went (a vague gesture performed with her eyes upon the door) and Wanker bounded out after them. They were suddenly gone, the autumnal Atlantic air blowing in along the hall. It occurred to Elle that they trusted her entirely with their home, sensing no danger from a wandering cook, well of course, there was none. Even Marianne did not fear her intrusion, joined to Ben for all time by a small, unseen presence. She should worry though, Elle surmised, for she knew how selfish she could be, she had proved that already. Finding herself some toast, she mused a while and chose her clothes for the day with care, arranging her worldly goods tidily, along with the bedding so as not to cause annoyance to her hosts. What a blessing she could leave everything there! She reveled in her lightened load, just her small knapsack, jumper and coat and then hotfoot to the destroyer-pens again to see what, if any vessels had arrived since the previous afternoon.

Out of the old town gates and onto the long straight road, the wind was cool. The sea, a wonderful Mediterranean blue glistened in the sunshine which still held some warmth, even in November. How infinitely preferable to dank foggy days in the UK at that time of year. She could see some masts in the distance and felt a small wave of excitement. She was sure they were not there before and found herself walking faster almost jogging, in her haste to see any new arrivals.

She looked down on over a hundred feet of pure perfection. *Solstice*, floating gently with her sleek blue topsides and immaculate varnish. Please, please let them have room for one more!

A head of brown curls popped out of the main hatch and Elle recognised Lulu whom she had briefly met the month before in Mallorca, 'Hey Lu!' she called, and Lulu looked up with a big smile lighting up her lovely impish face. Lulu was so classically stunning, she turned every head with her perfect peach complexion, gorgeous smile and glossy hair, sometimes it was all Elle could do not to just stare at her in admiration. Her beauty came naturally and effortlessly and although she was almost square in stature and slightly stocky, her face was the face of an angel.

Lulu scrambled deftly up the nearest ladder and gave Elle a big hug on the quayside. 'Who are you with, how did you get here?' Her questions came faster than they could possibly be answered and the girls dissolved into laughter.

'Is *Solstice* fully crewed?' Elle couldn't wait to ask.

'Yes,' she replied, 'I am employed for the season as stewardess as long as I behave myself. I was taken on along with the cook in Banus just three days ago so you only just missed out Elle, I am sure something will come up though. Don't look so sad,' she added as she noticed the downcast face of her friend. It would have been hard to miss the change in Elle's demeanour, or the drop in her shoulders. 'There is something fairly large coming alongside now in the next pen, look!'

Sure enough they could see two large aluminium masts moving in close to the wall, and Elle's hopes lifted again.

'Catch you later' she squeezed her friend's arm and headed on eagerly to take a peek.

El Guero, she would have to look that up to see what it meant, but her guess was something like Warrior or rather The Warrior? She looked brand new, the shape of the windows made her look fierce with the dark perspex giving her a mysterious countenance. She was probably about eighty feet long, definitely a strong enough looking vessel to get her safely across to the other side. Elle perched on a bollard (her favourite seat of late) and inspected every detail of the boat before her as *El Guero* came alongside. A fairly elderly bearded gentleman brought her in skilfully, so neat in his manoeuvre that he could almost place the mooring line himself over her seat. At the last moment he chucked it towards her without a word and by some fluke Elle caught it and made it fast with a quick bowline.

'You done that before,' he shouted up, and she was not sure if that was a question or an observation, so she just shrugged by way of reply. She studied him carefully and decided that he was probably older than she had first thought, his head appearing to wobble involuntarily as he spoke, giving the impression that he was shaking his head in exasperation at everything that was happening around him. There were two men on the foredeck, one youngish and obviously a fairly able crew member, who had made the bow fast with apparent ease, and the other a portly middle aged man with glasses who looked to Elle to be lost, bewildered and curiously out of place.

'Come on you arseholes, get another fender down on that bow will you.'

An onlooker would have noticed the bewilderment on Elle's face on hearing this command from the skipper. What sort of man would command his crew so rudely? A few more words and she caught a distinct American drawl. She hardly knew anything about Americans and in that moment she was not sure she wanted to discover more. There was a girl now coming out from below and Elle thought that if that were the whole crew then they probably would have room for one more. A feminine companion being already on board made the whole idea of joining more attractive. The mooring process was complete and the skipper was on his way up the wall to check the springs. There was no time like the present and Elle took a deep breath. 'May I talk to you sir?' she ventured, suddenly keen to show off her polite British way.

'Sure,' he said, still with the head shaking which was a trifle disarming, but also with a hint of a twinkle in his eyes, deep set in his weather beaten face.

'I am looking for a passage to the West Indies and I wonder if you have space for an extra or need of a cook?'

'Took on a cook here two days ago, could do with another watch-keeper but I never take on two crew in the same port.'

'But I thought you just arrived?'

'No we just went out for a sea trial.'

She didn't really know how to reply to this, but after a moment she found the courage to blurt out, 'I don't know any of your crew, I never met them or even saw them before!'

'How do I know that missee?' he countered, but he did seem to be taking a fresh look at the small person who appeared to be arguing with him over his own strict principles.

'Well you could trust me,' she said, braver now.

The old seaman took a deep breath and Elle looked down fearing she had pushed too hard.

'Okay Princess welcome aboard, we leave in two days for Antigua via the Canaries, I hope you have funds, I will feed you on passage in return for watch keeping and deck duties but there is no wage for you as we are already crewed.' With this he disappeared down the ladder swiftly and below decks leaving his new crew member completely speechless.

She had successfully landed herself a ride to Antigua. Should she accept or hold back in case something better turned up?

There was nothing unsuitable about the vessel for sure, but the crew threatened to lift her out of her comfort zone, not the sort of travelling companions she was used to at all.

She felt it would be churlish to back out especially after persuading the skipper to trust her. Now she had won him over she decided to go and fetch her luggage, and move on board. She could help prepare for the voyage and thus get to know the others while the boat was still tied to the shore and the escape route was still open should she feel uncomfortable. A yacht becomes a small world when out at sea, not a place to be confined with people you fear or dislike.

Such a long walk back to the town again and in the heat of midday, she found herself starving and thirsty. The piece of toast she had eaten for breakfast seemed a very long time ago, especially after the events of the morning. A quick decision to grab a sandwich en route at "Head Office" proved to be a good one as Wanker was sat in the door way wagging his tail to greet her and who should she find sitting at the bar having his lunch, but Ben.

'I did it,' she started to tell him excitedly, 'I have found a ride.'

'What do you know about them exactly, and what is the boat like?' He seemed both suspicious and a bit protective immediately, knocking her enthusiasm.

'Not much but if I join them now, I'll have a couple of days to find out before we leave.'

'Well you don't have to rush it you know.'

'I do because it may be the only offer I get, and the boat looks new, well equipped and fit for the trip.'

'I'll take you down in the van with your gear I'm on a long lunch,' he volunteered. Such was her relief at the thought of transport for all her belongings down to the destroyer pens she almost kissed him. Ben took her in his small white works van and they were quiet with each other, both sensing a heavy cloud over them of things best left unsaid.

'Say a big thank you to Marianne won't you?'

'She's cool,' he replied, eyes fixed on the road ahead. Placing her bags carefully beside her on the quayside Ben spoke out as if an idea had just sprung to mind.

'Meet me tomorrow at the marina at seven.'

'Okay,' Elle replied, about to ask the reason but with a nod Ben pulled away and the van disappeared into the distance.

The skipper was there in the vast, raised cockpit and he shouted below. 'Hey, Carl get up here and help the Princess with her bags will you?'

She climbed aboard. 'My name is Elle,' she said firmly and, somewhat formally, she held out her hand.

The skipper shook it briefly, 'I'm John, pleased to meet you Princess, this is Carl my deckhand. Claire is below, she is the cook and Mike up on the foredeck there, he is the boss's chauffeur who just fancied coming along for the ride.' He shielded his mouth with his hand before adding, 'he is supposed to be a bit of an engineer but I have my doubts.'

A fairly strange crew she thought to herself, but she took note that John had shared a confidence with her about another crew member ... maybe in this instance, it was a gesture to help put her at ease.

'We are sailing to Nantucket to deliver *El Guero* to her new owner via the Canaries and Antigua to catch the trades and then heading north. You can stow your gear in the cabin forward with Claire and I will have your passport please, whilst you are aboard, for safe keeping.'

This seemed a fairly normal request and Elle went down the hatch to see the accommodation and meet Claire who was busy in the brightly lit galley below.

So it was a delivery, this information explained the strange mix of crew and the atmosphere, which was a bit unusual. She found *El Guero* to be roomy and spacious, too modern to be her cup-of-tea, but none the less comfortable, and definitely in need of a good clean up. Claire greeted her heartily and seemed very pleased to see her. Elle put this enthusiastic welcome down to the increase in ratio of females to males on board.

'Will you help me with the provisioning?' she asked and having stowed Elle's gear roughly away, they sat down in the saloon and started to go over the endless lists Claire had been making.

Elle glanced at her new shipmate with interest, a brown haired smiley sort of girl, not pretty but with a kind face. From Martha's Vineyard she had said, wherever that might be. The galley was equipped with two electric ovens and a large hob. There was plenty of freezer space but of course everything was dependant on the two large generators for power when at sea, or shore power when alongside. Elle preferred gas for cooking but she was used to old boats without the luxury of generated electricity.

Claire had firm plans for the large cuts of meat she would buy, but had neglected the need for plain biscuits, cereals and comforting snacks for those struggling with nausea in rough seas. Elle proceeded to add another list to which she gave careful thought to each item added. They both agreed that they would buy some fruit and vegetables in Gibraltar but restock again with the wonderful produce rumoured to be available in the markets of the Canaries, before the longest leg of the trip.

Claire showed her around, she inspected the shower and toilet opposite their cabin, which was cramped but adequate, and at least they did not have to share with the boys. The top bunk was to be Elle's as Claire had already taken the lower. The boys' bunks were up in the bow and the skipper slept down aft in the biggest cabin she had ever seen with a full-sized bathtub as well as a shower. The two girls, feeling like intruders in the strange old captain's personal space, quickly left his quarters.

'So how are we going to get all this shopping back here then?' Elle asked.

'John said to walk to Liptons, the new supermarket on the marina, and then get a taxi back when we are done.'

She was warming now to this girl with her soft accent and things were becoming less daunting. They had a plan, something to work on, together. John came below and he appeared more cheerful too, probably realising that having two girls on the job was more effective than one. He gave Claire a wad of cash, making her sign in a book on receipt in a professional manner. They set off up the road with Elle wondering how many more times she would go up and down that stretch of road before they finally set sail for the Canaries and beyond.

They chattered amiably on the way to the supermarket. Elle found out that Claire had been cooking for an American family in a villa in Spain and now needed to earn her passage home. She had never really sailed at all and had certainly not been out on the open ocean, so she would be in for a few surprises. Elle decided to keep this thought to herself. Wandering around she felt relieved that she had no responsibility and that she was just there to help if needed, as it was a huge task to provision for a possible three weeks at least out of sight of land. Claire had planned that if she made a roast nearly everyday then they could have cold cuts for sandwiches, which was a fairly sound idea as long as they had plenty of greens and fruit available too. Elle loaded some soup cans and beans in the trolley as the weather could turn against them making the preparation of a simple meal a difficult, almost impossible task. Plenty of tea, coffee and hot chocolate, water biscuits, cream crackers and digestives, Claire watched her as she gathered all of these necessities for life on stormy seas, her eyebrows often lifting in surprise.

'Did you ask the others if there was anything they particularly liked?' Elle asked, trying to think how she would have planned the shopping.

'No not really.'

'Well we could have one more shot at this tomorrow if there is anything we missed okay?'

Claire appeared to agree with this, as she did not respond.

Strange people yanks, Elle thought, and they made their way pushing loaded trolleys to the checkout. They boxed it all up and Claire paid in cash. She gathered up the receipt and several others from the floor as well.

'What on earth are you doing, you have the right ticket?' Elle was mystified.

'Well a spare one or two to account for missing cash never goes amiss,' she grinned, 'get wise Princess!'

Elle was silent, hating to be a party to such blatant dishonesty but powerless to intervene not wishing to lose her only ally at this early stage. Back they went in a taxi and with the help of a reluctant Carl, loaded all their purchases on board stowing as they unpacked. Elle realised she was exhausted and with the intention of reviving herself she hunted for the ware withal to make a cup of tea for everyone.

Scanning around the galley she asked, 'So do we have to run the generator to make a cup of tea?' This did not seem ideal. John over heard her request and showed her a one-ring primus stove with a small blue gas bottle stowed under the sink. Happy to find something she was accustomed to using, Elle made a much-needed cuppa and broke open some chocolate biscuits, already raiding their carefully stowed supplies.

'We have a fair amount of battery power for lights and pumps,' John explained, 'but we will have to run a generator or the main engine for a while each day to keep it topped up, so lights should be used sparingly and not left on. Also, obviously we must coincide the oven with the use of the generator, and on the longer passage we have to carefully monitor fresh water and fuel consumption.'

She could see Claire looking increasingly confused about all this information and she longed to escape for a while to see Ben or catch up with Lulu, but it was inappropriate to disappear right now during this briefing time.

'Shall we all go into town and grab some tucker?' John

suggested, the guys did not look bowled over by the idea but thinking they could do with some bonding or team building, Elle offered to introduce them to the delights of "Head Office" for a drink. Carl bounded off to look for a taxi and she felt hugely relieved, as truthfully, she did not think she could face the walk again.

The dank stale smell had vanished from the pub, a buzz with Gibraltarian working class people having a beer at the end of the day. Elle sat down next to Carl feeling she had given him little or no attention at all since she had joined the team. She decided he had the sort of features that she would not be able to recall in any detail if she were to not see him for a few days and she suspected that his character would hold no hidden depths at all. Elle could be cruel and dismissive of people who were of no interest to her but at least she recognised this fault in her own character. He was just an American to her, she had no idea which part he hailed from and if he told her, it would mean nothing. America was a big place and she had hated geography at school, but John fascinated her and as he was to be her custodian for a few weeks that could be fraught, or even dangerous, she thought it was prudent to try and find out a little more about him. So she had decided to question Carl, as Mike fell even lower on her scale of likability.

'So how did you meet up with John?' she probed.

'Well,' Carl considered his reply for a moment, 'basically he knew my Dad, they met way back'.

'So what did John do before he retired?' I presume he is retired?' she tried another tack hoping he might be a bit more forthcoming.

'He skippered whalers out of Nantucket.' A short reply with which he virtually turned his back on her, passing a quick comment to Claire that Elle missed. So it became as obvious to her as a slap across the face that she, the small, British hitchhiker was not entirely welcomed by all of the crew.

Some fish and chips and a couple of beers at *The Star* and they were on their way back to the destroyer pens. All Elle wanted to do was to collapse into her bunk after such an eventful day and she missed her friends, notably Ben, who was nowhere to be seen and even more still, Don and Janie. She resolved to phone them in the morning and tell them all her news.

The next day dawned, the final day in port so Elle made a break for it and collecting Lulu they set off for the marina to walk around the yachts, and have a coffee. As they ambled into town in the bright windy sunshine, Ben's van slowed alongside them.

'Morning ladies,' he greeted them with a smile, and Elle could see him absorbing Lulu's beautiful face shining out from under her woolly scarf and parka cocooning her from the chill morning breeze.

'Don't forget later,' he threw the words in her direction as he drove on with a thumbs up in the mirror. She wondered what brought him down towards the pens. Was he looking for her or just going about his work?

'Who was that?' demanded Lulu, 'Do you have friends in Gib then?'

Feeling defensive Elle replied too quickly 'Well I have spent quite a bit of time here on and off when I was crew on *Talisman*, and we hauled out to paint in Algeciras.' Of course that had nothing to do with anything as Algeciras was the other side of the border with no access to Gibraltar but she wanted to move the subject away from Ben.

'But you obviously like him I can tell!' She was like a dog with a bone her eyes alight with the scent of a scandal.

'Yes but he has a lady who is grossly pregnant and I am going to the Caribbean okay, enough said?'

'Oooooo touchy,' she laughed and finally at last she let it go but could not resist adding parrot fashion, 'don't forget later 'tho!'

They inspected the marina, full of long stayers, people living on all sorts of craft. Maybe they had been on their way to somewhere once but lack of funds or fear of the open sea had trapped them in the no-mans land that was Gibraltar.

'Look at the smugglers boats,' Lulu pointed to rows of study inflatables with huge outboards on their sterns. Elle nodded, that is exactly what they were, with their powerful engines to speed them away from customs patrolling the Straits between Europe and Morocco. They had their coffee in the new marina bar and talked about the excitement of reaching the other side and the possibility of meeting up with friends from the Mediterranean in Antigua, and the mystic of the islands they longed to see.

'My grandfather is in St Lucia you know,' Elle said proudly.

'How long has he been there?'

'About forty years.'

'He won't know much about you then.'

'Well he will when I find him won't he,' and they laughed with no idea why.

Elle phoned Don from the call box in the bar. *Talisman* had a phone on board when they were holed up for the winter in Banus.

'Stupid girl,' he said, 'at last, we have been worried.'

The sound of his voice and his affectionate tone made her own voice wobble. 'I am fine,' she said trying to sound braver than she felt, 'and I have found a passage across.'

He pushed her for an exact description of the boat, whether she had seen life jackets, flares and life rafts and instructed her to investigate the credentials of the skipper as much as she possibly could without seeming rude, including his navigational skills.

'It's difficult, they are Americans ... like aliens from another planet, you should hear their language! But I will try, I promise.'

Elle knew she had been less than thorough in her enquires concerning the safety equipment on board *El Guero*. 'Try not to worry and I will send a card from the Canaries and another from

Antigua and if there is no job for me there I will be back anyway. You know I have my open ticket safe.'

'Okay, well be wise and and safe Elle.'

'Will do, love to Janie and Dammit.'

'Yes to you too.'

'Bye.'

'Bye.'

A click and that was that. She wondered about her parents for a brief second, frowning as she replaced the receiver. It should have been them caring about where she was and the path she was following but sadly it was not and never would be.

'Right,' Elle announced, 'Don has quite rightly suggested that as the Atlantic crossing is a delivery *El Guero* could be seriously lacking in safety equipment so I am going to go back and will check right away.'

Lulu's lovely eyes grew wider. 'Mrs Sensible all of a sudden?'

'Yes well, needs must, come on.'

Back on board it was as though John had eaves dropped on her conversation with Don as all the life jackets were laid out on the deck to air and a man was bringing back the newly serviced life raft, lowering it down on a halyard to be strapped back in its place on the top of the saloon roof behind the main mast. So some of her pressing questions were answered straightaway without her saying a word, which was reassuring.

'I was going to ask about all of this, mind reader,' she said to John.

'Ah, not just a looker then Princess,' the head wobble more marked today. (Was it disapproval, contemplation of the moment, or the onset of some terrible disease, who knew?) A shrug from Elle. 'Not even,' she replied.

John waved his arm in the general direction of the rest of the crew on the foredeck ... 'The others haven't even asked, just taken it all for granted I guess,' and he set about checking dates on the flares in a box at his feet.

'Here, that's something I could do, I am sure there are more important preparations you need to see to,' Elle offered.

'Gee thanks, yes I could do with making sure Mike is sorting the oil change on the generators.'

So gradually it felt as though they were becoming a team in the build up to casting off the shore lines, with Claire organising her galley stores and Carl dragging sail bags up on deck to see what they would have to work with on the crossing.

'It would be good if we could get *vaseline* on most of the bright work too before we leave to protect it from the salt, although we could do this under way.' With these words John chucked a pot at her which she almost dropped, caught by surprise.

She had never heard the description 'bright work' before, so she stuck her head down the hatch to ask Claire. 'It's all the chrome and varnished woodwork, I think,' she said, and Elle realised that she would learn a fair amount of American terminology on the trip.

If all were ready and the weather was fair, after a brief visit to the fuel quay for diesel and water, they were to leave the following day. Her evening assignation with Boyd was heavy on her mind, a quick goodbye would be the best and on with her new life outside the waters of the Mediterranean at last.

At 6.55, showered and fresh, Elle arrived at the marina bar.

At 7.25, Elle still showered and fresh was still waiting at the bar!

At 7.45 when she was just about to go Ben sauntered in.

'Sorry,' he said, with no explanation.

'Come on.' Taking her hand he led her down the first pontoon in the dark right to the end where he climbed onto a small motor cruiser and started lifting back the cover to the cockpit revealing the doors to the main cabin. Pulling her down to sit on the bench seat in the small saloon he spoke almost in a whisper. 'I thought we could talk here without prying eyes.' Elle was abruptly reminded of his circumstances, and she decided that a last shot fumble in the dark before she left was not how she intended to behave.

He put his arms around her and just held her tightly, stroking her hair as he would a child. 'I have to come clean,' he said.

She leaned back to see his face, 'About what exactly?'

He took a deep breath before speaking quickly as if the haste might lessen the impact of his words, 'I know Peter and I knew you were coming and he asked me to look out for you and help you if I could.'

'You what?' Elle could not help but raise her voice at this revelation.

'He worked in Gib for a while last year and we have been friends ever since.'

She was quiet now, stunned, the information sinking in and a million questions churned around in her mind. She felt tricked and betrayed by the boy in whose arms she was firmly still held, as he had been acting solely at Peter's request, and not because he felt any connection with her at all. Her cheeks were burning, and fury rose in a bubble to the surface in her head and burst silently with the knowledge that Peter did actually still care what happened to her.

One question escaped in a whisper ... 'So do you know everything that occurred between Peter and I, all of it?'

Shaking his head he replied, 'No, not all of it, but I know that whatever happened to separate you, he is still fond of you.'

'I saw him recently in Ibiza, did you know that too?'

'Yes I knew and I know as you do that he is back with Sally in Mallorca now and that they plan to build a life together, but it doesn't mean that you are forgotten, Elle, it's not that easy for him to let you go'.

'Well I am glad about that,' she said and she could feel tears coming now, tears of humiliation that these two men should know each other and discuss her and the things she had done in the past, maybe talked about all the hurt and pain she had caused Peter and others too. The situation catapulted her back into feeling like the badly behaved child she was trying to leave behind.

Turning her face away from him she said 'I need to go now, it's a good thing I am going away.'

'Yes but you will be fine and meet plenty of new people and it will be good to leave it all in the past.' He kissed her hard on the lips and they climbed back out onto the pontoon. With another quick hug, she managed a smile and walked away without looking back, needing to assert her strength and independence, after her close brush with tears. Elle ran most of the way back still angered by the apparent conspiracy between Peter and Ben! Ben and Peter, their two names and their two faces swam maddeningly around in her head, too much to bear, she could not wait to set sail.

3

"The winter day broke blue and bright
With glancing sun and glancing spray
As o'er the swell our boat made way
As gallant as a gull in flight."

W.W. Gibson, *Flannan Isle*

The advantage or perhaps disadvantage of a first class education, coupled with a huge pleasure in all things literary, is that chunks of poems learnt or prose studied remained wedged in Elle's mind only to pop out when they suited the day or the mood. Although written about Scottish waters Gibson's poem totally described the picture around her as they headed out of the Straits of Gibraltar in the sunshine with a stiff prevailing breeze from the west.

Elle could see John relaxing into his element as they crept away from the land and all the pressures it placed upon him. She could relate to this man, a kindred spirit found, as all they had to contend with now was the weather, and the boat itself. They must try to find their way, keeping body and soul and crew together until they reached their destination.

Carl was watching John's face, awaiting orders, he reminded Elle of a crouching dog attentive for a word or signal as they sat in the cockpit acclimatising themselves to the bouncing motion of *El Guero* as she headed out into the wind under motor.

John eventually looked aloft and said, 'I think we will hoist main and stay sail and put one reef in and then see what wind strength we get when we turn the corner and make our course for the Canaries.' Her confidence in him was slowly growing as she watched his slow ponderous decisions. The importance of trusting one's captain at sea can never be underestimated.

Moving around carefully on the foredeck, attaching themselves with their chunky harness clips, Carl and Elle removed sail ties and hoisted stay sail and main, pulling the latter down with a slab reef to reduce the area they would present to the wind when the course was set. Carl nodded to her and she could see that he was more than a little impressed that such a skinny, useless looking girl could in fact find her way around the sheets and halyards, and that she might prove her worth as a crew member after all.

They retreated to the safety of the cockpit and then sat to wait until they cleared the straits and had made their way out into the open Atlantic.

Watching the others she was beginning to wonder how John would organise the watches. She did not have long to mull it over as he had already begun to discuss it with Carl raising his normally soft voice above the wind and the sound of the engine. 'We need engineering skills on each watch so I guess that makes it a forgone conclusion that the Princess and I will take one watch and you and Mike will take the other leaving Claire to concentrate on making sure we all eat? Six hours on and six off, with everyone on deck for night time sail changes,' he looked around his crew. 'Everybody okay with that?'

They all nodded and Elle was relieved that they had the first short part to the Canaries to get accustomed to the pattern, because she knew it would be hard to settle into this sort of routine. How would it have worked without her? John would have taken a solo watch which could have proven dangerous, so this meant that they were definitely better off with her than without her.

John continued, 'So today we will eat some tucker at five and

Elle and I will take the first watch from six until midnight, so you guys get you heads down after some grub okay?' Everything he said sounded like a question as if he feared some argument from them, some challenge to his leadership, but none came, not yet, time would tell.

There was not much protection in the cockpit on the cold November day but Elle decided to get her book and sit in a corner in the air, not trusting her sea legs to kick in just yet if she retired below. No one seemed to be expecting her to do anything so she just read and dozed, keeping her thoughts well away from all she was leaving, and losing herself every now and again in a trance watching the waves as they hit the bow and broke away beneath the hull. How she loved the calming of her spirit at sea. She could not explain why she felt so at peace, studying every breaker that rolled, and echoed on splitting into tiny wavelets, chasing each other with a fizzing sound, across whirlpools that caught the light with a myriad of colour beneath the momentarily oily surface that lay between each wave. The sea portrayed a new character every time she sailed, lumpy some days with the waves never quite breaking, choppy others, and occasionally, wonderfully glassy and smooth. Life was like that too, she decided, sometimes she fell down a trough and other days she was lifted and cast high in a cascade of froth and floated on carried by a stream of bubbles. Often she was nauseous with the turbulence within her stirred up by all her concerns, akin to seasickness. The sea would always be her comfort, her place to be and her security. The water held all the answers.

Claire came up through the hatch and looked about as green as the Granny Smith that Elle was munching on. She patted the cushion beside her, 'Come sit here a while in the fresh air, it will be less bumpy when we bear away and start sailing.'

Claire looked confused, 'You mean this isn't sailing?'

Elle smiled and shook her head, 'No, when we turn more sideways on to the wind the sails will be full, and although the boat will lean over a bit we will have a smoother ride.' She tried to show her how it would be with totally inadequate hand gestures, and had the curious sensation of trying to explain the wind to a child when in fact Claire was probably eight or nine years her senior. 'John is plotting our course right now and soon we will be starting to turn.'

Carl was on the wheel and sure enough, the skipper's voice came up from where he was seated at the chart table. 'Bear away a bit now can you, and Princess take the helm while he lets the main and stay sail out.'

'Okay Skip,' they were glad to have something to do and the change of motion was a welcome one. Carl hoisted a medium sized jib as well, winching the sheets in tight giving them a fresh burst of speed.

Suddenly all went quiet except for the swish of the hull through the sea and Elle realised that John had shut down the main engine. How glorious, they were sailing at last. Elle knew that they had absolutely no automatic steering at all which seemed like a huge omission on somebody's part and also meant that three hours of each six hour watch had to be spent on the helm. For all her modern interior *El Guero* was a bit lacking in equipment obviously having changed hands with a rather skimpy inventory.

John came back up. 'Do we not have an auto pilot?' she asked.

He smiled, 'What's the matter Princess, don't you like steering?'

'On the contrary I do, I just thought it would be helpful sometimes.'

'Well I have been a whaling captain for forty years with no fancy auto pilot', he said, 'so I guess we'll manage.'

Why did she feel he was laughing at her almost all the time? Worse than that he was even succeeding in humbling her in a strange way. Why would she think they needed more than a basic crew, hull and sails to get them across the vast stretch of open ocean that they faced? She concentrated on keeping the boat comfortably on course with the sails full, as if to prove to him that she was more than capable of helming all the way to Antigua if necessary.

Claire was a little happier and went down to rustle up snacks, but Elle could sense that for their inexperienced cook this trip was to be a lot more than she had bargained for when she had impulsively signed up in Banus on some sunny Spanish day. They sailed along through the swells that passed beneath them as the waves continued their journey to break on the shore of the distant African Coast. Elle fancied she could hear the roar as they hit the beach but of course the land was too far away.

At six the guys went below to rest and she was left alone with John for the first of many watches. Darkness had fallen already as he tested out the deck lights for night sail changes and she loved the way she could not see the sea when they were switched on, just the deck and the sails, their own island in time as if suspended, floating in the blackness surrounding them. Elle sat quietly for a while concentrating on the helm, and then she started to think that the passage would be a long and silent one to Antigua if she did not make an effort to chat with this old whaling captain. The endless hours they faced together were intimidating. She wondered how old he was, deciding he must be nearly seventy at least and she was not keen on that thought in case his powers of deduction and navigation might be waning. On the opposite note they were probably excellent given his experience and sea miles. She decided not to ask his age as it would surely be a rude question and quite tactless. Starting with the subject of herself was, without a doubt, a wiser idea, 'What's with the Princess label anyway?' she said.

Not turning his gaze from the dark horizon he answered, 'Well you are the only British person aboard and you have princesses over there don't you? Anyway you have that slightly superior sort of aloofness about you and the name just fits from where I'm standing'.

She thought about his reasoning. 'I try to be aloof to give the impression of confidence.' she said.

'Well it doesn't work Princess,' he answered and there it was again, the flash of amusement flickering across his features. He looked more serious then as he asked, 'What do you think about the others, will we sleep while they have the con?'

She supposed this to mean while they were up there in charge as it were, she had never heard it called 'the con' before. Thinking for a moment she said cautiously 'I think Carl is a good sailor he reminds me of the racing crew I have met in the Med, boat niggers, we call them, guys who are strong and do as they are told quickly without question, but Mike, the chauffeur? What exactly is he doing here? Already he looks fairly uncomfortable to me and we are not even a day out of port yet.'

'The boss, as in the owner in Nantucket, thought it would be the trip of a lifetime for him, which it most likely will be, but whether he enjoys it or not, well there's the rub.'

This first watch passed quickly with their light chat and she was glad to find her way down to her bunk, grateful too that it was on the lee side on their tack, so the angle of the boat and bounce of the waves kept her firmly against the side of the hull, and she had no need to fiddle about with tying the lee board designed to stop her falling out. She slept quite well for almost exactly the first hour and then the motion started to change, with the boat coming on the wind again and then bearing away with short, sudden, course changes. Of course there was one member of the crew who had no idea how to hold a boat steady on track with the sails set fair ... no prizes for who, and she could only hope he mastered it before they were running with the trade winds with the gigantic swells of the Atlantic right behind the boat chasing them to Antigua.

Two days on and they were all a little tired but Elle could see from the chart that they were over a quarter of the way to the Canaries, well almost, and making good speed. Although they came out of the Straits into a westerly wind, it had veered to the north west now being much more on the stern and with the current in their favour this increased their apparent speed to average nine knots at least. It was about seven hundred miles to Tenerife from Gibraltar and Elle was determined to acclimatise herself to being at sea and to enjoy the experience rather than counting the hours until landfall. Going on watch at six pm and then to bed at midnight gave her and John a fairly normal night's sleep pattern if a little short, and she was sure he had done this for her benefit. Although he had indicated that the pattern would shift to share the "dead watches", as yet she saw no sign of change. She could already see a crack in the crew, which could easily grow if he did not choose to share the worst watch of the night between them. But John had the responsibility of the navigation too and the lions share of keeping a check on all things mechanical and so the choice of hours had, quite justly, to be his. Besides it seemed to work well. Claire was still using the pre-prepared meals she had bought for the first week along with ham and cheese for sandwiches so, although she did not look a healthy colour, she continued to achieve a hot meal for them at the change of the early evening watch and Elle was able to help her.

On the third night at sea she took the helm from a very tired Mike after supper. John appeared not to be taking star sights, maybe it was too overcast, for he came unexpectedly and sat beside her in the corner on the cockpit bench.

'Tell me again Princess why you are here, maybe I forgot or perhaps I didn't listen hard enough the first time?'

Elle was totally unprepared for this direct interrogation preferring to be lost in a dream helping the boat find to her way through the dark waves. 'There are several reasons,' she said, 'would you like them all?'

She could see the motion of his grey head shaking in the dim light shed by the instrument panel as if he meant no, but his answer was the opposite, 'Yes,' he said, 'I would like them all, all of the reasons why you are sitting here.'

'Looking for my grandfather?' she ventured.

He shook his head, now a definite negative, 'No more than just that? I know it's more than that. I want to hear all of it.'

So Elle began somewhere near the beginning, haltingly at first and then she started to explain and his apparent interest in her story all gave her confidence in the telling.

'Have you been to the UK?' she asked.

'My first visit to Europe,' he replied quickly, and he threw his arms wide as if to embrace it all, 'and I haven't come across many of you British guys yet either, so you are all new to me.'

No one had ever made her into an alien or a foreigner before.

'Well,' she said and the words began to slide out with the trace of a sigh behind them.

'I grew up in a small village in the country, my father scraping a living with a small accounting business for farmers with my mother's help, when she felt inclined. My father mowed the lawn at weekends while my mother picked scented pinks in summer and wrapped earthy snowdrops in ivy leaves in early spring, for some financial return from a nearby florist. I think she imagined this small toil to be earning a living.'

Like a stone skimming the water with a powerful throw, Elle stayed on the surface of the dark that swirled beneath her words and she avoided John's gaze in the darkness, keeping her eyes on the bright compass light and the tell tale ribbon for the wind, fluttering above her. She edited her story as she spoke sorting through the details to give him a picture but not the complete one, an artist's sketch, an outline without the shading and colour needed to fill between the lines, and make the picture whole.

I stood in the shallows of the river watching the weed, such a vibrant green with small white blooms, the water ice-cold around my trembling toes waiting for father to dive from the weir, while mother lay languidly in the grass, filing her nails, sunning herself. She was always playing the lady wherever she was, on a muddy riverbank, dancing the stage boards of Oklahoma *or portraying the love struck glory of Maria, in* West Side Story, *her sweet call, caught in the cobwebbed corners of the village hall.*

My father had a dream as full as a hot air balloon but none of the fire beneath, for struggling flames were quickly beaten down by the dampening agonies of raising his small family, and pleasing his demanding wife.

Primary school was a bus ride away, one full hour of stopping and starting, swaying and rolling along in a red double decker, every gear change of the journey leaving an echo in my mind forever. My best friend was gathered aboard in the next village and on reaching our destination we would wander the river path and up the road to the school kicking our way through the layers of leaves in autumn, gathering conkers and sweet chestnuts, brimming satchels, recorders peeping out at the side.

My brother was sent to boarding school far away when barely seven years old.

Something woke me, late in the evening, and I stumbled along the corridor to the spare room where my friend's older sister was sleeping, babysitting us while father and mother dined with friends. Gently pushing the door, just for reassurance that she was there I suppose, I saw my father's head raised from the bed, with her, just a shape in the dark shadow beneath. Comprehension was impossible. I struggled to sort out an explanation from muddled sleepy thoughts but failed. I needed to get back to my bed and hide. I had to have been mistaken, dreaming even. I hoped I hadn't been noticed, scared that I might be to blame in some way for my discovery.

The words are easy to find, the sounds simple to make, but like a pencil pressed too hard upon paper, the scorch mark on my childhood would be never be erased. A black hole appeared and I fell in, but I was no Alice and this was no fantasy rabbit hole with potions to solve each problem. I clung to the edges which broke away under the grip of my small hands and I plummeted, crashing against the sides as I fell down and down, spiraling out of control, crumbling clods of my life as I had known it following me into the dark beneath. From the edges of the crater cracks began to radiate slowly, spider lines that would forever disfigure the cheek of my life.

Everything began to change … my mother ran down the stairs and I saw tears. I had never seen my mother cry even when the whole family had wept over the demise of the dog, she had remained tough, practical and completely devoid of emotion.

There were rows, more than just niggling arguments, these confrontations were bitter, doors were slammed and my father disappeared, the mower was silent, the grass grew long. There was talk of boarding school for both brother and sister. We had become a burden, an inconvenience.

Boarding school. How wonderful to have friends around me all the time to bounce on the beds and giggle away the nights. Some girls wept for home and this infected me quickly, as surely as the spread of a common cold, and I became sad and homesick, weeping uncontrollably on my brief exeats at home, infuriating my mother who snapped and shouted.

The first weekend I was due to go home at the start of the autumn term, I was full of expectation for promised riding and fun. The shock of the change that greeted me left me numb and drowning. Home was gone, sold, my bedroom, my sanctuary, my life … all lost. "We must stay with your grandmother now", was the only answer I heard, from the closed, resolved face of my mother. My father was nowhere to be seen.

Quietly all the teasing mockery quite gone from his voice, John said 'Don't tell me any more if you don't want to.'

'I will,' she answered, wondering if he could see through the brief account she had chosen to tell, she thought perhaps his gruff ways hid a sensitive man, after all.

'Time is something we have plenty of right now Princess,' he answered, and with that he went to the stern, torch in hand, to read the log as they did every hour to recalculate their approximate position and speed, from the last mark on the chart that he had made from the sextant sights he had taken earlier in the day.

Next day John and Elle took over their watch in heavy rain and she realised just how little shelter there was for the helmsman. Even with her new recently acquired sailing coat and waterproof trousers, sitting still in the rain for six hours one is unlikely to stay warm, and coming off watch at midday she shivered, chilled to the bone. The generator had been running for Claire to heat soup so there was hot water. She plucked up the courage to make a request, 'Could I have a hot shower please John?'

Her watch-partner nodded, also visibly cold and wet. 'Don't get used to the luxury though girl as when we leave Tenerife we will be on rations so it will be sink washes and very careful water usage.'

'Message understood,' she replied, thinking she would sort out that problem with him later. Meanwhile Elle felt like a new person after her shower although a little bruised from attempting to wash with the motion of the boat. Claire was in the galley and the generator was still running.

'I'm not trying to steal your job,' Elle said carefully, 'but shall I have a go at making a cake for tea, cheer everyone up?' Far from looking put out, the cook looked ecstatically happy at this suggestion and disappeared quick as a flash to her bunk. Elle had made sure they bought what was needed for simple sponges in Gibraltar so she set about mixing and ten minutes later her creation was in the oven wedged with bits of foil and a saucepan lid to keep the tin level and in one place. The cake, covered with a butter icing, was hugely appreciated and for once they were all smiling, and she saw how such a simple thing had lifted the morale of everyone aboard.

That night as soon as they were alone John spoke out, 'Before you carry on telling me a bit more about why you are here, thanks for today Princess, that was a good move on your part.' Inwardly she smiled as praise from John was hard to earn, she had learnt that much about him. He found it easier to show displeasure with the actions of his crew than to praise them.

A while later when she was settled for her stretch on the wheel, John urged her on with her tale. 'So what happened next after your parents divorced?'

'Well, my mother moved in with my grandmother and went to teacher training college, and my father moved into a rented cottage with his new girlfriend who was soon to be his wife. So as our families were friends, my mother being close to the parents of the object of my fathers desire, and her sister being my closest childhood friend, the whole affair was a sad and sordid one for everyone, excepting, of course, for the two at the centre of it all. They appeared blind to all the upset they had caused. My schoolwork went downhill quickly and eventually I became ill. Not wanting to return to board at school any longer, I went daily from my grandmother's house. My mother meanwhile, chose a man from a varied selection of suitors. William wooed us both with lavish gifts and had a catamaran which appealed to me immediately.'

John smiled at this, 'So you liked him because he had a boat?'

'Yes there wasn't much else I liked about him at first if I'm honest. He took me sailing, out from Mudeford to look for mackerel on Christchurch ledge, my first real taste of sailing along the Dorset coast. My mother hated being on a boat so although she came the first few times to sunbathe after a while she didn't come at all, complaining of seasickness and cold. I've never told anybody all of this,' she added. 'Are you seriously interested?'

'Yes Princess I am seriously interested, where is Mudeford? You will have to show me on a map. Dorset too, all these names mean very little to me.' Did she see a smile lurking in the dark of his face? She could not be sure.

There was no place for me in my father's new life, no slot that I could slide into, no hole to fill, the photographs were full. I was an awkward cuckoo in a tidy nest. My new stepmother already had three girls and soon there was another on the way. I watched the profound toll this took on my brother who retreated into his shell, squashed, as he often was, in the back seat of the car with four more sisters he had never asked for. Pushed firmly to the back of a line, not even comprehending why he was queuing. I began to experience pain that manifested itself physically as the insecurity and emotional confusion of my new life took it's toll just as I became a teenager and I was alone. No one was close enough to listen. And I fell ill and missed important schooling time when crucial exams were due. A flash of joy came unexpectedly from behind the dark clouds as I began to sail with my new stepfather, my mother insisting it would strengthen my health. Although he was a difficult, damaged man, we formed an alliance and found companionship enjoying a mutual pleasure on the sea aboard his ramshackle catamaran, fishing and sailing. I found a sweetheart on the Isle of Wight, magical moonlit walks with a boy who adored me and I quickly learned to tempt and tease him with his eager hands and intimate probing kiss. Then a thunderbolt fell from a summer sky when my stepfather took on Peter, the son of a lifelong friend to be our crew, and I cast all other suitors hastily aside. I was hooked as firmly as a mackerel on my line.

'I went to college to finish my studies but I was a teenage nightmare back then who cared for nothing and no one, I have grown up a lot now,' Elle added quickly.

'How old are you Princess?' he asked.

'Twenty three.'

'Wow that is old,' now he was really laughing.

'Don't tease,' she returned.

'So when I finished at college I went to Jersey and moved in with this man Peter, who you must understand, completely stole my heart.'

'Does he still have it?' John asked,

'I think he does, maybe for ever,' she replied hesitantly, 'but it's complicated. Anyway I think I totally broke another boy's heart, a boy much more suitable who adored me and I just left with this man whom every one disapproved of as he was eight or so years older than me.'

'Just to change the subject girl, it's gusting up a bit, I think we should get Carl on deck and put in another reef and change the head sail.' John studied the white horses forward of the beam on the port side as they danced away from the bow. Elle felt awkward immediately realising she had become so engrossed in relating her past that she had failed to notice the change in the sea and the strengthening wind.

So they worked by floodlight with the sea picking up behind them and spray in the air, and in the glare of the mast lights the waves were hidden from them in the inky blackness around the bright deck. They were a team on the isolated, pitching and rolling platform that was *El Guero*, and this was at last, a pure, crazy and exhilarating joy.

They were past the half-way mark now, Elle frequently looked at the chart wishing away the miles. She loved being at sea but longed to arrive in the Canaries, Spanish islands that she had not seen before, not that there would be any time to explore. Landfall, such anticipation, she was already tempted to scan the horizon although she knew it to be far too soon. What would she be like after the twenty or so days on the crossing? Claire was really struggling with seasickness. How would she cope on the main passage? Perhaps she would jump ship in the Canaries. She didn't really open up to Elle about anything or to anyone else on board for that matter. Mike and Carl often muttered together and it made her think of *Mutiny on the Bounty*, as she guessed that they grumbled about John but he just simply ignored their whispers and kept his attention on the weather, the boat and to a certain extent his watch partner. She decided that she probably provided him with light relief in the long windy hours.

A better day followed. At five thirty am Elle was eating cereal with new optimism. The weather was improving and that was always reflected in her spirits, lifting them away from dark waves, and potential storms. They were heading south and by the following night, after dark fell, they should see the loom of light from the northern tip of the Canary Islands. They would leave Lanzarote, Fuerte Venture, and Gran Canaria to starboard on their course and sail on through to Santa Cruz on Tenerife. Apparently this port was the closest thing to a bustling Spanish city in the islands and she was excited at the prospect of stepping ashore. John too was cheerful especially about the fine fish restaurants he said they would find. With new found boyish enthusiasm he prepared to start the main engine which they customarily ran for the first couple of hours on their morning watch to charge the batteries. He pressed the button and nothing happened, and again, still nothing. Checking that the engine was in neutral and with everything seeming to be in order he pressed for a third time. Still nothing.

Ellie looked at him quizzically, he shrugged and dove below to the cramped engine room, the words, 'You have the con Princess,' hung in the air behind his disappearing figure.

A couple of hours or so went by with Elle so lost in sea and sky that he startled her with his reappearance. He moved in beside her to take the helm.

'Make us a coffee I have given up with that for a while.'

The sound of defeat was in his voice and the image of the crew walking ashore in search of a fine fish dinner suddenly faded. Elle was wondering how they could possibly bring such a huge piece of fibreglass safely alongside the quay with no engine but she did not think it was an appropriate question to ask, not yet anyway. They sailed on through the day and sure enough by the time she and the skipper were settled on their watch the following evening, they could detect the feint loom of light and life on the shores of Lanzarote.

The structure of their days at sea was calming and therapeutic, with Elle looking forward to landfall but almost dreading the change that would inevitably occur. Routine was something that she had learnt within a few days of her arrival at school. She washed her hair on Saturdays at lunch time, changed her sheets and penned letters home on Sundays after attending the church service of her choice. It suited her to have her life thus organised. Ever since she had left, she had tried to keep a pattern to her days whenever possible, as in a strange way it made her feel happier and able to accomplish more.

Everyday she rose at five thirty, made a hot drink for all and took over with John at six. They checked for chafe and weakness in the rig, worked out their position, wrote the log and in this way the early watches passed quickly. She dozed and read the afternoons away, helped with the main meal and by the time the clearing up was done it was the hour for the long evening stretch. Tales were to be told although she noticed the story was nearly always hers, as John gave little away always pushing her to carry on until she had finally narrated almost her whole life leading up to their meeting on the quayside. This unburdening had given her some relief in a way so she did not resist, spilling out all her secrets, gradually, as they pressed on through endless sea miles of lonely waves.

On arrival in the Canaries this routine would be broken whilst they stopped for a couple of days, shopped for provisions, filled the tanks with water and fuel and allowed crew members to let their hair down before they embarked on the next stage of their journey. She half feared this would destabilize her, and she knew it would take them all a few days to settle again when they set off for the major part of their voyage across the Atlantic.

By the end of the following day they were approaching Santa Cruz harbour but still without engine power to take them into port. When they were approximately an hour away from the entrance and the dusk was creeping around them, John called them all to the cockpit for a crew briefing as to how they would attempt to come alongside the fuelling berth in the harbour. Mike and Claire were to be in charge of fenders and to make sure that no damage occurred as they reached the wall. Elle was to be responsible for getting a line ashore as soon as it was possible. With the skipper at the helm they were to drift to the quay under a small head sail, swing into wind to allow Carl to drop the canvas as if the eighty-five foot Camper and Nicholson yacht were just a dinghy, and then they would calmly glide up to the dock.

They tacked in, the light evening breeze filling the sail. All of them were excited and pleased to have come in to the calm water of the outer harbour, and to be able to breathe in the smells of the shore. John pointed out the wall in the distance with the fuel pumps and they readied themselves with fenders and lines. Elle could not believe they were attempting such a manoeuvre but there was no alternative. As they came closer she could see a figure standing on the quay. She hoped that with some sign language and cooperation this stranger would catch a line and wrap it around a ring or bollard and throw it back to her thus securing at least one end of the yacht. Attempting a risky jump was to be avoided at all costs. Carl was to take the second line ashore to pull the stern alongside.

They were approaching the wall now at quite a speed, the bow cutting through the dark, murky harbour water, and Elle's stomach churned with nervousness, not for danger to life or limb because there was none, but for fear of disappointing her crew mates and skipper with a badly thrown line.

John, although in command of some rather unusual vocabulary at times, practically never raised his voice except to make himself heard above a howling wind or a restless sea. His complete air of calm enveloped them as they progressed towards the wall and Elle began to feel confident about the task, or rather the rope, in hand. At the very last moment when it seemed as though the bow must strike the quay he threw the helm to port and motioned to Carl to drop the thrashing sail to the deck. Elle chucked her line to the bewildered onlooker shouting in her limited Spanish with the aid of wild hand gestures, for him to pass the rope through the iron ring on the wall and pass it back to her so that she could pull the bow in firmly. Carl had already jumped ashore with a line to the stern. Those in charge of attaching fenders had done their job and the yacht bounced onto them with a resounding squeak and they were securely moored alongside with no engine power at all. Elle's face glowed with huge admiration for the old, bearded whaling captain from Nantucket and she grinned at him, her trust increasing with each day and every problem they encountered.

That same evening they had Spanish engineers, the best to be found in Santa Cruz working on the engine and as long as the parts they needed arrived the following day as hoped, they would be ready to be on their way again. They wandered as a crew through lush gardens in the sweet evening air with flowering cacti and Elle relished the almost tropical environment after the rain over the dismal rock of Gibraltar.

4

"Compromise brings harmony to both, happiness to none."

Amit Kalcintri

'Hey guys,' Elle detected nervousness in John's tone. 'How about we find a fish joint and some good wine?'

Carl replied too quickly, obviously speaking for the others and thus revealing a previous discussion amongst themselves. 'I think we are just gonna wander and have a few beers thanks.'

Well that's that then, Ellie surmised, she could hardly leave the skipper to eat alone, it just did not seem fair of the rest to behave like that. 'I really fancy the fish idea,' she ventured brightly and John looked pleased. She decided that good manners were definitely called for in this situation. So the elderly skipper and his watch partner, wandered away from the others in search of a glass of Spanish wine and some local fresh fish.

'Do you not want to call your folks?' he asked once they were seated.

'Actually I spoke to them from Gib and I think I will leave it now 'til we get there, then I might let them know I made it.'

'Do they not worry?'

'I really don't think they do,' she said and a small sad silence engulfed them. 'I will tell you more about everything when we are back at sea but tonight I am enjoying being spoilt with excellent food and wine and I thank you for all you have done to get us this far.'

'This is only the beginning the hardest part is yet to come,' he answered, the shake of his head exaggerated perhaps by the wine. 'Welcome aboard Princess,' he said, and he raised his glass to her.

The morning was a bright, sunny one and the girls found a fresh fruit market and a friendly local merchant who was delighted to deliver their purchases to the fuel quay where they were still ensconced, immobile. They bought wonderful fruit and vegetables by the case, and Elle reflected that they would not succumb to lack of vitamins and subsequently scurvy like the sailors of old. Such huge oranges and tomatoes, she had never seen produce that was so succulent and fresh in such abundance.

'Where are we going to stow all this?' the skipper's eyes were wide with concern, but he was smiling so they knew their booty met with his approval. They loaded it all aboard and distributed the boxes in every spare corner they could find. They packed the fridge carefully with the most perishable items, not that there was much space there to fill as they had already stowed a stack of dairy produce in Gibraltar. There was a festive air about the preparations that day, better than the feeling ashore the previous evening, when the crew had been divided and the atmosphere uneasy. The engine was running sweet as a nut and John intended to set sail literally into the sunset at the start of the evening watch.

After an early dinner they left Santa Cruz behind and Elle wished she had had more time to explore the island, but they had an ocean to cross and trade winds to catch. As they set out into the dark tossing seas, she watched the cosy lights of the harbour shrinking to a flicker behind them. One minute they were there, the next they vanished, obscured by a rising wave and the pitching roll of *El Guero* as she struggled to set her path through a troubled beam sea. Elle was excited. The hunt had begun to find the missing family member whose genes she must have inherited in order to embark on this mad voyage. She reached out towards John and moved to take the wheel from him, as if by being in control she could somehow hasten their arrival in the islands. The motion was uncomfortable and they would have to wait to pick up the following winds for this to improve. Claire had gone a shade of grey and retired to her bunk already and Elle too was struggling and glad to be out in the air.

'So what happened when you moved in with this man then Princess? Come on, we have quite some hours to pass now between here and Antigua. I will not judge you, only listen, your story intrigues me, and maybe I can help with it all,' he folded his arms, a listening pose.

'Help?' Ellie retorted, at once bristling and defensive. 'What exactly do you think you could help with?'

'Well I don't know advice, support, comfort anything you might need I guess, I don't mean to be intrusive but maybe I could offer my thoughts.'

Yes, she thought. Why is this abrupt, rude old sea captain interested in even hearing the story of an exceedingly confused twenty something, let alone offering advice and support? She would probably not take a blind bit of notice of anything he had to say anyway, or would she?

'I met a guy in Gibraltar I really liked.' She offered this snippet to try and switch to a completely different tack, 'His name is Ben and he has a dog called Wanker.'

'And you could see a future for yourself trapped on the rock with a boy named Ben walking a dog called Wanker, I hardly think so!' He was almost singing his words at her with a touch of hilarity. 'You are worth so much more than that.'

'How would you know what I am worth?' she snorted, 'But put like that it doesn't sound like an awe inspiring life no.'

'So come on what happened with this other guy the one you reckon means so much to you?'

She glanced at his face in the dark catching a touch of envy in his voice, for a man he had never met and a situation he knew nothing about.

'I went for the summer and stayed there in Jersey where he lived. He wanted me to go back to continue with my studies and perhaps go to university but I just wanted to stay and make a life with him. It was the only future I could envisage. Career, qualifications none of it seemed important to me at eighteen.'

'And is it now?

'Well yes, now that I am confident that I can be good at something, I want to do well and prove that I can make my own life and not depend on anyone else, but back then I didn't really care.'

I had totally ignored my lover's protestations and stayed. Peter reasoned with me far into the night but his good sense smacked of rejection and I could not accept the idea of leaving his side. This was how I wanted things to be and I was very stubborn, determined to hold onto the security he provided, not able to envisage stepping back out into my own life and the future of building a career on my own. I would surely lose him if I turned away. Why did he not want me to stay and be with him forever? I could not and would not understand, not then and still not now.

He bought an old boat on the South coast and I accompanied him to make sufficient repairs to sail it home to the islands. Our own adventure together. Swigging brandy for breakfast just to keep warm in the freezing sea air of winter. We were mad and wild and I was happy.

I hated his nights out drinking with the boys, back on the island. Excluded and rejected. I knew they had competitions to see who could bed the ugliest girl … pig pulling, they even had a nickname for their fun. I thought their amusement was somehow gleaned at my expense. I retaliated by going out with the girls. Men liked me, I could see their admiring glances but everyone knew I was spoken for, untouchable. I took a job in a bar needing to prove I could be grown up and capable.

'Although Peter's family were wealthy retailers with a chain of shops throughout the island, he was not obliged to work all the time, having fleeting spells in a managerial role, with his uncle primarily holding the reins. He had however learnt the hands on skill of his trade in London on leaving school so was versatile and capable of stepping into any role when needed. His passion was to sail and whether it was mine or not I was determined to follow where he led. When he began to deliver yachts on a semi-serious basis I was determined to tag along. It was Peter's dream to have a yacht delivery business and after going into partnership with a friend, he secured their first job. I begged to be allowed go with them to provision and cook, although I had not a clue what that would entail.

So we set out the three of us to take an old motor fishing vessel from Jersey to Ibiza via the Bay of Biscay with the wheelhouse high off the deck, in a rolling oily sea with thick fog enveloping us. It was a horrible journey. No gimbals on the stove with a small oven in which my pies flew from side to side. In the end we were limited to sandwiches for meals, cake, fruit and little else. I was a childish failure for my part on that unbearable journey and was relieved when we reached Gibraltar. On reflection I knew it was an ugly pig of a boat and ill equipped but I felt that some of the fault lay with my naivety to cope with such a situation. We walked the long path to the town in Gib., exhausted from the motion and lack of sleep, and while we were gone the customs impounded and stripped the boat to pieces suspecting us to be drug smugglers. They even dismantled the bunks and took away all our clothes and belongings. The experience really shook me. No one had ever gone through my personal belongings before in my whole life.'

'What did they find?' John leaned toward Elle with real interest.

'Nothing at all, of course, but it took us days to retrieve our belongings and the boat was a mess of broken wood and forced panels. At any rate, delayed by a week or so we finally set off for the final part of the journey to Ibiza. I loved it there as soon as I arrived, sunshine and blue sea, the farthest I had ever been from home and I never wanted to go back.

We moved into a hotel and had a blissful little holiday and I was sun burnt from top to tail and I was in love.'

With a deep sigh she carried on. 'When I had Peter to myself, every difference of opinion that we may have had vanished and we were close. We met a couple in the marina with a beautiful, small, wooden boat and after dinner and a few bottles one night they persuaded Peter to buy it, which wasn't difficult as we both adored the little, cosy floating haven we had stumbled on. A few days later Peter flew back to Jersey leaving me to stay with them, whilst he collected the cash, and *Moonstone* became our new home. Life should have become a dream come true but our problems temporarily forgotten in the excitement of the boat purchase soon rose to the surface again. That's enough for now I'm going to make us a hot drink and wake the other watch.'

'Hey Princess your bedtime story is just getting interesting, all that sun and island love.'

'Yes well I am tired and my bunk is calling,' and shutting him out with her firm reply she swung down the hatch to make hot chocolate in the gloom of the galley.

Twenty-four hours later the sea was starting to build behind them and the wind to creep more and more to push the boat from the stern. The sky was changing and one of the things she had come to admire about John was that he could read the clouds, predicting whether they held rain or strong, dangerous winds inside them. He was always, somewhat annoyingly, right. That morning with the wind starting to gust up on their stern. Everyone was on deck and they lashed the booms to goose-wing them, with the main to starboard, and the stay sail to port to balance the boat and catch all the wind.This rig called for concentration from the helmsman to keep the yacht steady.

Later John had said they might try a spinnaker, which sounded like fun and games in the growing swell. A sudden shout came, and they watched from the cockpit helpless spectators of a drama unfolding. The stay sail boom careered across from one side of the foredeck to the other, a clean sweep to hit Mike squarely on the forehead, before he could react to the warning cry, which came just too late. He was semi conscious as he was brought back to the cockpit and his glasses were smashed. What is an elderly chauffeur even doing on this trip? Elle had to ask herself. After a brandy, a spare pair of glasses, and all of them bombarding him with questions to try and find out if he had sustained more than just the huge egg which rapidly grew on his head, he retired to his bunk with a small bag of frozen peas. How quickly things can go wrong, she thought, he could have easily been knocked over the side. Let the incident serve as a warning to all of them to be super diligent, observant and careful, as this was no seaside picnic on which they had embarked. Elle gulped, a mouthful of fear of the sea, and the voyage that they had only just begun. As they were not very far out on their course she wondered if there might be some suggestion of going back to Santa Cruz to get Mike checked out properly but John seemed satisfied that he was not concussed so there was no talk of returning.

5

> "So I must be taken as I have been made. The success is not mine, the failure is not mine, but the two together make me."
>
> Charles Dickens

The next few days were uncomfortable with a turbulent swell on the stern quarter and heavy rain. The cockpit offered no refuge as the wind drove the rain across them and even the windscreen did not serve any purpose in such conditions. It was horrible below, close, with the stench of wet oilskins as they attempted to dry them and themselves between watches. Every hatch was tightly shut against weather and spray and the stale air made Elle's stomach heave. Off watch in the afternoon she wedged herself in a corner behind the windscreen where she had fresh air and a packet of cream crackers for sustenance. Maybe she slipped in and out of a doze as she listened vaguely to the banter between Mike and Carl.

John kept looking at her, concerned she guessed, by her change of habit. Usually she would tuck herself in her bunk for a while in the afternoon to catnap, but she had no need to offer an explanation for the place she had chosen to sit and would certainly not admit to a bout of seasickness. She was shivery and withdrawn, the recollection of the details of the last couple of years had caused her some confusion, refreshing her distress and misery and, more particularly, the horror and remorse at her own behaviour. Her self-examination went on and on in those days where there was little to distract her, lost in thought in the grey waves around her. The stone skipped on across a mirror sea in the version she told to John across the long night watches. No one could see down, deep below the surface, or stir and poke amongst the weed and crevices, in order to make a fair judgement of her crimes.

My promiscuity was not driven by the desire for sex alone, I know that without any doubt, but more by my often conscious and overpowering need to feel loved and cared for, cherished and protected. I realised that in making desperate choices I drove away anyone who would have been close to me. All I probably needed was a hug or two and the whole calamity might have been averted. I had so wanted Peter's admiration and affection but he seemed to drift away from me as we began to live aboard our perfect home in the marina. I wanted our life to replicate that of the Belgian couple who had filled the little boat with comfortable detail and their love for each other.

All the brass hinges on the wooden cupboards were burnished with their daily polish, and inside, crockery and pans nestled for every meal carefully cooked on the shiny gimbaled stove. Our clothes were folded neatly to fill the small hammocks made of netting that lined the spare space above our bunk seats. We began to make friends in the marina and we both undertook small maintenance jobs on other yachts to give us food and beer money. I scraped, painted, scrubbed and varnished as hard as I could to the best of my inexperienced ability, but at the end of the day after our meal around the little varnished table, the sex and affection slowly dwindled to nothing. Peter often took to the aft cabin bed before me and fell deeply asleep as soon as he lay down. Comprehension for the cause of this rejection was beyond me. I knew I was looking pretty with my public school fresh peach look, sun kissed by my first encounter with the Mediterranean. Other men were unsubtle with their admiring glances cast in my direction. I could only conclude that his wish for me to go back and continue my studies and to leave him to his bachelor ways was still hanging over us, although the subject had not been mentioned for sometime. He was pushing me away and I could feel the poison of his intention. What had I done to be so unwanted? He avoided taking the same break as me at lunchtime in case I should want to share a brief half hour with him while we ate. That he preferred to share his meal with the men folk on the marina, was a dagger in my heart, to eat alone a terrible humiliation. I worked on with no respite at midday, preferring to hide amongst my tins of varnish and brushes.

One day an Australian called Aiden turned up on our patch, a wiry tanned man with a full beard, curly hair and an appealing smile. Having spent a year travelling in Australia, Peter took to him immediately, arranging for him to sleep on a yacht that I was helping to varnish, and inviting him to eat with us and play backgammon far into the night. With his broad, quirky accent and huge laugh, we became firm friends with him and trusted him. I still hold him responsible for what happened, the boys blamed me entirely and their united stand against me, shook away the last piece of faith I had that Peter would eventually understand me. How could he have joined forces with this intruder and be so unforgiving and ruthless to condemn me? I have been over the evening of my downfall so many times in my mind, and now huddled in this draughty wet corner surrounded by tossing, angry waves, the sequence of events still haunts me.

We had finished our game after dinner one evening and I had been left to clear and wash-up with our guest as Peter had fallen asleep once more at the table and so had hastened to bed when the sound of the dishes had briefly roused him. Aiden was watching me closely when he said, 'Why do you stay with him when he so clearly does not appreciate you? You are completely taken for granted.'

I was not slow to answer him, I needed no time to find the reason, 'I love him and have done since I was fifteen. But I do hate the way he pays me less and less attention and sometimes I feel as though he really doesn't want me here with him at all.'

'I am sure that's not true, you are so lovely,' and with this declaration he pulled me gently at first, then harder towards him and we had the first fated kiss that became and deeper and more passionate as it continued, until he pulled me down alongside him on the bench seat of the small cabin. I had only ever made proper love with Peter and he had made me believe that I was little more than a silly child who had no idea about the ways of men. To find myself astride this exciting foreigner who had all the right things to say was exciting and therein lay my plight. Night after night I went to him while Peter slept until someone saw me climbing out of the wrong hatch in the middle of the night and my world crumbled around me as I walked back to the sleeping man I loved. How could I have betrayed him? I didn't even really like Aiden, the guilt began to stifle me, a thick, black blanket of shame. Why had I committed this treacherous act? Just as awful in secret as in discovery.

We planned to sail the boat back to Jersey through the canals and to my horror Peter invited Aiden to join us. I was a shameful disgrace. I was the betrayer, the whore amongst honest men. There was no rescue package for our relationship from that point on especially with a constant reminder of my infidelity by Peter's side day and night, and when we finally arrived back home I packed silently and left them. I had decided to make my way via England back to Spain, this time totally alone.

She edited the painful parts, ready to present John with an abbreviated, adapted version of her story. She would tell him only about her arrival in Spain and maybe not all of that either, as her life got worse before it got better.

At least when she had left Peter he had given her a gift and in doing so had told her that he had never loved anyone except her, which made her grieve even more deeply. Why could he not have shown her, told her, or made her feel treasured and worth something after all? That was all it would have taken to change the path of events. Tears pricked her eyes now as they did on the day the little plane flew her away from him. She rubbed hard at her eyes full of rain and salty spray.

John's strident tones broke into her sad reverie, 'Come on you are going to catch your death sat there all day.'

'I am not cold and I am quite comfortable thank you,' she replied, when in fact her limbs had locked to stone in the dampness. She really wanted to be left alone buried in her mood that reflected the weather around her.

'Well we appear to have a generator problem and Claire needs help with dinner if you could spare the time.'

He had resorted to sarcasm now to shift her, so rather unwillingly she made her way below. Stripping off her wet coat she suddenly shivered uncontrollably, cold to the core, her limbs aching with the effort of always moving carefully around trying to avoid too many bruises. Claire promptly collapsed onto the saloon bench relief clear in her face, as Elle looked as though she might take over from her in her attempt to prepare a hot meal. They still had light to see what they were doing, but the fancy electric ovens and hob were all rendered useless by the lack of generated power. She had pointed out to Claire when they were shopping, somewhat proud of her greater seagoing experience, that the cooking of large roasting joints was completely dependant on the normal functioning of the generators. When one takes to sea in a yacht nothing mechanical or electrical should ever be relied upon and sadly the people with the parts and the know how to fix things would not be travelling with them.

A large, formidable leg of lamb was lying, partly defrosted, wedged in the sink, surrounded by vegetables in various states of preparation. Elle decided to boil up some water and make a hot drink before attempting to shove all the ingredients into one pan and cook them on the emergency gas burner that had only really been added as an afterthought in Gibraltar.

Thank goodness for a skipper with foresight and wisdom! She hoped there would be no more disasters to challenge his abilities. She set about hacking (an appropriate description as the knives on board were all blunt and hers were packed away) the meat off the bone and loaded a plate with smallish chunks, rolling them in flour and herbs from the store cupboard. Certainty increasing with every piece, she could, and would succeed in making a satisfactory meal. She fried it all until it was a uniform brown as she had learnt in her not too far distant cookery classes in London. She then added some wine and a stock cube dissolved in water and put in all the vegetables including the potatoes that Claire had been planning to roast, dried herbs, salt and pepper and finally, with the lid firmly on, she secured it back on the gas with the flame as low as she could to ensure a slow simmer.

Tidying up quickly Elle was quite pleased with herself, almost smug, so she wrapped up again and scrambled back to her spot on deck before the queasy feeling in the pit of her stomach got the better of her. Claire looked like she was probably asleep or doing a good job of pretending to be to secure her exemption from culinary duties.

Well there we are, if they don't like it they can have a go themselves next time as I have done my best. She decided that if she embarked on a passage of this length officially as cook, to prepare and freeze stews and casseroles would be prudent.

John was on the foredeck seeing to the change of a rope that had almost chaffed through. He saw her resurface and made his way carefully down the deck to her. 'How is dinner Princess?'

'Cooking for a while,' she answered with a sleepy grin.

'Well you seem to have cheered up a bit anyway,' he observed.

'Maybe I needed to feel a bit more useful to everyone, and not just like some sort of hitchhiker,' she added carefully. As he turned his face to the breeze, she found it hard to catch his words. 'I never doubted your place in the team, even if you did!'

Dinner was a resounding success, a welcome change from the endless roasts, a touch on the chewy side, but with bread from the freezer, no one complained. John was extremely happy in his non-committal way, so much so that later that night he informed her during their watch that she was now on a wage of one hundred dollars a week. He would buy her an open ticket home, so the money she had safely set aside for that purpose could be used for other needs. This came as a complete bolt from the blue. 'Thank you, thank you, thank you,' she shouted to him and the waves alike, and he merely smiled and shook his head.

Nearly a week into their trip and the wind was definitely picking up behind them now, full dead astern. The trade winds, how exhilarating! Elle's thoughts tumbled about in a head that had cleared, so much lighter now than the damp corner she had been trapped in just a few hours ago, both in body and spirit. She was in charge of the galley officially, Claire being only too happy to relinquish her role as she continued to be terribly seasick and was not coping at all with the uncomfortable surprises that passage making was throwing at them.

The previous evening, after dinner, they had been sailing along steadily, when John called for all hands on deck with a sudden urgency. The guys who had just settled in their bunks were a grumpy and stumbled up with sleep in their eyes.

'Get the canvas down, all of it and fast.' A crisp, no nonsense command, and they all jumped to releasing halyards and gathering the sails into their arms as they fell, lashing the heavy, obstinate fabric as best they could. Within minutes they were struck by hard fluky gusts from all directions and Elle was frighteningly aware that if they had been carrying the rig as it was moments before, they were at risk of a disastrous knock down or even losing the mast.

'How did you know that was coming?' she shouted above the howling wind, clinging to the stays as the lack of sails to balance the boat made the rolling intolerable.

'Saw a cloud I didn't like the look of Princess.'

What could she say, she was simply astonished and impressed by his perception and grateful for it too, they could have so easily have been flattened. The following day was better and although there were clouds about, the skipper the skipper assured her that they might have showers, but they would not be subject to the strong gusts of the night before. Everything had changed for Elle, she had more to think about than just the weather and what it might bring, she had to plan the nourishment of her fellow crew. She had earned respect and had her place and a job to do as well as watch keeping. She was tired but buzzing with the thrill. That night they were to change their wrist watches by one hour in order to gradually reach the time zone of the "other side" and Elle eagerly followed each mark on the chart with welling anticipation. She could see their progress, although they still had a long way to go.

6

> "Remember you are half water. If you can't go through an obstacle, go around it. Water does."
>
> Margaret Atwood, *The Penelopiad*

Elle could not stop herself from endlessly imagining Peter relating all of their sad history to her new friend and ally Ben. How could the world be so punishingly small? She could hardly bear the idea of the conversations that may have passed between them, and was overwhelmed by her shame and foolishness. She had to try to put all of that behind her as going over and over it and trying to guess how others might think of her was a futile pastime. She was finding her feet now amongst this strange foreign crew. She had to believe that her uncomfortable past would not catch up with her, and that new acquaintances without any knowledge of her previous behaviour, would let her start afresh.

The swell was developing behind them steadily driven by the wind, like some fierce beast determined to overpower the yacht. Elle kept her eyes firmly on the bow, not daring to look back. Each wave towered over the stern and just as she thought it might flood over the cockpit submerging them, the boat was lifted as a mountain of water passed beneath, breaking under the hull, carrying them surfing down with an acceleration of speed into the watery hollow that followed each wave. This made controlling the helm exhausting as *El Guero* corkscrewed as she flew before the next one took her. Needless to say there was a fine line between maintaining their course or being turned completely upside down in a tangle of ropes, masts and canvas, not for the feint hearted sailor at all.

Lewis Caroll came to mind, perhaps his 'Snark' was after all quite simply the spirit of the sea, who when disturbed from his lair would pursue with a terrible wrath. She had never understood the poem perhaps.

> "Then the bowsprit got mixed with the rudder sometimes:
> A thing as the Bellman remarked,
> That frequently happens in tropical climes,
> When a vessel is, so to speak,
> 'snarked.' "
>
> Lewis Carrol, *The Hunting of the Snark*

Elle, having taken over all the cooking, was released in part from her morning watch to sort things out for the day. She was fairly tired as sleep was frequently disturbed and fretful. That evening, she had achieved a really tasty meal, a pot roast of chicken with plenty of vegetables, olives and wine and everyone seemed happy. Claire surfaced and managed a small plateful and then disappeared again quickly. If she had planned on losing weight during the trip she would certainly succeed for she hardly seemed to manage to eat at all and Elle felt sorry for her. The others ate hugely as on passage nourishment tends not to be just about appetite but also about the comfort that hot food can provide in testing conditions. John had been checking levels of fresh water before dinner, and there were nervous glances around the table, as they feared a water consumption lecture. Sure enough it came.

'I think we should all start to be more conscious that our fresh water is limited,' he began.

'Can we still shower?' Elle asked, fearing the worst from the look of his stern face.

'Be better if we switch to stand up washes in the shower with a mix of salt from the sea water tap in the galley and a quick rinse in fresh, and just a cup of fresh water for teeth. Never leave a tap running please. Washing up can be done in salt water for sure with just a rinse in fresh at the end.'

It all sounded pretty grim. The thought of washing her hair and smalls in seawater was not a comforting one at all, neither was staggering about with buckets of salt water in order to wash. They were all quiet for the rest of the meal and she guessed the guys were thinking that they probably had enough fresh water to continue with modest showers if they were careful.

As if reading their minds, John added, 'The problem is, we are not really sure how long we are going to be out here.'

'Point taken,' mumbled Carl, 'but perhaps the situation could be reviewed as we get further on, past the half way point for example?'

John nodded, 'I shall keep monitoring it of course, but in the meantime it would pay us to be prudent, that's all I am trying to say.'

Elle had observed that during some of the heavy rain storms they had encountered, water funneled along the main boom and ran off the end like a gushing tap. She secretly decided to find herself a bucket or two for the morning to catch this supply so that she could have a really luxurious wash in fresh water, and then use the same to wash her clothes. Knowing her luck though it probably would not rain significantly for days. She kept her idea to herself in case someone else beat her to it, although she guessed that she cared far more about hair washes than anyone else aboard.

It proved difficult washing up in salt water and even after a rinse in fresh, when dried the crockery felt sticky, in fact everything she tried to clean was tacky and dirty. Falling around trying to do any but the basic clearing up was exhausting and depressing. It did not seem to really bother anyone but her. Elle hated struggling around in disorder in the small airless living area.

Later that evening on watch, John pressed her for more of her story, so she carried on, relying on her narrative to keep her awake as having had no time for a nap in the afternoon, her eyes were heavy. She had spent her off watch time struggling in the pitching and rolling galley to sort things out and plan the meals for the next few days as best she could.

'I went home briefly to my parents, staying a few days with each, stirring up the old anxieties of homelessness, listening to all the 'I told you so's' and enduring the obvious silences when I entered a room. The weather was cold and I longed to feel the Spanish sun again. I wasn't interested in any of the advice or direction they continuously suggested. None of my family had any idea how I was feeling or what I had been through and worst still I knew they didn't really care. I knew they wanted me to disappear and not be an embarrassment or disrupt their lives in any way. My father took me riding over crisp, frosty fields in a last ditch half-hearted attempt to make me stay. Was it guilt behind his endless reasoning? I rather suspected so, he could not possibly or truthfully wanted to have changed my mind and risk me staying around spoiling his new life. I sold a few things, books, musical instruments, the trappings of my childhood that I had packed safely away and from this I managed to raise the air fare and a bit more besides in case I didn't find work immediately.

With strained goodbyes I flew to Majorca and strolled bravely (well I thought so) down the Passeo Maritimo where all the yachts were moored, in glorious windy sunshine, the familiar clack of halyards on masts was a homely sound to me. Life is all about where you feel you belong after all?' Having turned her statement into a question she looked at John for an answer but he remained silent.

'I knew I had learnt a good deal about paint and varnish under Peter's careful instruction and that I would make a reasonable deck hand.' She felt she had to make John realise that she did, even at that time have a plan even though it was rather reckless behaviour for a girl completely on her own. 'I had penned a letter to the owners of an old gaff schooner that I had greatly admired during her refit in Jersey, knowing that soon they would be chartering in the Med. and would possibly be in need of crew. I resolved to post it as soon as I secured a return address in Mallorca.'

John butted in, 'So when did you do your cookery lessons?'

'Patience,' Elle sighed, 'I haven't nearly got to that yet.'

'I love the way you are so serious in your story telling Princess, like you are reading to me from an old fashioned book or something.' John butted in again, breaking her train of thought, he didn't seem to realise how much effort and concentration was needed on her part, to be carefully selective and omit any information of which she was not particularly proud.

'You are making fun of me, my life is a serious business from where I am standing.'

'And so it should be and I didn't mean to make fun, it was not intentional, I enjoy your cute British way that's all.' He looked concerned, for an instant, as though he might be sorry to have upset her.

'I have always been called solemn and serious, unless I am actually smiling,' she complained. 'I have spent my whole life being to told to cheer up, but it is just the way I am. I have a sad sort of face.'

'I can't argue with that,' he folded his arms and smiled, 'but it's enough for me that you talk to me and I make you laugh sometimes. So what happened when you landed in Mallorca, did you get a job?'

'Yes I did, that very first night I met Mac the Smuggler. He simply sat down beside me and took my hand and shook it quickly, raising it to his lips with a quick bow, cheeky yet endearing all at once. A well-known character in the Balearics, he was nicknamed 'the Smuggler' because he got caught smuggling something, I never did find out what. He was not a flamboyant figure with an eye patch, in case that's how you imagine him, not a swash buckling type at all. He was a quiet man from Manchester, quite thin and looked like he should have had someone to look after him really, charming enough, but not someone who attracted me except as a friend and job prospect. By all accounts he did have quite a reputation with the ladies and he must have been in his early fifties when we met that evening, fast cars and many women were in his past. I was soon well informed by the barman in *Harry's Bar*, of Mac's life as a successful gambler until he had suffered an almost fatal car crash that had triggered a personality change. Serious head injuries had left him withdrawn, a reader, who never touched alcohol, preferring an early night instead of clubs and bars. Mac had a mate in Manchester who had bought a steel ketch, *The Sparrowhawk*. He had asked him to skipper the boat and oversee the work that needed doing on the hull.

So there it was, my first proper crew job, Mac said I could do the varnish work and help with the hull as well as getting things up to scratch below decks. A small wage, food and my bunk in return, it seemed fine to me. The Smuggler had a small motor launch that was his home tied alongside *Sparrowhawk* on the Passeo. He bought me supper and we shook hands on our little deal.

This is a good moment to stop, it's starting to rain and thank goodness it's the end of our stint. Look there are drips landing in my bucket!'

As she jumped up and danced about, she would never have imagined she could be so excited about collecting rain, but she was triumphant. Long days and nights at sea tend to focus the mind on simple things when all the complications of life ashore have disappeared. She could hardly wait to go to bed so as to wake up and investigate the bucket again in the morning.

She slept badly sensing the sea building and it had to be Mike on the helm. He could not hold the boat steady at all as the hull fell off the back of the enormous waves. She had worked out that if she was tossed sleeping out of her bunk (the lee boards not being high enough to prevent her flight) she would land on the toilet the other side of the corridor. Eventually she drifted off with this worry uppermost in her dreams, with memories of Mac the Smuggler beneath.

Morning brought two things, one bad the other good. No hope for the generator was the bad thing. John had worked long and hard in very testing conditions to try and affect a repair but he informed them solemnly that he had given up. They could continue to charge the batteries enough for light and use of important pumps, that is to say bilge and fresh water. The refrigeration could only be switched on whilst the engine was running. So they had to continue with no oven, no electric hob and the electrically powered toilets that used a huge amount of power had now to be flushed with a bucket of seawater. This was fine for the guys who relieved themselves 'willy-nilly' over the side, and were discussing happily about making a toilet chair astern. Elle resolved to keep filling her bucket. Her heart sank at the culinary challenge the rest of the trip presented.

The good thing about the morning was that the sun shone, with the air feeling noticably warmer and her bucket was full, slopping with the ungainly bouncing of the boat. She had a plan to wash herself and her hair and then rinse her clothes all from this one bucket, which would at least make her feel better if not entirely clean. How could living rely so much on electricity, she wondered as she chopped vegetables to make soup. She was determined to use the fresh consumables as they would deteriorate with a fridge that would not be as cold and a climate that warmed with every nautical mile. The tins she would keep until all the rest was gone. She reckoned her planning kept her sane, she was so glad to have something to occupy her. Later, she hung her washing as high as she could reach, she hoped it would dry. It would be sticky from the salt spray and initial wash in sea water, but clean. She feared for the zips on her jeans as they were all stuck, which seemed to be of enormous amusement to the rest of the crew. Elle was glad she had provided them with something to laugh about.

There was a ship that day, the first one they had seen in the seascape wilderness surrounding them. Far away on the horizon astern to port, it steadily crept up, threatening to pass quite close to *El Guero.*

Coming up on deck after lunch the ship was alarmingly near and John observed that it appeared to have altered course purposefully to take a look at them. Sure enough they were attempting to make radio contact asking if they needed anything! Elle was tempted to say 'a hot bath in fresh water,' but she held her tongue, water being a touchy subject. John replied that they were fine and requested that the ship held her course at a fair distance as they were struggling to steady their own track in the overpowering, following sea.

'Request understood Captain, safe passage for you and your crew,' was the return and they altered their course to pass a fair way from *El Guero*, which was certainly enough excitement for one day, although it was comforting to know that there was at least one other vessel not too far away. The feeling of isolation and venturing into the unknown grew with every passing day, alongside the prospect of arrival, which was still possibly weeks away, depending on the wind strength, governing their speed.

Evening watches were shorter now as Elle was spending the first part of the six o'clock take over serving dinner and trying to commandeer help to clear away. The washing up was losing its charm when one had to use seawater to do the major part of the job. Life had become more like camping than luxury-yachting.

John was bursting with enthusiasm for his evening of her story telling, so Elle was compelled to continue as soon as they were alone, although she feared some of the next part would cause her some more disquiet in her recollection of events.

7

> "When human beings love they try to get something. They also try to give something and this double aim makes love more complicated than food or sleep."
>
> E.M. Forster

'So we took *Sparrowhawk* to a small cove further up the coast where there was a shipyard of sorts with a travel lift. A Spanish company there had agreed a price with Mac to do the work on the hull. The workers chipped and banged at the rust and sang like wailing cats from early in the morning until the end of the day. For me, the blissful quiet that fell when they went home could never come soon enough. Peter somehow found us, probably from information gleaned from *Harry's Bar*. Mac was friendly and hospitable and he stayed with us on board for a few days, nothing serious was said about anything and I was a little shy of him but happy. When he came to go he said that he had met someone else. A gentle admission of the facts that landed on my head like a shovel. I wondered why he had sought me out at all. Was it politeness to tell me face to face, or did he owe me this revelation? Was it a planned revenge, or did he think that after all I didn't care?

I was ill for a few days, a virus I suppose, but I could barely descend the ladder to reach the toilet block on the other side of the yard. I was stricken with a melancholy fog, carried on a southerly breeze from the cold, stormy waters of the Channel Islands. Mac looked after me although I never really told him the whole story, he became unexpectedly a good and caring friend and never asked for details of my relationship with Peter.

When I felt better I made friends with a German scuba diving club that was based in the village. Mac never wanted to go for a drink or a meal ashore, and I was lonely. They were a friendly crowd with whom I felt safe, often dancing late into the night in the small bar within walking distance of the shipyard. Their company made me feel happy, desirable and normal again. Although they all spoke in German most of the time it didn't seem to matter, they laughed with wide smiles on their handsome bronzed faces. One of their company was a boy called Gunter, we became inseparable in the evenings chatting about everything and anything, occasionally pecking on the cheek on parting but nothing more intimate. After we had known each other for a couple of weeks he said he had to return to Germany to see his fiancé as they were to be married at the end of the summer. I knew it was foolish but I really liked this boy and although we were only friends, I felt broken hearted that he was promised to someone else. I thought that in some ways he had led me to believe that he liked me enough for our friendship to develop into a relationship. Was I just a game, a diversion for the handsome German Romeo? We talked into the small hours and I fell unwittingly asleep in the spare bed in his room, so I didn't return to *Sparrowhawk* until the following morning. When I turned up, Mac was as cold as the steel of the hull, in fact he would not even look at me, avoiding my eyes whilst calmly telling me that he was taking me that same day to Palma. He said he had found me a job as a stewardess on a motorboat belonging to a man he knew. I tried to explain that I was only friends with Gunter, and that my banishment was a huge over reaction, but he insisted that my behaviour was appalling. He was jealous of course, he couldn't bear my friendship with the German. He coped with my feelings for Peter but that was different, that was before, and he knew that our relationship was over, but this new competition for my affections was not to be tolerated, in fact worse than that he had decided to punish me.'

'That wasn't very fair,' John chipped in.

'No I didn't think so either, I was only finding a friend my own age rather than sitting in, night after night while Mac read his book. You don't think my behaviour was appalling as he suggested do you?'

'No, not at all, it was a perfectly normal way to behave, and I really don't think you even owed him an explanation of where you were or who you were with.'

'Mac had up to this point been very kind to me though, so I suppose I should have explained and that would have been the end of it. He never gave me a chance to even try.

Anyway he marched me down the quay at the marina in Palma like a naughty child and all I could think about was the letter I hoped to receive offering me the job I wanted so much. The motor boat was horrid and the owner, a self made millionaire sporting gold chains around his neck and wrists, was probably in his sixties. He was not someone I took to at all, or trusted on first impressions. His wife appeared some twenty years younger and had a baby on each hip, so she had her hands full. There was a fair bit of winking going on between this podgy, well-indulged man and Mac that spoke volumes. What did they take me for, some sort of stupid bimbo? When Mac was gone he showed me to a cabin and informed me that I must share the space with him. You can guess what I did at that point.'

'You left,' John said, his voice almost a whisper.

Of course I did, running, tripping and blinded by tears, back down the quay to the marina office as fast as I could dragging my suitcases, wounded and scolded, just exactly how Mac wanted me to feel. He had thrown me to an animal, a horrible, disgusting, and perverted man with a taste for abusing young girls, in front of his pregnant wife. Making them share his cabin and ordering them to his bed.

'Yes, I fell gratefully into the fold of a family I knew, right there on the pontoon where their small day launch was moored. I had met them previously through Mac and I blurted out everything to them. They were kind, but admonished me a little for not being more cautious of the Smuggler in the first place as they knew him of old. Luckily they insisted that I stay in their apartment until I found another job, in exchange for some babysitting and help with shopping and housework. So I moved in immediately and spent happy hours at their finca in the centre of the island, gathering almonds and oranges straight from the trees. I was ill again brought on by the upset of it all and was glad to be safe within a family. Some weeks later I had a letter about my dream job, finally, at last. Basically, the skipper, Don could not think of a better way of stopping my begging letters than sending me a ticket and an invitation to join them in Puerto José Banus, as soon as I possibly could.

John interceded, 'How wonderful that must have felt, someone was watching out for you and helping with your plan then.'

'I suppose maybe the same someone who put *El Guero* where I would find her? Perhaps tomorrow I will tell you a bit about life on *Talisman*.'

'Did you see Mac again after that?' John asked.

'Yes he came to look for me in England when I was in London doing my diploma, to set things right, and to apologise as best he could, admitting that he cared for me. I told him that I could only ever be his friend and I never saw him again. Maybe he will reappear who knows, somewhere along the line, but I never really forgave him for that cruel business.'

'Nor should you, he was not much of a friend to you in the end, he betrayed you and I don't think you deserved that treatment.'

'Thank you, I know you would say how you truthfully feel, even if your opinion is not necessarily what I want to hear.' Elle replied.

'I care for you too Princess and I would never treat you badly, so what is your answer to me now?' he announced.

She answered slowly for fear of his anger, but a tiny trace of her own slipped into her tone of voice. 'I should hope that your feelings are just those of a caring friendship and nothing more inappropriate.'

'Well and what if they were as you call it, "inappropriate" although geez I am not sure why I should be condemned, we are man and woman are we not?' He was getting cross now and his tone was changing. How could she reply without making this worse?

'I would lose all the respect that I have for you, it's as simple as that. Those misplaced feelings of yours would threaten the wonderful trusting friendship that we have built, and that would be sad.' He looked a long way from understanding what she meant on this subject so she moved on quickly. 'It's time for the change of watch so I'm going below to make everyone a hot drink if that's okay with you.'

'Count me out Princess,' came the answer and she thought it might take a while to repair this rift of watch keeping partners, for Elle was angry and hurt too. He should never have placed her in this position, what was he thinking of, at least fifty years her senior at a guess, not even a father figure, grandfather more like!

The early watch dawned with a soft orange sun and new excitement, the unsettling mood of their conversation of the previous night carried away by the trade winds. Surely they were almost the other side of the world for there were flying fish, (Elle had always thought them to be imaginary) rising, multicoloured from the crests of the waves, the sunlight catching their wings as they leaped and soared. She and John stumbled dangerously around the pitching deck to try to save those that lay gasping for breath on the wet teak, casting them quickly back into the spray. Elle feared that those on the boat would not survive the shock of impact nor the duration of time out of the water.

She enjoyed real warm sun on her face and for the first time shed her big coat in favour of a shower proof top against the spray. She climbed through the back of the wardrobe into Narnia but in reverse, leaving the winter season behind her and finding herself suddenly in summer. How could she ever cross the ocean by air, after the gradual achievement of sailing across, the bruises, challenges, and sheer joy of the weather and the sea? Time to mull over the promise of arrival in another land, a different season, and the completely unknown culture of the islanders, all would be new to her.

'Hey guys, look here.' A shout from Carl verging on hysteria, as he adjusted the chaffing sheets on the bow. Clipped on to the pulpit, he made an amusing sight shouting, pointing and waving to them.

'A whale, I think it's a whale!'

John set off to the bow to look and Elle was quick to follow, noticing his worried glances as she ventured onto the side deck moving her clip as she went.

'It looks like an outsize black and white dolphin.'

'Killer whale,' John answered her. Of course he would know.

It appeared to be playing under the bow and they were all kneeling in the spray, clipped on, but holding tight as they leaned perilously far out over the stanchions. She had seen dolphins but this was the most amazing thing ... this great fish actually enjoying itself in the frothy waves breaking under the bow. They were stunned into silence, marveling in having the chance to share the extraordinary sight.

The creation of a main meal continued to be a challenge but the crew were appreciative and grateful, as they knew that conditions below were taxing and the lack of the generator to provide the hob and oven was nothing short of disaster. That night she managed a pretty good macaroni cheese. Of course to achieve a sizzling brown top to any dish was impossible using one sole burner, and involved a relay of saucepans to keep things hot, wedging things in corners all around the galley to stop them escaping with the pitch and roll and glide of the yacht. No more attempts at cakes either so watching their supply of sweet things diminishing, she had taken to putting a rationed amount out for each watch to make them last. Elle wished she and Claire had envisaged this turn of events when they were in the supermarket. At least her insistence on large quantities of fruit being purchased in the Canaries, (purely for selfish reasons) was a successful move and the produce was lasting well.

As soon as they had settled on their evening watch, John started the conversation, maybe to set the subject and avoid the awkwardness of their uncomfortable discussion the previous night. '*Talisman*, tell me then, what was it like?'

'What was it like? It was quite simply like coming home,' she said. 'From the moment they met me at the airport in Malaga it was as though I was safe. This couple that I had never met before simply wrapped me in their warmth and care, opening their home to me and folding me inside. I had never experienced such a sanctuary. Don taught me so much, about varnishing, painting, sailing and generally maintaining the sort of boat that will always be my favourite choice, old and wooden with as many gaff sails as possible!

After my season with them I went back to the UK determined to cook like Janie, more certain of an ambition than I had ever been. Up until that point I had lived in a day to day blur, not really having any idea of an ultimate goal. I found a cookery school in West Kensington where after six months of lessons, I attained a diploma specialising in the cooking of the French Provinces. Of course it was expensive and I had no money or parental support, (although I was silly enough to ask only to be firmly refused). I managed to secure the job of housekeeper in a residential hotel in Bedford Square that was almost wholly staffed by foreign students. In return for my board and lodging and a token wage, I had to organise the young foreigners and ensure that the hotel was clean and that all the laundry was processed efficiently. I was able to go to my course in the afternoon and in the evening I cooked steaks in a restaurant to earn some cash. Sometimes I got back to the hotel very late and tired out, the only part of my day that I enjoyed was my time writing out recipes and learning to cook them in West Ken. I was almost chubby on *Talisman* but in London turned I into the skinny thing I am now! Mac the Smuggler came looking for me to ask for my forgiveness for what he had done to me and although I was lonely and secretly pleased to see a friendly face, I made it clear that I was still upset with him.

In a city of busy people I was isolated, the students in the hotel barely spoke English, and every time I met a man he just seemed intent on dragging me to a bedroom. So I threw myself into working and cooking and when I eventually found my way back to my room I was exhausted, often too tired to eat anything other than bread, cheese and fruit.'

'Mac must really have been fond of you though,' John pointed out the obvious that she had already worked out for herself.

'Yes that's why he did what he did I suppose, frustration and jealousy.'

'Complicated old life, isn't it Princess? So that's your tactic then to catch sea captains in your web and then spurn their honest attentions?'

Elle was not sure she liked the way the conversation was going again so she quickly laughed it away.

'He nicknamed me his Sea Witch. I haven't seen him since our cup of tea in London and I wonder when he will appear or if he is back on the Passeo Maritimo whistling at the girls, his usual old self. When I had finished my course I went to work for a Dutch baroness in a house in Essex, cooking and helping with the horses. It was fun but she didn't pay me very much. Although I had a sweet cottage to live in, all I wanted to do was get back on the sea.'

There was a boy there. Should I tell you about that? Brother to the stable girl I shared the cottage with, and husband to a comely Essex lass with his baby on her hip not 6-months-old. We held a cottage party in the summer and I cooked my first big spread. As soon as he came in the door I could not look at him for our mutual attraction was fierce, and ugly given the circumstances. We snuck out to a bank by the pool the other side of the main house. We lay there spooned together for a while with his face buried in my hair. Gently he raised my dress and began to wriggle his hand inside my silky underwear and to touch me, softly, intimately. We still had not even kissed each other but both of us knew what had to happen, without question or delay. I pushed against him feeling my desire quicken, as he felt for the core of my passion. The rising tide inside me had burst like a wave upon the shore, followed by the fan like sprays upon the beach that follow, translucent mother of pearl, lacy effervescence. I pushed his hand away to find he was far inside me then seeking, his own pleasure close. Afterwards we had lain innocently there and looked at the stars, knowing we would have been missed but powerless to think up a suitable story to explain our joint disappearance. In the weeks that followed, he just appeared, on his bicycle, or in his car, having left some lame excuse for his absence at home. In the warm straw of a stable or on the damp grass again by the pool late at night, we simply could not deny ourselves. Everyone knew, of course they did, and his sister left her job before the season end, and moved out of the cottage to try and sever all connection with me. I was a terrible destructive force and I wreaked havoc on a whole family, driven by some unknown motive because it certainly brought me no pleasure, apart from sexually, I had disgraced myself again.

'I flew back to *Talisman*, and helped Don with the varnishing and we discussed what I should do to get to the Caribbean and that's how I ended up sitting in the destroyer pens next to *El Guero*.'

'So glad you did too,' John admitted. This was an unexpected sign of appreciation from the hard old sea captain. She was getting to know a little more about him with each long night watch.

With a rope tied firmly around her waist Elle climbed down the swimming ladder, rung by rung, waiting a minute or two at each level. She was not sure about the wisdom of a swim at all, but she needed to be distanced from the endless, wallowing motion of *El Guero* as they drifted becalmed in the Sargasso Sea. The others all leant over the guardrail to watch her go bravely into the wrinkled, weed strewn glass that was the surface of the water that day. The sea has so many moods and this smooth calm was a favourite of Elle's, although with the combination of the sails flapping and the inevitable huge mid Atlantic swell, the boat was far from comfortable. The ladder dipped in and out of the water on each roll of the hull, giving her a taste of the temperature, which was surprisingly warm, so having reached the last rung she let go. She panicked immediately feeling alone in the water. Floating away from the hull, the movement of the boat became hugely exaggerated and far worse than when standing on deck. With each roll she could see a sizeable area of the keel before the boat, like a giant pendulum went back the other way. Elle was overcome with terror that she might somehow be sucked beneath.

Claire, instructed to be on diligent shark watch, shouted down, 'Imagine how your little wriggly, white legs look, tasty and tempting to the fish that might be looking up at you.'

'That's enough for me then,' the swimmer said, 'I'm coming out now'. Grabbing the ladder she was quickly back on deck, amidst the guffaws of her fellow crew members.

'Well at least I was brave enough to do it, more than you lot. I shall now treat myself to a fresh water wash down and be cleaner than the rest of you put together.' Just as she set off clinging on in search of her bucket the one cloud that none of them had even noticed directly above their heads, produced a heavy burst of tropical rain. The others dashed below for shelter, but Elle grabbing her sponge had a blissful wash, clipped to the guardrail for fear she should fall over, still in her bikini while the others reappeared in oilskin jackets. 'Why are you putting more clothes on, when you should be taking them off?' She came to the conclusion that she was definitely the odd one out amongst them.

John shouted, 'Come on you guys, stop messing about, the breeze is coming back.' Sure enough with the whitecaps on the tops of the swell reappearing, the sails were straining to be let out and reset. Up went the genoa again in double quick time and with the wind came a bit more stability. Elle went below to tackle the galley and fix a feast, the short swim having improved her appetite.

They were all happy to be firmly on the move again at supper as with each nautical mile and each adjustment of the clock coupled with the exciting feel of tropical sun on their faces, their destination became more real. The following day she resolved to enthuse everyone into polishing and sprucing everything, including themselves, so that when they came into English Harbour in Antigua, they did so with flourish, proud of themselves and the boat, although *El Guero* had let them down spectacularly in the engineering department. She and John laughed about this on their early watch. 'Lets see if you can get the others motivated. Potential mutineers the lot of them,' he said.

He was right there, she had been well aware of grumbles, mainly concerning water rations and distribution of chores, but she supposed this happened on most vessels. At sea a boat becomes the entire world for a crew, an island where conflicting personalities are trapped together. When Carl and their valiant chauffeur took over at eleven, she attached a rope to a bucket and gaily tossed it over the side to pull up some water to start to give the heads a good salty scrub followed by a fresh water wash. She was well aware that this particular chore was a bone of contention with no one particularly wanting to volunteer. Elle was no angel of cleanliness, but she hated a dirty heads more than anything. She leant over towards the turquoise waves, and when the bucket was brimming full she tugged. John grunted a warning but too late, she was, as always, determined in her purpose. To pull up a full bucket of water with the boat doing six or seven knots down wind was a stupid idea and she sensed something go in her back with a sharp, knife like pain and the bucket was gone, riding on the last wave into the distance, surprisingly enough still full of water.

'You were very lucky you didn't go overboard with the bucket, you stupid, stupid girl.' John was angry but concerned. 'Whatever were you thinking!'

'Well I don't suppose I was, thinking I mean,' she said piteously. 'And now I think I hurt my back a bit.'

'I am not at all surprised,' and with that he left her and hurried below to scrutinise his charts as if his show of concern had exposed a weakness.

Elle was possessed with the spirit of a twenty two year old, stubborn girl who thought she could never make any errors concerning the practicalities of life at sea (a know-it-all). This time she knew for sure that she had made a big mistake for the punishment was swift to ensue. Lying awake the morning after the day before, it was as if she was encased in a box, moving her head to either side, or up and down caused excruciating pain. She knew the best thing she could do was to move before she locked up, solid. So she slowly slid down her ladder to the cabin sole and started to quietly rummage in one of her bags for the anti inflammatories that she knew she had packed somewhere. Claire woke up.

'What on earth are you looking for at this time of day?' she asked, cross and sleepy.

'Pills, I hurt my neck okay, pinched a nerve or pulled a muscle or something, anyway its really painful and I need to go on watch.'

'Some in my drawer here,' and she reached out to open it. Grabbing the packet with a yip of thanks, Elle went slowly in search of tea. The pills were numbingly effective and she hoped to have enough until things improved. John said nothing about it but she could see him watching, and she knew he had observed that she being very careful in the way she moved about and it was pretty obvious that she was not moving her head very much. He came back up into the cockpit after a session at his chart table, grinned at her and then announced, 'We should make landfall on our early watch tomorrow Princess.'

'Brilliant, that's really good news, well done with all your navigating and stuff.' Even from inside the painful box in which she was imprisoned this was such fantastic news.

'We'll save the celebrations until we see something on the horizon okay.'

Neck or no neck she would be up tomorrow, well before her watch, straining her eyes for the loom of the lights from Antigua, should they make landfall where he predicted. She could hardly believe it and cursed her injury.

PART TWO

The Caribbean

8

John…

"I didn't have feelings for her in the wrong way, she completely misunderstood me … I have always been hopeless at finding the right words to fill a moment. I had simply wanted her to understand that we had a special bond, nothing more complicated than that. Without wife or offspring, at seventy-three years old, I could have been the grandfather she so longed to meet, although I believed him to be considerably older than me. How old is old, at my age I don't have so many years in front of me now. Apart from the occasional romantic dalliance ashore, there has only ever been the sea and I. In Elle I recognised the same awe and respect for wind and water, as we studied the tossing landscape of waves and clouds together, night after night. I dreaded landfall and the thought that she would walk away from me down the gangway towards whatever life had in store for her. There would be men there to corrupt and misuse her, to seduce and betray. I feared for her, that was all. I made a plan to try and forbid her from stepping ashore but I knew I could not hold on to her for long, as a butterfly against glass, she had to be free.

I tried my best to woo her to stay for the trip to Nantucket by endeavouring to make it sound exciting, but I knew the attraction of the chance to cruise around the islands with new friends of her own age would prove irresistible. And then there was her grandfather, I could not deny her that meeting, she had to achieve her ambition.

She was brave, charmingly naive and confident, yet irreparably damaged. When I had to let her go I could only hope that her choices in life would lead her on a safe, calm passage."

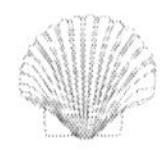 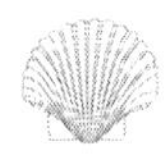 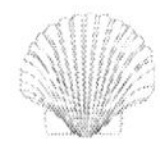

Bracing herself against the side of the cockpit with binoculars, sure enough, right on cue, Elle could detect a loom far away in the distance. A small bird had settled on the deck as if for a short rest, which after all the long days away from land was totally astonishing. Only the pain stopped her from dancing around with excitement.

'What's our ETA then skipper?' She couldn't wait to ask.

'English Harbour about what you Brit's call teatime, so the plan is to drop the hook in the outer harbour, and wait for customs to come out to us whilst having a leisurely meal and general tidy up. I think shore parties can wait for tomorrow,' he added.

The guys won't like that one bit, she thought, but said nothing.

'You have the con Princess, I am going to see how we've done with water and fuel,' John headed below.

'Well you must have a fair idea, you've been checking every five minutes,' she muttered but he had gone below and was luckily out of earshot. The engine started up, maybe, just maybe, there might be enough hot water for showers.

John reappeared. 'Seems like we did rather well as we have the port side fresh water tank more than half full and plenty of diesel.'

'Does this mean that my hair is like white straw and all my zips are ruined for nothing?' Her exhilaration dissolved into a pool of irritability.

'Well no, not for nothing as we could have been becalmed for weeks, or become completely lost, and been at sea for far longer.' John stated the case for the defense but Elle had not finished yet with her prosecution.

She came to a quick decision and after her watch before starting any food preparation she headed down to the sanctuary of John's aft cabin, passed through to the heads where the bath tub lay and locked herself firmly in, armed with bubble bath and shampoo. She was going to have a hot bath and no one on the ocean could have stopped her. Funnily enough nothing was said at the table later, probably for fear of causing a row, but Elle noticed all the crew appeared to have had showers, but it was only she who had dared to fill the bath. She felt so much better, all her anger washed away in the sheer luxury of real cleanliness. The heat of the water had freed her neck a little too and she was sure it was a trapped nerve that would release in time.

The rest of the day passed in a haze of happy anticipation of feeling the ground beneath their feet, seeing the beauty of a Caribbean island, eating different food, and in Elle's case, hopefully seeing familiar faces. The boys were talking nonstop of pina coladas and rum punches. Everyone had thanked her for the grand job she had done in the galley. She could not say it had been easy. She was covered in burns on her hands and bruises on her legs and she longed for the boat to lie still at anchor. She had learnt a lot about making a meal out of nothing on one single burner, something she had not envisaged on first sighting *El Guero*'s well fitted galley with two electric ovens and four hobs. She was perhaps grateful in one way as the rest of the crew now held her in much higher esteem than on their first meeting. She had gained confidence and felt proud. Some of the self-hatred swamping her since she had left the Channel Islands, was softening its grip. Maybe she would fare better in these new islands full of warm favourable winds, bananas, spices, pine-apples and the promise of meeting a long lost member of her family whom she had never seen.

On rounding the corner under Shirley Heights they suddenly left the swell behind them and glided into the blissful calm of the hideaway hurricane hole. Elle was overcome with exhaustion, pain and relief. She normally kept a remote distance from her other crew members excepting her watch partner, but she found herself joining in with their noisy exuberance.

'Come on guys are we ready to tidy the mainsail away and drop this hook or what?' John pulled them up.

Safely at anchor at last and for now Elle was content to sit on deck, nursing the ever painful back of her neck, absorbing her surroundings. Boston whalers and dinghies were buzzing around between the yachts and the shore and she searched eagerly for a familiar figure or hull. Most of the boats must have recently arrived but yet they had not seen a single yacht on passage. A surge of restlessness to begin her search for a job as cook for the charter season swamped her, alongside a desire to leave *El Guero* and her crew behind her in favour of more suitable companions.

John was holding firm in his decision to refrain from shore parties until the morrow. They would move early to the fuel quay, wash down, fill up with fresh water and then anchor stern to the main wall for a few days in order to provision for the trip up to Nantucket. He had already made several comments alluding to his wish for her to stay aboard for the next leg of the journey which she had ignored so far. Soon she would have to tell him that she planned to stay in Antigua, her priority being to find a suitable position amongst the charter fleet.

After quietly writing home with a glass of champagne beside her, Elle passed the rest of the evening curled on the genoa bag, listening to the others celebrating their arrival and watching her view change as they swung gently on the anchor. She decided her letter made the crossing sound more fun than it had been in reality. She sounded far happier and more confident than she actually felt, and she wondered if her father would read between the lines. The sounds lulled and seduced her, palm trees rustled near houses nestled in the greenery and out board motors hummed leaving the lap of their tiny wake breaking against the hull. She was both serenaded and bewitched by the chirping of the tree frogs. The gentle ambiance of the tropics soothed all and she fell asleep, the first proper rest in almost a month.

Elle's first letter home…

> *Dear Daddy and all,*
>
> *We docked in Antigua yesterday and after a long twenty days at sea, land was an exciting and welcome sight. We made on average quite a fast passage. For the first few days we zoomed along with an encouraging south-easterly – then we had some squally days of no wind so we motored all that we could afford in order to use fuel wisely and then inevitably the engine had to go off and we rolled the scuppers under literally for a few days. But I swam, yes only me, and we caught fish, played backgammon and pulled the sails up and down like maniacs at every sign of a breeze. The winds played tremendous sport with us. In the end the trade winds, accurately predicted by the skipper, hit us and with a force eight or nine behind us we flew to Antigua, carried along by the most tremendous waves, which frequently threw themselves into the cockpit. The motion of the boat was the most exhausting thing making life such hard work and oh so many bruises and aches and pains I feel like an old granny!!. I now still find myself gently swaying and this is not entirely due to the champagne since our arrival.*

The boat made a staunch trip – no leakages or disasters EXCEPT the loo broke so we made a rushed repair on the one in the crew quarter but it had to be flushed with salt water, so it seemed fifty percent of my time off watch was spent struggling to fill small jerry cans in all weathers with salt water. I have severely wrenched my back trying to pull up a bucket when we were sailing fast down wind. 'Stupid girl' doesn't change!

The generators packed up too, the main problem with that was the loss of the oven so we had to cope with a gas burner, which was ok but no bread making which was sad. I invented yeast type muffins which I sort of baked in a frying pan. After a few interesting attempts I got it down to a fine art, filling them with jam, cheese, honey, raisins and God knows what else. Anyway they were exceptionally popular amongst the midnight galley mice raiders. We didn't really run out of anything – the green bananas I had so carefully chosen ripened in about twenty four hours so I threw them all in the deep freeze in a desperate attempt to save them and you should try it – they were really delicious if a little mushy, surprising how the skin protected them.

I found it really was a skeleton crew, six hours on watch was a long time. We tried to keep as industrious as possible as a horrible lethargy slips over one at sea. So we washed the boat and spent time attending to chafe, mending sails and splicing ropes. I showered and washed my clothes in rainwater as the salt made me so sticky, and broke all my zips.

Well here we are, over 2,500 miles on the log in all.

Antigua harbour is beautiful, – lusciously green right to the waters edge, like a freshwater lake. Totally unspoilt, there don't seem to be tourists like in Mallorca. It is the end of the rainy season here and in-between the huge thunderstorms, the sun is the hottest I have ever known. It is strange to think of you all shivering in November weather. I hope you are all suitably jealous but be comforted by the fact that the mosquitoes are atrocious and starving hungry to eat me. The tree frogs are weird they sort of sing and bleep as dusk falls.

I still really can't believe that I am here and I may soon find John.

I have more money then when I set out having been paid for the crossing, also an open ticket home so I feel a bit more secure, although I don't know what my next plan is yet. I will write again soon hopefully with news of grandfather.

All my love

Elle

Waking with complete surprise at the calm, her neck solid from an awkward sleeping position, she lay still. Would Peter be proud of her now, had she redeemed herself a little by her crossing of the Atlantic? Must she do everything she did in order to imagine he might be pleased with her? Was he truly all that mattered? To her horror she realised she had been well and truly eaten by mosquitoes while sleeping. Served her right for falling asleep on their dinner table.

As they came alongside the fuel quay Elle was numb, shocked by the strangeness. The heat, odours and sounds of the Caribbean made her dizzy, along with the confines of the gripping pain in her back and neck. If only that would ease she could cope.

'Missee! Hi there! Look at me missee! What's your name, I am Norman, you want a taxi? You need laundry doin?'

'Hey Girlie, I take your laundry, I'm Josephine, remember me?'

A sea of black faces rushed up to her as she stood on the deck while they tied up. Bewildered by their friendly, demanding approach she wanted to answer all so as not to disappoint, but tongue tied she answered none. The tree frogs grew deafening with proximity, a background to the scramble for her attention.

Elle's neck was worse and she struggled to help the guys with a wash down while they were tied up to the fuel and water berth. Claire was off, lining her bags up on the quay, desperate to leave behind an experience that had been a nightmare for her. To fly out, away from an island that she had already christened "this godforsaken dump." Each to their own opinion. She was desperate to find friends, see Lulu and familiar faces, but was forbidden to step ashore until John deemed it to be the right time. Later they were to move over to take a berth stern on the main quay with all the other yachts, so she had high hopes of escape. She respected John for his abilities as a skipper and excellent seaman, but this imprisonment on the yacht was totally bizarre and she was not sure how to react. Patience, she told herself, he had to let her go soon, he was not her keeper after all.

The wash down accomplished, they cast off and moved into a convenient gap stern to the main wall. She still couldn't see any yachts she recognised, just a group of black faces again, calling and clamouring to provide them with anything they might need.

'Hey Skip, here, over here, Skip, Skip.' So confusing and distracting from the job in hand of tying up and dropping the gangway down. Within minutes the boys were off to *The Admiral's Inn*, and now Elle felt wary after all of stepping ashore on her own. She didn't want John to notice this sudden fear of the unknown, but he was watching her closely and saw his chance to keep control of his fast disappearing crew.

'Wait Princess, how 'bout we get scrubbed up and I take you for a special lobster diner at the Ad's to say thanks for all you did. It's not been the easiest of crossings and you surely stepped into the breach there in the galley.'

Elle was exhausted, the relentless six hours on and six off taking their toll perhaps and the dreadful pain, worse since the wash down, nagged on. To be chaperoned ashore this first night was not such a bad idea, certainly better than being confined by either the skipper or her own nervousness of venturing forth alone. Maybe he was worried about her for the right reasons, the caring supervision of a father figure.

She gave in, 'Yes okay, I might have a rest before, if we can go ashore about six as I would like to see if my friends are here.'

'Sure thing, I shall go fix us a table for seven or so and we can have a rum punch first.' He had turned back into a gentleman, her jailer no longer. Maybe she had imagined that situation and she could forgive him for trying to cling to the camaraderie that was theirs.

They wound their way through the mangroves along the short path to the pub, the tree frogs deafening, and surreal. Standing in the doorway to *The Admiral's Inn* were Harry McNamara and his girlfriend Marie, two of her dearest friends from Mallorca and as they threw their arms around her, she found herself crying. She half expected Mac the Smuggler to be the next to appear.

'We made it!' They all chattered at once and John stood in the shadows clearly taken aback that his Princess was thus enthusiastically welcomed so far from home shores.

'I must go have a drink with my skipper AND he has booked us a lobster dinner, I'll catch you in a bit.' Elle could see them looking John up and down and wondering. 'Don't worry it's just my duty to do this right now okay, but later I need to ask you about work and stuff.'

'Go on then, but you must come and stay with us, soon as possible, soon as you pack your stuff,' Marie whispered urgently.

Marie's sixth sense had warned her that Elle needed to leave

El Guero and she was right. Elle made a plan to tell John politely over dinner that she would be jumping ship the following morning leaving him free to hire new crew to continue on with the journey north to Nantucket. John had gone in and Elle followed to find him sitting at a table set for dinner with two pina coladas in front of him. What a strange pair they must have made. There were many faces at the bar turned towards them.

'Thank you,' she said. An awkward silence fell between them as she sipped the sweet, thick, cold drink which had to be the most delicious cocktail she had ever tasted in her life. Ice-laden flavours of coconut, pineapple and spices, she could barely detect the hidden rum.

'I thought I hated rum,' she blurted out.

'That's because you never tasted *Mount Gay*,' John informed her and she had to agree.

'Total nectar, absolute bliss, even my neck feels better for it.'

He laughed throwing back his bearded head and those at the bar grew even more interested not attempting to hide their blatant stares.

'I have a confession to make Princess,' he said solemnly.

'Okay, and what's that all about?' she asked nervously.

'You look so cute and tanned with all that blond hair bleached by the sun, I feel as though I am throwing you to the wolves bringing you here, and I can see all the guys looking at you and I can't bear what they might be thinking, which is why I wanted you to stay on board and not come ashore at all.'

'I sensed that,' she replied kindly, 'but John I have to leave now and find my own way, that was always the plan.'

'Not coming to Nantucket then?' he asked sadly, anticipating the answer.

'No, I must find a job here, as a charter cook, just as I intended and then probably cross back for the summer in the Med again. I will be fine, I am tougher than I look.'

'Oh I know that Princess, I just worry for you that's all.'

'Well don't,' she answered with a laugh, but he was not smiling.

Later at the bar they met a nurse. She was prepared to visit early the next day to manipulate her back to try and free the trapped nerves or whatever it was causing all the pain. John walked her back after dinner with little further discussion, and Elle was happy in her cabin to start packing her things. The space she had shared with Claire was strange and empty, she missed her, although in the end they had not bonded, having little or nothing in common. After the days of anticipation and the hardships of the passage, finally the silence was an anticlimax.

9

> "There are worse things I could do,
> Than go with a boy or two"
>
> Anonymous

Stiana, the wonderful old wooden ketch that Harry McNamara skippered was moored just up the quay and it was no problem for Elle to move her things down one gang plank and up the other, but not so easy to say goodbye to John. He seemed sad, almost cold and business like that last morning as he gave her not only her wages, but also an open ticket home as he had promised. For her part Elle was glad to be moving back amongst her own breed, with Marie's open chatter hard to beat. The nurse came early as she had promised and Elle was beginning to feel the therapeutic healing effects of her rough treatment already.

She wondered if she would ever see John again, but knew their paths would be unlikely to cross, and she allowed herself a little sadness too. She had learnt so much from him, not only concerning the weather and good seamanship but also about herself. *El Guero* disappeared at dawn a couple of days later and there, for Elle, lay a chapter closed.

She and Marie made a huge bowl of rum punch, thick with Caribbean fruits and spices to celebrate the arrival of more familiar faces and vessels as they docked after passage from the Canaries. Her friend's sister was amongst them so Elle shared her excitement and began to accustom herself to the relaxed haven of English Harbour.

A name like McNamara befits a sturdy Scot, but Harry was a wiry, bespectacled New Zealander, with an oversized laugh for his short stature. An excellent seaman but fond of imbibing more than a few ales when tied to the dock. He had quite a temper as Elle discovered after a beating him several times at *Monopoly*. The board, houses, hotels and money were dispatched swiftly over the side to float away across English Harbour. Petite, lively Marie completely adored him. In the fierce Caribbean sun, the arrivals were safely moored and the planter's punch was ladled to all from the stern deck of *Stiana*. The crews wandered on the quayside, glasses in hand and the banter was joyous yet friendly and calm. Elle was realising the beginning of her dream of island life amongst her kindred spirits, and looked forward eagerly to the arrival of Lulu who was already out on a charter but was soon scheduled to return to English Harbour.

All was serene, until Harry took his shirt off.

'Excuse me mon but you must keep your shirt on, please.' The two local policeman seemed to materialise from nowhere.

'I'm too hot.' Harry grinned at them, which didn't really help at all. He took a step back from their slightly menacing proximity and the next part happened quickly and inevitably. Being more than a little wobbly from the rum he fell backwards over the edge of the quay and into the water between the boats. Elle could only presume the two officials had figured Harry's plunge to have been intentional and disrespectful for they hauled him from the water, scraping the skin off his legs and promptly handcuffed him.

His knees were bleeding and grazed and he had somehow managed to secure a nasty cut to his forehead. Marie ran to *Stiana* and gathered up the first aid box pushing through to attend to his injuries. To Elle's horror the situation escalated as the two policeman now proceeded to arrest Marie and ignoring her protestations concerning Harry's bleeding legs, they led them both away in the direction of the police station. There was no quicker way to dampen a party. Elle and Marie's sister tidied up quickly and followed the path to the station. On arrival they were told they were not allowed access to the prisoners who were to be held separately until the following morning when conditions of bail would be discussed. Elle felt terrified for them, it all seemed unjust and unreasonable. This was not home territory and apparently there was no room for argument or discussion.

Sadly they returned to *Stiana* to wait. Elle felt uncomfortable in this suddenly hostile environment where she feared for her friends.

After little sleep they returned and were allowed in to see Marie at her sister's firm insistence for reassurance of her well-being. She was sitting on a wooden bench in a cell with straw upon the floor and a bucket. Her face stained with tears she told them that in the night one of the men had promised her freedom in return for sex. At this revelation she began to cry afresh and neither of the girls could calm her. Having decided not to broach the subject of this disgusting behaviour with Marie's jailers, Elle demanded of the man who appeared to be in charge what could be done to free her friends.

'Two hundred US dollars each Miss, before midday, are the terms of the bail, otherwise they must serve the sentence given.' Elle knew to argue would be futile and more than likely she would find herself locked up next to Marie, so studying his unrelenting, weathered, black features she turned away determined to raise the money long before noon. She was learning fast, these locals were not to be messed with. It was their island after all. John could maybe have given her an insight before all this had happened and saved them the distress. Clearly the commonplace antics of the yachting fraternity in the Spanish Islands were unacceptable in this part of the world, although the atmosphere had led them to believe otherwise.

Elle could have raised the bail money from her own personal funds but it would have left a huge hole in her emergency kitty.

After discussions on the quayside she discovered to her relief that everyone was prepared to chip in small amounts and placing a note in the housekeeping cash box on *Stiana* she took the rest to make up the four hundred dollars. Her friends' release was secured without much ado and although she understood the authorities needed to make a point about the behaviour of visitors to their island, she wondered if it all was a cover up for an easy way of fund raising for the local constabulary.

Unsurprisingly Harry and Marie had had enough of English Harbour for a while and so planned to sail on down islands fairly swiftly as their first charter was booked to begin in St Lucia. Nothing was to be lost by being there early. Luckily Elle stumbled upon Ted, a man she knew from her days in Jersey, who was skipper of a comfortable yacht called *Bonaire*. He invited her to stay rent free in exchange for some cake baking and took her in with a rather fatherly, even proprietary air, having an inkling of her troubled times in the Channel Islands.

Elle was thin and even more waif like than when she had arrived in Gibraltar if that was possible. She found the roasted peanuts in the islands irresistible and was barely ever seen without a bag tucked in her pocket. These and the thick coconut and pineapple shakes served in the marina bar, without the rum, kept her sustained, and the occasional cold beer but Elle had never been a drinker. She went to *The Admiral's Inn* in the evenings for the sociability and to look for work. Pushing her way through the intrusive undergrowth she remembered her first impressions of the place that represented everything that enchanted her about the Caribbean. The tree frogs had competition with the steel band playing outside the terrace doors of the pub leading out onto a decked area, where people were sitting softly talking and small black children were dancing to a rhythm that spoke directly to their limbs. Cheery bartenders, whizzed blenders mashing bananas for daiquiris, and crushing the ice to a milky white, frothy pulp. The air was steeped with the scent of fresh spices from the islands, sugar syrup and golden rum. She was aware of the open stares of so many crewmen, blond and tanned Peter look alikes, whose hungry eyes she tried to avoid, by lowering her own.

A cheeky Australian managed to catch her out on more than one occasion. Not unlike Aiden he had the most engaging regard when he looked at her, with his full ginger beard and mop of uncontrollable curls. A naughty small boy. They became firm friends, and he would take her in the blistering afternoons, the air shimmering in the heat, to walk to lonely breezy beaches, where they would hunt for lizards. He left her sitting high upon the rocks whilst he dived for lobsters. He had an invention all of his own, a mad, novel lobster-catching apparatus in the form of a shaggy floor mop attached to a long wooden handle. Entering the water awkwardly with this tool, he would dive down deeply amongst the rocks on the seabed and plunging the mop between the cowering lobsters, he twisted it violently back and forth. Trying to protect themselves they quickly became entangled firmly in the fronds of the mop and he simply drew them out, returning to line up his catch on the rock in front of his applauding companion. Geoff adored her and was triumphant when he made her laugh and smile as Elle had always been inclined to be in the shadow of the solemn side of life.

On one of these occasions he caught her eye and the air between them changed. Feverishly they tore off each other's swimwear and made happy, passionate love on the rocks, he having carefully placed a bundle of their towels beneath her. It was gay, abandoned bliss, and luckily no one saw them there, for their behaviour was surely breaching island etiquette. They washed each other in the sea and Elle felt drugged by love, sunshine and the warmth of the water on her naked body.

No tension existed between them, no discussion of past or future. Geoff was on holiday using the villa belonging to his aunt so soon his vacation would end and he would fly away back to his home and work in the States and leave her with their memories. They spent hours there at the private house tucked away from prying eyes. His aunt had installed a water bed for remedial purposes for her bad back, but Geoff and Elle had found another use for it other than sleeping in their endless hours of fun.

'I will write to you, I promise,' he said in those last few hours before he left. 'I don't want this to be the end of us.'

Elle shook her head as if to agree. It could not be the end, but she knew it would be. Their time had been fun and carefree but he was not cast to reappear in her life. She saw his sincerity, it shone from his face, but she would forget him. It was her way. He was a brief but shiny stone in her path and she could sense John shaking his old grey head in exasperation.

'Geoff gone then?' Ted gently inquired, 'not sticking around for Christmas?'

'Yes he's gone, oh my gosh it's Christmas next Tuesday,' Elle replied, 'I suppose it's time I seriously came down to earth and looked for work, if that's possible in this distracting place. It certainly doesn't feel like the week before Christmas, no one even seems to mention it here.'

Ted winked at her.

Robin, a short, mousy haired crewman aboard *Bonaire*, butted in, 'I heard the Ocean charter fleet are in looking for a cook or two.'

'Thanks Robin,' Elle grinned at him across the cockpit table, taking a look at him with fresh eyes, thus singled out in being able to help her. He seemed to grow taller with his pride.

Elle knew that Harrisons, the main charter company operating from English Harbour, had a small fleet of these spacious yachts. Ocean 71s, being of course seventy-one feet long, had specifically been designed and built in England for the charter market. Fast sailing sloops with luxurious accommodation and large deck saloon and cockpit, they were an extremely popular choice for groups of Americans to charter in the islands and were normally fully booked throughout the season.

After making enquiries in the office on the quay, the following day she scrubbed and brushed before making her way to an eleven o'clock coffee appointment with Chris Ryll, the skipper of *Ocean Sun*. He had, according to the girl in Harrisons, a French fiancée, who was an exceptional, out of this world sort of cook but finding it hard to work together without arguments, she had taken a job and gone north to St Barths with another vessel. All a little bizarre Elle thought, especially if they were planning to marry. Anyway that state of affairs had nothing to do with her.

She scanned the bar from the door having a slight advantage as he would have no idea what she looked like. There was only one man sat by himself with papers and forms in front of him and she was ninety nine percent sure it was him. Dressed in white uniform style shorts and a pale blue shirt, he had to be a skipper. She was right as when she approached he stood, she saw he had *Ocean Sun* embroidered on his shirt pocket.

Elle caught a whiff of body odour and noticed the dark stains beneath his arms as he pulled back a chair for her and introduced himself. Not an unattractive man with his neatly trimmed beard and blue eyes but the underarm problem and his slightly shifty nervous manner were both decidedly off putting. Greetings were exchanged awkwardly, and Elle sat down.

Chris began. 'As I expect they told you in the office, *Ocean Sun* is one of the most popular of the Harrison fleet with back to back charter throughout the season with quick changeovers. What I am trying to say is mm, it's very hard work and the cook has to be well organised and professional, with all her menus planned and the boat always well stocked and ready. My fiancée, Florence was brilliant at this so she will be a hard act to follow.'

Elle felt defeated before she had even opened her mouth but she was not, absolutely not, going to let him realise this. He was so insufferably smug.

'I am more than qualified, although I am obviously not as experienced as Florence. I took over the cooking on the crossing having to be adaptable to a variety of testing situations including total loss of generator power mid Atlantic.'

'Yes Elle,' and so saying, from his paperwork, he produced a hand written letter. 'I have a letter here received by Harrisons, in which the skipper of *El Guero*, John was it, mm, praises you highly.'

Elle was visibly shocked as she had no idea John had done this for her to facilitate her finding a position.

'I have another reference here,' she said quickly as if to confirm the genuine content of the other, 'from the Dutch Baroness for whom I cooked and kept house last summer in Wiltshire whilst she was busy showing her horses around the country.'

He took it from her and read studiously which gave her an opportunity to look at him more closely. His hands were pudgy, Elle always studied people's hands and often their feet as well, should they of course, be barefoot. She suspected that his palms might be sweaty like his armpits as he did appear to have rather a nervous air about him, frequently emitting a sound, not really an 'um' but more just a 'mm' both when he was mid sentence and when he was reading. His stature also suggested he probably loved his food and wine as for a young man he was distinctly on the chubby side. She did wonder what Florence was like and why an engaged couple who were presumably used to working together, had chosen not to carry on doing so for the forth coming season.

Chris broke into her reverie, 'Mm, well, you do seem to be what we are looking for, if a little inexperienced, but I expect you will learn quickly. We are going up to St Barths next week, probably setting out on Boxing Day or thereabouts, for a shake down cruise and you could meet Florence and gain a few tips from her as she has done the last two seasons aboard *Ocean Sun.* Mm. So you could move aboard next weekend if it suits, and start to find your way around the galley. In fact come around tomorrow morning and have a guided tour, mm, there's a plan.'

'Yes Chris, how exciting, I would like to do that,' Elle said and rising she took his proffered hand and gave it a firm shake, confirming the dampness of his palm just as she suspected.

'Until tomorrow then,' and she took her leave.

As she walked back to *Bonaire* she could not help but feel a little pleased with herself. A job on one of the busiest boats of the Harrison fleet, but with the pride came a shiver of nerves. She would go back now and spend time going through recipes, menus, and making stock lists. She could do it, she knew she could but a certain amount of homework was essential.

At least, knowing the existence of Florence, she was confident she would not have to suffer the advances of Captain Ryll but with her feeling of slight disdain, would she in fact have any confidence in him as a skipper? This would come in time, or not as the case may be. She needed to feel safe at sea. There were plenty of reefs, rocks and gusty winds around these islands. Back on *Bonaire*, the crew was ecstatic on her behalf and Robin even more proud then ever, for having been the one to give her the tip. Ted gave her a hug but made a face showing he was sad to lose his little ward so quickly.

A commotion of shouts came from the jetty as the locals gathered to offer their services to a new arrival, and Elle and the others piled on deck to watch.

'*Solstice?*' Elle squeaked unable to sustain her normal quiet composure at the sight of the navy blue hull and gleaming teak decks with Lulu trotting down, fender in hand, her glorious brown curls shining in the dazzling brightness of the Caribbean sun.

10

> "The sea has never been friendly to man. At worst it has been the accomplice of human restlessness."
>
> Joseph Conrad

Later they met in *The Admiral's Inn*. The two beautiful girls were happy to see each other.

'How was the crossing with your Yanks?' Lulu was feverish to know.

'Well,' Elle began, unsure of how to put the strangest, probably most exhausting few weeks of her life into a sentence or two. 'We did watches six hours on and six off, the cook was horribly sick so I took over in the galley, and the best part was I got paid!'

'That sounds amazing, how did you manage all the cooking and stuff? I was terribly sea sick too so I wasn't much help to anyone at all. I hope it isn't going to be so rough all the time when we go out on charter or I shall be the worst stewardess in the islands! Gosh Elle look at that stunning Rastafarian at the bar. I think I am in love.'

Elle shook her head in exasperation, 'Lu you never change do you?'

All questions concerning their crossings were instantly set aside, Lulu was off on another tack now for the young man in question could not take his eyes off her, no man ever could and he made his way to their table, drink in hand.

‘Ladies,’ he said with a low bow, ‘may I join you.’

They both nodded, Lulu rather too enthusiastically.

‘Boogie,’ he said with a grin, showing his extremely white teeth often found in handsome men with dark skins.

‘What about Boogie, what do you mean,’ quizzed Lu totally non-plussed, twisting a curl about in her fingers, which made her look all the more fetching.

‘It’s his name silly,’ laughed Elle, Lulu was not always the sharpest, ‘this is Lulu and I am Elle.’

‘Wonderful girls,’ he said, still grinning as he looked from one to the other.

‘We work on charter yachts,’ volunteered Lulu, ‘we have just crossed the Atlantic and met up again, we last saw each other in Gibraltar. Do you live here, what do you do?’

‘Yeah I look after a yacht for a guy an I do varnishin’ and stuff around de harbour, I have a first class team for the all general maintenance jobs on de yachts so you can tell your captains. Give us a recommendation.’

The girls were entranced by his lazy native drawl and his dreadlocks. Elle could not stop staring at his hair and wondered what it would feel like to touch it. Boogie was totally smitten with her companion she could tell. He saw only Lulu.

Suddenly an idea came to Elle that being a local he might know something of her grandfather. Surely the old man would be a celebrity having lived in St Lucia for forty years and people would know of him.

‘You don’t ever go down to St Lucia do you? Only my grandfather lives there and I wondered if you had heard of him.’

Boogie scratched around in his amazing head of hair, ‘No I don’t really ever go down to the other islands, I got me everytin’ I need right here in English Harbour.’

So that was that. Never mind she would hear of him from some other source if she persevered, she knew she would. It was only a question of time.

'You girls fancy a row boat ride out to my yacht?' Boogie was pressing.

Lu spoke up, 'I suppose we could for an hour or so, Elle do you have to be anywhere?'

Elle was torn then with not really wanting to go and play gooseberry, but also not happy with Lu going on her own. They had only just met this guy and neither knew anything about him.

'Okay,' she said reluctantly, 'just for a bit.'

So they found themselves being paddled gallantly across the harbour towards the mangroves on the opposite side where there were a few yachts on deep water moorings away from the hustle bustle and comings and goings of the charter yachts. Elle could not help but notice the beautiful varnish and polished fittings on the dinghy and if that was anything to go by the boat itself would be amazing.

'I bet the mosquitoes are even worse over here,' mused Lulu as Boogie skillfully paddled past the vessels lying in the still, dark water overshadowed by the leaning undergrowth.

'This is a real hurricane hole, isn't it?' said Elle.

'Yes you all safer in here when it's blowin' mon,' and with this he swung the dinghy on a paddle to bring her neatly alongside a smooth varnished wooden hull, with a well designed gangway so they could simply step aboard.

Tying the tender deftly, Boogie motioned them down the companionway and followed the girls into the deep belly of the yacht. He sat them around the table and busied himself in the open galley area making tea, leaving them to take in their surroundings. Elle was stunned. The combination of acres of varnished wood and Persian red fabrics on bench seats with masses of cushions everywhere certainly gave the yacht the luxurious feel she deserved. Boogie put Bob Dylan on the stereo and lit the oil lamps to give a soft glow all around. Elle suspected he was a master of seduction and hoped her friend would not fall too hard. Having served them with tea he produced a joint that

Elle firmly refused, and Lulu too but in the end she gave in and agreed to a tiny puff. This was all she took much to Elle's relief.

Boogie and Lulu chatted quietly, they seemed to have a lot to talk about. Elle allowed herself to snuggle back into the cushions and weirdly she began to be able to recall and piece together a few more fragments of her dream she had had the previous night. It should have been Geoff romancing her in the dream but no, it was Peter.

She had felt him all around her when she awoke, his touch, and the feel of him, the security of his love she had always craved was there in the colour of her sleep. They were sailing together, being as one, living entwined and then horribly he had pushed her away again, leaving her to awaken to just the aching trace of him floating about her. His presence hanging like a ghost.

Elle guessed the dream must have been inspired by the last time they had been together, for shortly before *Talisman* brought her to Gibraltar he had come to visit her in Jose Banus, having left his new girl in Mallorca. He had visited especially to be with Elle, just with Elle. She had cooked him a meal with her newly perfected culinary skills, impressing him and although he was somewhat distant, they had loved each other again for one night. Then he had gone, delivering her back to *Talisman* with uncomfortable politeness. Would this one night of joy haunt her forever now and taint her dreams. The line between dream and reality grew paper thin with sleep and on awakening she struggled to separate them.

'Hey sleepy head, you are far too comfortable there and you look dozy to me,' Lulu crashed into her reverie. 'We should get back don't you think?'

'Yes we should, I have homework to do, I am inspecting my new galley tomorrow so there is loads I should be thinking about!'

Outside the day was closing in already much to their surprise as neither of them had sensed the time passing. Boogie skimmed them back across the calm of the harbour and kissing them on both cheeks, was gone with a wave and his broad signature smile.

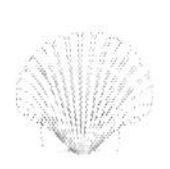 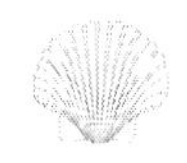 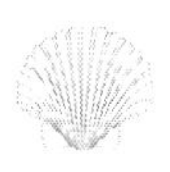

Darling Daddy,

Thank you for your telegram, such a lovely surprise!

I am at the moment transient between boats but I have been offered the cook's job on an Ocean 71 called Ocean Sun. She will be based here whilst chartering for the season, which is ideal for me. El Guero's plans were so undecided and so much work needed doing before she was fit to cruise or charter. I left with no hard feelings except a sad skipper who is sorry to lose my fish smoker. He insisted on giving me the money to fly to find John, if he is indeed in St Lucia as we suspect. So that's a fantastic bonus.

Ocean Sun is the cream of all the charter fleet here, and I am the envy of all the other cooks seeking work.

I am slowly becoming accustomed to this paradise, such a sleepy way of life and the black people are different in their ways. Last night I smoked a local fish called a dorado on the quay here and collected quite a crowd of fascinated crews. I couldn't have brought a handier gadget with me, perfect to amuse the charter guests. Ocean Sun is virtually brand new. The galley is out of this world and fully air-conditioned.

I can't believe it will soon be Christmas, black children are already caroling at the end of our gangway.

I miss you all so much…

Yes she did miss them, it was true, but she knew within two days or even a few hours of arriving back there she would feel, left out, unwanted, a burden on her parent's busy full lives. This was her place now, she was building her new life.

The next morning with the strain of looking for work off her shoulders, Elle walked confidently down to *Ocean Sun's* gangway, and climbing carefully she kicked of her shoes on the stern deck, knocked loudly on the teak, and called out a hello.

There was a crew member wiping down with a chammy in the centre cockpit who she had not noticed until he stood up.

'Hi, you must be Elle,' he called. 'Welcome aboard!' Dropping his cloth he sprang to the aft deck to shake her hand. Elle immediately took in his height and slenderness, as well as his hair, so blond he could almost have been an albino. His skin was freckly and not particularly tanned and she guessed he must burn easily in the fierce sun and wind.

'I'm Gray,' he said with no preamble. 'I am to show you around as Chris is in a meeting over in the office, and before I forget we are invited to the Harrison pre-season Christmas drinks at the house on the hill tomorrow. If you come around just before six we could all walk up there together.'

'Thank you, thank you very much,' stammered Elle as she looked around her trying to take in the yacht that was soon to be her home for the winter.

'How many crew are there?'

'Just the three of us, she is quite easy to sail and the guests sometimes join in or get in the way, one of the two! Chris is the lazy one, plots a course and then feels he should have the rest of the day off, while I clean, sail and wash up!'

Elle already had the impression that the long, white haired man, was full of resentment towards the skipper. She followed him down into an enormous saloon with a large dining table to seat six on one side, with the chart table and instruments tucked neatly opposite. There were two steps down to the galley on the port side with a hatch to pass food through to the dining area. To starboard was a small guest cabin, and further towards the bow were another two smaller cabins, one of which was he informed her, was the skipper's lair. In-between there was a heads and in the forepeak there were two identical bunks.

'One of these bunks will be yours and the other mine, although when we are empty you will be able to have one of the guest cabins for a bit of privacy.'

'So we are the only crew then, no stewardess at all?' The situation was slowly sinking in, and Elle needed clarification of her duties. 'All the housekeeping jobs, laundry and things, do I have to do all of those too?'

'Afraid so, but I help with bed making, changeovers and general tidying and cleaning, it's up to us really. You send the laundry ashore wherever we are, uniforms, the lot and if we sometimes have to wait a day to collect so be it.'

'It sounds like too much to do, but I suppose if Florence managed I will.'

'Well there were, let me tell you, masses of rows, which is why she has gone to another job. She is one fiery French lady and Chris can be, dare I say it, an idle pig not paying any attention to the work of his crew.'

Elle was surprised at his willingness to tell her all the bad things at this early stage. Could life on *Ocean Sun* really be that hard?

'Come I will show you down aft.' he said ushering her through a door at the stern end of the saloon.

They passed through another heads, which seemed a strange layout, to reach the double cabin aft, making up a total of six guest beds in all. On the other side was the access to the engine, which lay under the cockpit.

'The boat sails really well, and we often have races with other sister vessels, so we have a good time, even though it is hard going when we are constantly on charter. They are nearly always Americans who come and they really know how to enjoy themselves when they are on holiday. Most have them have been before as well so we know what to expect. They send a list of food preferences on booking which makes it easier for you to stock up and plan your menus before they arrive.'

'Sounds helpful. Could I please have one more quick peak in the galley before I go?'

'Of course.'

Gray showed her the galley again opening all the drawers where plenty of saucepans, baking tins and a food processor were neatly stored.

'Florence was a top class cook, I hope you can manage.'

'I do too,' replied Elle thinking thanks for the vote of confidence, Gray, give me a chance! With that she took her leave assuring him she would be there on time for the drinks party the following evening.

That night Ted cooked aboard *Bonaire*, he really was an extraordinarily good cook and Elle knew she would be sad to leave this gentle sanctuary. A raft of young locals attached themselves to the side of the hull in the dark to sing carols, and she marveled at the strange novelty of Christmas amongst tropical rainstorms and hibiscus, when there should have been cold, grey days and holly. Elle was happy, and Peter was almost forgotten, for the first time in ages.

Christmas in England had always been the worst time; everyone celebrating bringing the reality of her fractured family home to her even more. There had been no place in which she belonged, she was always the awkward, difficult one. On this side of the Atlantic she was both liked and appreciated.

The following evening Elle met with Chris and Gray as arranged and they walked up the hill behind English Harbour to the Harrison family home hidden in the trees overlooking the port.

'Who will be there tonight?' asked Elle.

The other crews of the Harrison charter fleet plus a few friends, usually,' said Gray.

'You have obviously done this before then?'

Yes they hold the same drinks every Christmas before we all set out with guests.'

Chris was notably silent, glancing about him as he walked in his own kind of nervous way. Elle preferred people who were open and easy to understand like Gray. She was not at all sure about the skipper. They arrived at the door of the disguised wooden dwelling, which was delightfully camouflaged amongst the mangroves. Mrs Harrison welcomed them to a huge living area, which to Elle's fascination seemed to have gaps in the roof to let the rain in to water the vegetation growing inside the house as well as out. A simple dwelling, but luxurious and stylish at the same time.

Mr Harrison was an elderly man, Elle guessed he must be eighty or more. He remained seated in his comfortable armchair, simply raising his hand to greet the familiar faces, and enquiring gently the names of the new.

Elle was in awe of the friendly chatter of all these crew whom she had never met nor seen before, excepting the occasional face she recognised from the bar. Mrs Harrison, who seemed to have taken her under her wing, introduced her to a friendly chap called Freddie. Tall, dark, loose limbed and fidgety he had an engaging smile. A little boy in a grown man's body.

'Which boat do you work on?' Elle asked.

'*Fandango*,' he said, struggling to drink his punch through the mass of fruit floating on the top. Elle feared he might choke he drank so awkwardly.

'If you look down there you can just see her through the trees.'

Elle followed his arm and could just see a large, steel ketch on one of the private moorings.

'I like the look of her round stern, a lovely shape, what design is she? So stately and important.'

Freddie laughed at her description, 'She's a Phillip Rhodes, there are a few about, not that many though. She is privately owned so not a charter vessel at all. We are just three guys on board, the skipper never takes on girl crew sadly,' he added, 'but you are welcome to visit.'

'I am on *Ocean Sun* for the season, but I have a secret mission to find my grandfather who sailed over here forty years ago and bought some fishing boats in St Lucia.'

'Well then you should ask Mr Harrison as he came over here at about that time and he might know of him, or have known him in the past.'

'Thanks for telling me I might just, if I see an opportunity.' On glancing over she saw that there were people chatting, entirely surrounding the elderly gentleman's chair.

'You have a slightly local accent, if you don't mind me saying. Did you grow up here?'

'Sort of,' Freddie grinned, 'Bahamas, well spotted.'

He was struck with her, she could tell, he too was extremely likeable, with almost a stutter as he chose his words, and a definite charming air.

'Perhaps we could meet at the pub for a drink sometime?'

'Perhaps we could, oh look, no one is with Mr Harrison now, would you introduce me?'

They walked across and Freddie motioned for her to follow his example and sit cross-legged on the floor next to the old man's chair, so they could command his attention without standing over him.

'Geoffrey, this is Elle, the new cook for *Ocean Sun*.'

'Pleased to meet you Elle, and good luck for the season.' He bent down to shake her hand.

'I was wondering,' Elle began, nervous now, 'if you knew of a John Mathias who might have arrived in the islands about the same time as you?'

'I most certainly do remember him, young lady, and yes, he did arrive here the same year as myself, but he sailed on down islands to St Lucia and took up with a Doctor fellow named Snoddy as far as I know. Intent on fishing they were, the pair of them.'

'How exciting, I shall just have to wait patiently until I have the chance to find him which I am sure I will at some point. Do you remember him, what was he like?'

'Yes a tall, striking man with deep blue eyes, not unlike yours now I come to think of it.'

'My father's sister my Aunt Anne is the only one to have been out to stay with him but that was quite a few years ago, and she spoke of fishing trips in rather ramshackle craft.'

'That sounds like the John Mathias I knew,' and he laughed softly. 'Look after this one Freddie boy.'

With this they felt themselves dismissed and taking her leave of her new crewmates Freddie accompanied her back to *Bonaire*, with a promise to seek her out in the very near future.

Elle caught sight of Boogie paddling Lulu towards the beach with her hand trailing in the water, she looked dreamy and content and Elle hoped she would not have her heart broken by her fascinating new beau.

11

> "It's life I think, to watch the water.
> A man can learn so many things."
>
> Nicholas Spark, *The Notebook*

The day had come to join her new yacht and crew. Christmas had been strange. Elle wondered if any of her family spoke of her at home. She had managed to telephone her mother to say they had arrived but had regretted the effort and expense as her mother's limited response of 'that's nice dear,' or something similar had left her sad and disappointed. She had attempted quickly to describe the thrill and excitement of landfall and arrival in the islands after the harrowing Atlantic crossing, but she could tell her mother was not really listening. She never did.

They had opened champagne and eaten well on *Bonaire* thanks to Ted, whilst sitting in the shady cockpit watching dinghy racing in the harbour. All the yachts owning small sailing tenders of any variety and there were many, were joining in, and Elle wished she could borrow one.

Afterwards there had been drinks in the Inn of course, which lively though it was, lacked something, and for the first time since he left, she missed Geoff. They were writing to each other but the post was slow and the distance between them made it difficult for Elle to believe she would ever see him again.

She found herself placing her trusty cookbooks on a small shelf in the galley of *Ocean Sun* and arranging her sharp little knives in a drawer. Ready for action. Chris had shown her to the small guest cabin she was privileged to use until the first guests arrived and she stowed all her belongings neatly wondering how many times she would move in the forthcoming months. Already from *El Guero*, to *Stiana*, on to *Bonaire* and now to *Ocean Sun*. Not bad in less than a month, but hopefully she could stay put now for a while.

'Gray will go with you to town tomorrow to stock up a bit before we set sail for St Barths,' Chris shouted down. 'Tonight we will eat at the pub.'

'Lovely, thank you,' Elle replied.

Opening the hatch above her new bunk wide she lay down for the afternoon with the collection of recipes from her cookery diploma that she had kept all together in a big blue binder. Time to think about what to cook.

Whilst engrossed in studying fish dishes and lunchtime easy meals in case they were sailing, Elle fell asleep. The soft breeze on her face, through the hatch, was delightful and the mosquitoes during the quiet of the afternoon, were sleeping too...

She was sailing again through calm, crystal clear, Caribbean waters with Peter. A calm intimacy enveloped them as if they had been at sea for months and would be forever, on a small wooden boat. The cosy interior as she looked down was too spacious for length of the craft. Dark wood, a chiming clock, cushions everywhere. Then suddenly, a pontoon, suitcases and he was telling her she had to go, had to leave. When she looked at his stern face it was not Peter at all but Mac the Smuggler, standing there. The mist of her dream cleared and Elle awoke with a start. Anger, hurt and humiliation, all combined to form a cloud that suffocated her previously optimistic mood. Why must she keep dreaming these situations when she never thought about them during her wakening hours? Gradually the recollection of the dream faded and she let it slip away, until she was left with only the hollow emptiness of rejection and bewilderment.

'Would you like a shower Elle?' Gray's head appeared down the hatch, 'before me and Chris snaffle all the hot water.'

'That's very gentlemanly of you, I will,' she said reflecting as she said it that Gray was not a man's man, in fact she would not be at all surprised if he was gay. He was quite womanly in his ways and comments, most men would just dive in and use all the hot water without a second thought. She had to build a strong friendship with him, as they were to share not only a cabin but also all the chores throughout the long season. Somehow Elle knew any problems she would have on board *Ocean Sun* would not be instigated by her crew mate.

After a pleasant dinner with her new team, Elle had a drink with Boogie and Lulu who were sitting on bar stools or practically sharing the same one, much to Elle's embarrassment. After she had listened to their amourous flirting for a while she excused herself to Chris and Gray and returned to her cabin to read. She lamented that she had only had her friend to herself for a very short time because since Lulu met Boogie she never had any free time, for girl talk. Elle was never a party girl, always secretly preferring a comfortable bunk and a good book. By the end of the day she was past her best, she was a morning person and always would be.

Dropping off to sleep with a chirping lullaby of tree frogs, she tried not to listen for one mosquito in particular because once she started that, she would be awake all night. She had lathered herself in deterrent, which would hopefully stop them bothering her. The first few weeks had left her looking like one big, itchy mosquito bite but she was now, she thought, beginning to build up a sort of immunity, or though some said it was the rum in the blood that was the best protection. One pina colada a day, Elle surmised, would hardly be enough so she resorted to the cream.

Suddenly she snapped out of her sleepy half awake state.

Someone was on deck, on the foredeck to be exact, she had not heard him or her come aboard and she suddenly felt terrified. The next thing she knew a pair of bare feet followed by two muscular brown legs dropped onto her bunk through the opening. It was Chris.

'What on earth are you doing?' I think you've got the wrong hatch. Your cabin is the other side isn't it, or am I in the wrong one?' she struggled on, trying to find an explanation for his behaviour. 'Are you drunk?'

'No I just came to kiss my new cook goodnight,' he said and lunged at her pining her down for there was not much headroom, attempting to kiss her mouth whilst tugging down the thin sheet, and grabbing roughly at her thin nightdress, with eager hands.

'Get off me,' Elle growled, and with all her might she pushed and kicked him over the side of her narrow bunk. There was only one way for him to go and he fell down awkwardly onto the cabin sole with a loud crash, knocking her book and an empty cup off the shelf as he went. The cup smashed making an ugly dent in the polished floor.

'For goodness sake, I could have broken my neck, you silly girl.'

'Me, silly? I would have thought you were the one who should be called silly. Attacking me in the middle of the night! I thought you were engaged!' Elle was furious now and grabbed for her dressing gown, wrapping herself quickly, defensively. 'I shan't be staying that's for sure so you can explain why to your precious fiancée and Gray or perhaps I should?'

She looked at Chris's face and could see the reality of her threat sinking in. He hadn't bargained for rejection or the consequences that would follow if his plan took a negative turn. 'Not at all bright,' she could hear her mother's favourite description when she encountered people who were darn right stupid.

'Please, please no, I'm sorry okay, I misread the situation and

I have had a few drinks. Sometimes girls like you will sleep with skippers. I didn't mean to cause offence.' He was groveling now.

'Well this girl is not one of those girls who automatically climbs into bed with the skipper. Just let me go to sleep and I will think about it in the morning, and don't think Gray doesn't know after all the noise or perhaps he's used to it. Maybe you have done it before.' With this last comment she pushed him out of her cabin and slammed the door, and reaching up she pulled the hatch down as well so there was only a small gap for air. Gradually, her anger subsiding, she fell asleep.

Breakfast was a solemn affair. Gray was quite obviously aware of what had occurred, the bulkheads of the yacht being little thicker than a double sheet of marine ply. He smiled at her a few times catching her eye when Chris was reading at the table, rolling his eyes and shaking his head. Elle went to the skipper later when he was seated at his chart table, planning the route north.

'I had every intention of packing and returning to *Bonaire* this morning, but that wouldn't help either of us. So I am prepared to carry on and give the job a chance, as long as you promise never to behave like that again.'

'Thank you Elle. Mm. I'm sorry. I assure you I won't.'

She walked away feeling she held all the cards with him now.

They sailed to St Barths, a fast sunny beat through bouncing seas. Elle could feel her skin burning and hair bleaching after the first day. She tried to attach a scarf around the latter tied at the back underneath to protect her head from the fierce wind and sun combination but Chris remarked that it was fetching so she took it off and shoved it firmly in the pocket of her shorts.

St Barths was a glorious island, quite a lot smaller than Antigua but full of colour, charm and French flair. Apart from the cow she spotted strung up near the beach so the blood ran into the sea, she was not at all happy about that. Such a disturbing, primitive sight that she looked quickly away.

They moored safely on the quayside, everything a touch more ramshackle than English harbour. A girl with flame-red, long curly hair and glasses in a long dress came flying along like some tropical bird. She ran up the passerelle almost before Gray had properly lowered it to the ground. Kissing him affectionately she then took Elle's hand and kissed her too, before turning to greet her fiancé. Chris kissed her on both cheeks and glanced to catch Elle's eye.

'*Mais cette cuisiniere*,' Florence turned in time to see him look. '*Elle est un peu trop jolie, non?* Gray, what do you think?'

Gray uncharacteristically blushed, 'Yes she is a very pretty cook.'

Florence and Elle cooked supper together. She was not at all how Elle had envisaged her. She resembled an academic type with her small, round glasses, until she took them off to rub her eyes and then she was transformed into someone quite striking, all green eyes, and auburn curls and oh, so unmistakably French. What could this beautiful and capable girl possibly see in Chris Ryll? Especially if she knew him well enough to know that he would probably try to be unfaithful with every new cook he employed, if anyone succumbed to his non-existent charms and sweaty armpits of course. This thought made her smile.

Florence made simple things for the table look exciting and tasty and Elle felt humbled. She showed her how to make the most delicious French almond tart, the presentation being so professional that the layers of light pastry with almond cream could have come straight from a patisserie in Paris. Elle resolved to do her best but knew the season ahead would be a learning curve whereas Florence was a master of her task. They went through menus, ideas and recipes together and gradually Elle felt more hopeful, inspired by the skills of the French girl.

Ocean Sun took her leave of St Barths after a couple of days and they sailed south for a few windy days and nights down to St Vincent in the Grenadines to pick up their first charter, a honeymoon couple. The passage making was strange, unlike anything she had known before. They passed to the leeward side of the islands, feeling the full force of the strength of the constant wind and choppy seas in the open ocean and then they had to motor as the yacht fell into the shelter of the land.

Elle was spellbound by the anchorage at Petit St Vincent. The rocky outcrop was lit as if by magic with twinkling fairy lights at night. Small sailing craft, with patched scruffy sails carried the steel band members and their drums as they sailed haphazardly from 'jump up' to 'jump up' on the neighbouring beaches by day to entertain the yachts in the evenings. She was often too tired after hours in the galley to go ashore but would sit on the deck in the cool night air enjoying the band from afar, or she would plunge into the clear, phosphorescent waters surrounding the hull and relieve the heat of the day from her tired body.

This first charter went well, there being only two guests swathed in each other's company and barely noticing their surroundings. Elle slipped into the swing of things, adapting gradually to the lack of fresh produce available, and contrastingly, the abundance of fish. Small craft rowed out to greet them as they neared every port offering them lobster and snapper and she drove a hard bargain while the guests looked on encouraging her. Gray was helpful and supportive but when they retired to the cramped forepeak at night she would fall asleep listening to his analysis of their day, as well as his continuous moaning about the increasing number of grievances he had with the skipper.

Tobago Cays ... they seemed to slip through azure water from paradise to paradise. A lagoon of translucent pale blue water, still fanned by the fresh steady prevailing wind, but the sea was calm, protected from the swell and chop, encircled by reefs and small, sandy islands. Elle noted Chris's skill in navigating them safely into the anchorage although sometimes he would ask her to stand on the bow to watch for shadows, for the reefs were all around them. The Cays was a haven for windsurfers, but she had declined to have a go, for fear of making a fool of herself.

Elle frequently touched the silver bangle Peter had given her. She had lost the original one whilst snorkeling in Ibiza, so he had bought her another, this time with solid balls of silver on each end so it could not slip off. She wore it all the time. She had some spare money now and she loved to buy clothes in the small quayside boutiques full of brightly printed Caribbean fabrics. She had found a long dress not unlike the one Florence had worn in St Barths. After a hot day wearing her uniform changing into a dress or tying a pareo around her with little or no underwear (being cautious in the wind of course) was so much more comfortable. Peter would be so proud of her now, she reflected, but then he probably never even gave her a thought. She could not bear to imagine him with his new partner.

One hot afternoon with the honeymooners and crew both indulging in a siesta, Elle noticed a pale blue hull swinging at anchor, a yacht she had not noticed before. This was unusual as she normally had tabs on every vessel in each anchorage, such was her passion for boat spotting.

There was a man on the side deck and even from a distance she noted his height, tan and handlebar moustache. On the foredeck was someone who she at first thought was a slight deck hand but when the figure turned her way she could make out that in fact it was a slim, topless girl who was working diligently oiling the winches. This was clearly a racing craft to deserve such meticulous maintenance. *Pandora's Box*, Elle caught sight of the name on the stern as the hull swung again. She heard the splash as the man dived off the bow and to her surprise he began to swim in a fast crawl straight towards *Ocean Sun*.

'Prepare to repel boarders,' muttered Gray, peeping through the stanchions from his prone position on the genoa bag. Elle watched the lithe figure crossing the distance effortlessly.

'Yo James.' Chris moved swiftly to lower the bathing ladder.

'Somebody recognises him anyway,' Elle said to no one in particular.

'How are you mate?' The two skippers shook hands, formally in spite of James' dripping state.

'Good Chris, I'm good, actually I came over ask for an introduction to your new cook.'

What was it about skippers and cooks, Elle thought to herself, as she stood up pulling her T shirt back over her bikini feeling appropriately shy at this newcomer's interest.

'We have met before, am I right?'

Elle studied his face, feeling a blush creeping. 'Have we? I'm sorry but I don't remember at all.'

'It was some years ago, you were going about, or should I say stepping out with a friend of mine in the New Forest and when I came to visit him one day, you were there, sitting on the sofa if I remember correctly. I thought him so lucky to have such a pretty girl on his arm and when he bent to talk to you, you reached up and touched his face. I thought what an affectionate and lovely girl you were and I have never forgotten the incident.'

Elle was now truly embarrassed. She did know the house and boy he spoke of, but as for remembering this man, not a chance.

'I am sorry but I don't remember you at all when probably I should, but we are going back several years. How could you be sure I was she at such a distance?'

'I should probably own up to having spied you in *The Admiral's Inn*, I never forget a pretty face.'

Elle decided he was full of himself and just a little smarmy, but she smiled anyway, at a loss for an apt reply.

With a grandiose bow he took his leave and returned the way he had come, back to *Pandora's Box*.

12

"Announcing the intended arrival of some people is kind of like issuing a hurricane warning."

Richelle E. Goodrich

There was one charter Elle would never forget. Three Texan brain surgeons and their who wives were determined to have the best time of their lives in the islands. The boxes came on ahead, they were mostly full of rum but one box labeled 'Grunt Essentials' was exclusively condiments and pickles. As she unpacked and tried to find stowage space, Elle had not heard of many of these delicacies for one thing, and for another she had no idea what type of dish each would accompany. And then there were the flags. Grunt flags, their own personal design with instructions to fly them at masthead and cross trees. Was this decoration legal under maritime law? Chris said they would treat them as house flags and take them down when near the authorities. T-shirts too, for guests and crew alike. No one could escape being part of the Grunt team. They were like children, Elle decided, playing a holiday game. They were all supposed to join in and she had never been one for games. Elle knew it would be a difficult two weeks mostly because she was intimidated by their dietary requirements but she did like the group, with their noisy, boisterous ways.

The first breakfast did not go well. Eggs sunny side, eggs over easy, for goodness sakes how many ways could one fry an egg?

Then there were the pancakes, she cooked literally piles of them which vanished under lashings of maple syrup in a jiffy, empty plates flying back through the hatch for more. One of the ladies requested scrambled eggs, just to dirty yet another pan, with the Jalapeño peppers they had brought with them in jars. How was she to know how hot they were and to only add a tiny amount? Elle had never seen them before and so had absolutely no idea how to use them. Sparingly would have been the plan if only she had known, but as it was she added plenty, in fact a bit extra in case she was skimping and the eggs were sent back. 'Inedible,' she was told, by a red faced Texan lady with a burning mouth. The mess and accumulation of dishes, plates and pans was just the last straw, and Elle was a desperate figure as she peered out of the forepeak hatch to try to attract Gray's attention to help her.

'Five minutes until we up anchor,' he raised one hand splaying five fingers.

'Not unless someone gives me a hand we won't be,' stammered Elle with a vision of all the wreckage of breakfast flying everywhere as they set out into a bouncy sea.

'Hang on then, I'm coming,' and finally he came down, to save her and everything was stowed away.

The week continued, wet bathing suits were dropped on cabin soles, sodden towels chucked on cushion seats, and although Elle had learnt a tremendous amount in London it was quite a different matter, using her knowledge without mishap to cater for six mad Texans in a cramped galley. Often she was forced to 'prep up' whilst *Ocean Sun* was either leaning over on one side or the other whilst lifting and falling with the waves. She gutted the fish they had caught sitting on the bathing ladder, and jammed them in the oven with spices and herbs and random splashes of wine because this seemed to meet with tremendous approval from her guests. Elle was used to having to plan a second easy dessert in case the first more ambitious idea did not turn out quite as she hoped and frequently it did not. Cheese-cakes burnt in the oven and mousses stubbornly refused to set. She was learning painfully by her mistakes and she could sense Chris wishing he had kept Florence in spite of the rows. The more Elle's confidence slipped away, the more disasters seemed to occur and she fell into her bunk at night exhausted and tearful.

One morning towards the end of the charter Elle woke up realising that it was her birthday. Not that it was going to make any difference to her day because as far as she knew no one else had an inkling. Then there was Gray coming out of the galley with a cup of tea, which he presented to her.

'Happy Birthday,' he announced, grinning.

'I thought no one knew.'

'Well you were wrong, there were forms you filled out remember. Get yourself ready because you are to have a Grunt breakfast before you are apparently, on their orders, banished from the galley all day. I must say Chris is not happy about it, but he seems to have been overruled whether he likes it or not!'

Sure enough they had prepared a simple breakfast for everybody and she could see as she glanced through the hatch that they hadn't made too much mess in her galley. Chris wished her 'Many Happy Returns,' with a fairly grumpy scowl to show his displeasure at his loss of control over the charter routine.

'Pack a bag for the day,' Gray instructed, 'swimmers, sun cream, hat, peanuts, beer and water, all those sorts of things, book to read or whatever, you are going ashore for a rest.'

'Ashore where exactly?' demanded Elle. As the yacht was at anchor in the Cays all she could see were reefs and tiny beach outcrops with at the most one palm tree, amongst all of them.

'That's exactly why you need a hat and sun cream because there isn't much shade where you're going.' He took her in the dinghy to the largest sandy island and helped her to bury her beer and water in the edge of the sea to keep it cool, with a marker so she would not lose it as the waves rose and fell over the shifting sand.

'Pick you up later Elle,' and with a wave he was gone.

For the first half an hour Elle felt strangely peculiar, all the rushing around, and then time stopped literally bringing complete calm. Nothing to do but swim, sleep and read her book. What joy. She spread out her towels and lay back with her hat firmly pulled over her face to protect her from the sun.

Elle dozed, swam and watched the goings on of all the yachts in the anchorage. She wished her family could see her now, marooned in paradise on her twenty third birthday. Some would call her lucky but was it luck that found her here? She hardly thought so, more like reckless stupidity! Elle hoped jungle drums would reach her grandfather to tell him his granddaughter was near.

Gray was making his way across the anchorage before she knew it, and she was not quite sure where the whole day could have gone … swimming, sleeping, reading and doing absolutely nothing.

'So what's been going on out there without me?'

'Well you'll have to wait and see,' he shouted over the noise of the outboard engine. As they drew alongside Elle could see balloons tied all around the cockpit.

Stepping carefully down the stairs into the saloon she could not believe her eyes, the whole area flashed and twinkled like a discotheque with Bob Marley blasting on the stereo. The table was laid not just for the guests as it normally would be, but for all of them, except for Chris who had his own place laid on the chart table. Just to make a point, typical. They all sprang from the galley singing a rousing chorus of Happy Birthday and brandishing a small cake covered in the sparklers that were normally used for cocktails. They all looked so pleased with themselves, totally oblivious to the skipper's plainly disgruntled air.

They had cooked some fish and made a wonderful meal, and although she had to be pleased Elle was embarrassed too. They made it perfectly clear that Chris had lost control of the proceedings and ignored his sulky manner. It was almost as if they knew everything ... maybe Gray had said more than he should have done about Chris's bad behaviour.

At the end of the meal, before the cake, to her increasing horror, Spiro began to read out a poem he had written in honour of her Birthday.

" 'Twas the night of her birthday
And all through the ship
The Grunts were toasting the fair Elle
With a sip.

The Captain was drunk and the first
Mate equipped
Lets pull off her clothes with a
Tear and a rip.

The crew all agreed and attacked
Poor sweet Elle
They stripped off her clothes and
Upon her they fell.

Off came the top and next came
The drawers
And Spiro defiled her on the aft bedroom floor
She screamed and she hollered and she fought
Tooth and nail
But when it was over
What a wild piece of tail.'

Happy Birthday and Thank You,
The Grunts."

It had been a strange day, isolated on the beach, munching on her monkey nuts, drinking her beer. The shock to her system of actually having had nothing to do was peculiar. From her birthday onwards she worked ceaselessly, charters back to back, falling into her bunk after fifteen hours or so on her feet. Sometimes she only managed to make her way to a sail bag on the foredeck where she would be lulled to sleep by a steel band on a nearby beach.

On a few occasions they were lucky enough to call in to Martinique where Elle rushed ashore to buy as much as she could carry, for the market there was almost like waking up in mainland France. There were avocados, fine beans, raspberries, ... things she had never seen in the other neighbouring islands. A glorious selection of cheeses and charcuterie, in fact everything she bought there made her work and her menus easier and more interesting. In some islands she had walked for miles in the heat to nothing but find a pile of oranges, sweet potatoes and christophene. There were always spices but she could not make a meal out of flavours alone. So she squirreled as much as she could in the cupboards and fridge to last as long as possible, before their next visit to the bountiful French island.

When they were tied to the palm trees under the Piton Mountains of St Lucia, Florence came to stay. The water in the bay was rumoured to be as deep as the mountains were high, perhaps deeper. So an anchor dropped would be ill advised, for understandably there would never be enough chain to allow it to reach the bottom. There were a couple of large mooring buoys, although Elle could not figure out how or what they were attached to either. After the bow line had been successfully tied to one of these, a long line had to be rowed ashore and tied firmly to a palm tree at the water's edge to secure the stern. The diving at the base of the Pitons was supposed to be the best in St Lucia with sponges, coral, an extraordinary variety of small fish, and also the larger hunting fish that came to feed.

Elle was not sure why Florence came. Was her visit intended to highlight the struggle she was having to keep the food on an even keel, as well as all the rest of the tasks she was supposed to do, or was her stay simply to spend time with her intended? 'I am going to be zee stewardess, to lay zee table and wash-up and help you with everysing,' she trilled.

Elle felt sick at the thought of her supervision. She often caught Chris and Florence talking in low voices only to look embarrassed as she entered and fall silent. She knew it would be a relief for Chris if she moved on, as she could easily tell Florence everything and in doing so could possibly sabotage their engagement. She guessed the sensible straight-laced French girl would not give him a second chance, but dropping him in the poo was not her intention; Elle was only interested in proving her ability in the galley. She knew their relationship was doomed anyway but she would not be the one to make him walk the plank. At teatime she scored better than Florence, her range of typically English afternoon cakes was inexhaustible and delicious. After dinner desserts, well they were infinitely more challenging, especially under the eagle eye of the French girl.

One evening she had planned a layered meringue of sorts, with a homemade fruit mousse between, decorated with all the Caribbean fruits, and a passion fruit glaze. It was decidedly ambitious, especially with everything else she needed to prepare for the meal. Elle feared that the mousse layer would not set, with the fridge misbehaving in the intense heat of the afternoon. Florence was popping in and out of the galley mumbling comments like, 'Zis is far too complicated for tonight,' and 'let me show you somesing simpler for your meringue cake'.

Stubbornly, Elle turned her back and carried on stirring her mixture praying for the latter to thicken to the right consistency. 'Calm, calm,' she said.

Florence was tossing her red hair, like a feisty mare and strutting around banging dishes. 'We must not disappoint zee guests, you know Elle, or we can lose the good reputation with one mistake.'

Elle chose to ignore this last attack, took a deep breath, and melting some more leaf gelatine in lemon juice she added what she hoped was a life saver to the mousse, and placed the bowl confidently back in the fridge, shooting a warning look at Florence as she did so. She made a quick decision to leave the mix there for ten minutes while she went on deck to stand in the breeze briefly, as the pressure had made her flustered and the galley even hotter than usual. To her surprise she came across James talking to Chris on the side deck with the tender from *Pandora's Box* tied alongside, bobbing in the waves. James's pleasure at the sight of her was evident, while Elle for her part found herself blushing and conscious of her overheated, somewhat sticky, appearance.

'Ah Elle, just the person,' James declared. 'I was just asking your good skipper if during the event of him having a replacement cook aboard, he would release you tomorrow night for dinner with us.'

Elle had longed for a night off but when it came down to the idea of Florence replacing her in the galley she was uncertain. This must have shown in her face as James continued, 'No excuses now, Chris has already agreed so I will pick you up at seven sharp.'

'Ok, thank you, if the plan is all arranged,' she said awkwardly.

'Arranged and agreed.' James smiled and kissed her hand, ever the gallant gentleman and climbed swiftly back down to his dinghy. Elle untied the painter and throwing into the boat she waved him away.

Chris was watching her closely, 'I think you have a keen suitor in James.'

'Nonsense, he is just being kind,' Elle said crossly and turned to go back down the fore hatch and thence to the galley. Opening the fridge gingerly, she pushed the spoon and to her delight the mousse was setting perfectly, so she cut paper to line the sides of the mould and layered the mixture with the meringue quickly, placing it back in the fridge as fast as she possibly could. An hour later when she turned her creation onto a serving dish, she reveled in the sight, for when she peeled away the paper the dessert was a total, impressive success and a lick of the paper told her the taste was sublime. All her worries disappeared, replaced instantly with the pride of achievement.

Of course Florence was watching discreetly through the hatch.

'Oh my goodness, I have to say your meringue looks won-der-ful,' she announced accentuating each syllable carefully.

'Thank you Florence, maybe I could share the recipe with you.' If Elle had a board in the galley she would have smugly marked her name with a point, against a zero for other team.

Every morning Elle woke extremely early and sat on deck with her first cup of tea, time to herself in one of the most breath-taking anchorages in the world. Lately there had been porpoises throwing themselves high out of the water at dawn and again at dusk. According to the skipper the males did this dramatic display solely for the purpose of seducing a mate. She sat and thought about her grandfather who was only a few miles away on the north coast of the island. She was sad that she had no time to seek him out but she knew the right opportunity would come, just a question of patience. Anyway he would be in complete ignorance of the fact that a member of his family was so near and so intent on finding him.

She mulled James over in her mind. His attraction to her was plain to see but she could not return the same admiration. He was 'nice'. What a terrible word, she would hate it if anyone described her as 'nice'. He was ... she could not quite put her finger on it, too posh, too public school, too stiff upper lip, and too predictable. He resembled a puppet with someone else pulling the strings. What ever he was, he never seemed real, and he was definitely too good to be true. Maybe that was the answer. He was a stereo typed British gentleman, no individuality at all ... I am really horrid, she decided and she resumed being amazed that the water in the bay could really be deeper than the two mountains were high. Imagine that!

The dinghy proudly bearing the board 'Tender to Pandora's Box', appeared alongside the boarding ladder at seven o'clock exactly. Elle had shed her uniform in favour of a brightly coloured pareo. She had treated herself to this in St Barths, and when she had tied it carefully over a similarly coloured bikini, she felt both cool and confident. If she had to swim home to escape James's manly clutches, she could tie the piece of cloth around her waist and make a hasty exit over the side. She hoped the evening would not give rise to such drastic measures but with her experience, skippers were not to be trusted.

The girl-boy person she had spotted on deck before came up from below to take the line.

'Elle, may I introduce Lara, Lara, Elle.' The two girls smiled and sized one another up unashamedly. Lara was boyish but attractive and completely naked except for a short flared skirt and a string of coral around her neck. Elle tried to be indifferent to this blatant, topless show, but she feared her expression would betray her. Lara was extremely small breasted but Elle could not help her eyes straying downwards from her face as she spoke to her.

'Have you cooked on *Pandora's Box* for long?'

'About three years, Jame and I used to have a bit of a thing going on, but we're just mates now, I have a Frenchman in my life who threatens to take me away from all this,' she laughed, a deep and somehow serious mirth. Lara had a strange way of twisting her mouth as she spoke, the words tumbling out, the sounds scrambled and then, at last, escaping to take their form.

'Do you charter her or is she just for owners use?'

'Mostly just the owner but we race, we did the transatlantic last year and I believe the boat is entered again, isn't she Jame?'

James shouted up from where he was mixing drinks in the galley at the foot of the companion way, 'Yes she is, but Lara is going to leave me for her gallant Frenchman so I have no cook as yet,' so saying he winked up at Elle, who did her best to ignore the inference.

'Are you two coming down for some nibbles then? Lara you best stir this fish stew of yours before it burns.'

So down they went into the belly of the boat and Elle was pleasantly surprised at how homely it was as she had heard that racing boats tended to be spartan.

'It's lovely down here,' Elle ventured, 'I would never have guessed.'

'Of course everything is gutted out when we race,' said Lara, 'to lose the weight and make space for all the different sails we have to carry, and the guys of course, usually a dozen or so.'

'Gosh I can't imagine how they all fit.' Elle was suitably horrified at the thought of all the sails and bodies squashed in especially through rough weather when all had to remain shuttered down mid-Atlantic. She knew what that was like, wet, salty, stinky oilskins, she could still smell the airlessness of *El Guero* in rough weather. Lara was standing at the gimbaled small stove stirring her fish stew and Elle wondered if she ever burnt herself bending over the flames half naked.

'So what do you cook for them all when you're on a race?'

'I prepare frozen packs and freeze them flat in layers in here in the order I want to use them,' and she lifted a lid in the work surface to show Elle a deep rectangular freezer. 'When full this one holds about twenty flat packs, makes the job really easy. Lots of tinned soups, beans, eggs and snacks, the guys are always starving but they only get one main meal a day.'

'Completely different to charter cooking then.'

'Yeah, I couldn't do what you do, all that fancy stuff!'

They laughed a little, a touch more relaxed, and Lara served up her fish stew, which Elle had to admit, smelt and tasted, delicious.

The evening passed easily and James took her back to a peaceful *Ocean Sun* as all had obviously gone ashore after dinner. He was the perfect gentleman, and she climbed aboard and sped wearily to her bunk glad to be alone with her thoughts.

The following day a tender from one of the other Ocean's that had appeared overnight to share the anchorage came alongside and passed Chris a note adressed to Elle. He brought it down to the galley.

'Lucky you received this as we are off today,' he remarked and stood there nosily waiting for her to open it. Just to annoy him she shoved it in the pocket of her pinny and carried on peeling potatoes.

Later, privately in her cabin she opened it.

Dear Elle,

I hope the season goes well and you are not finding the cooking too hard.

I have reason to believe that your Grandfather, John Mathias is still in VIEUX FORT, St Lucia.

I hope you may, at some point, have the time to see him.

Yours

Joe Harrison

English Harbour

Checking the coast was clear and the saloon empty, Elle ran up to the chart table and sat herself in the skippers chair, studying the chart in front of her. Vieux Fort, tracing with her finger, she measured the course. It was about a two hour journey, an uncomfortable beat to windward by the look of the prevailing wind direction. She surmised there was no point at all in requesting a detour for that day as they had to set a southerly course to drop Florence in Marigot Bay, a hurricane hole that the guests were also keen to visit. Unfortunately her Grandfather's home port was not particularly suitable for charter yachts on a cruise.

13

"The road goes ever on and on,
And wither then?
I cannot say."

J.R.R. Tolkien

Darling Daddy,

We really are having a busy season. On the last charter we went to Antigua, Barbuda, Saba, St Maartins and then to St Barths. (Look at a map) and you will see how we whizz around the islands. All the guests chuckle at me for my English ways, but however they tip exceedingly well and I bought myself a Minolta camera to try and record some of what I see.

We are going back to St Maartins to pick up another eight people, on to Antigua and then down to St Vincent again for another group. I hardly have time to breathe.

Ocean Sun is only 18 months old and is the height of luxury and I must say, tupperware tho' she is, she is fully mahoganised below and in my galley I have gas, gimbaled of course, electricity, microwave, 2 deep freezes, fridge and all the liquidisers and mixers I could possibly need.

We have just caught a Spanish mackerel, a big juicy fish which is great because if I can keep the crew food budget really low it means we can eat out occasionally. We have a windsurfer on board, which belongs to the crew. I now own a quarter share. We hire it to our guests by the hour, in a rather crafty fashion.

The skipper's fiancée cooked on board last year but found it too much. She is a French lawyer, very fiery, so the deckhand tells me. It is hard work but then I like a challenge. I haven't had a chance to go and find John yet but am saving the fare for the day I can go, and I look forward to it more than anything.

The northern islands are green and luscious, but I was shocked by the difference when we went down south. Shopping and feeding the guests is a real struggle for me, some islands have everything and some just bananas! I am learning quickly and have found some local cookbooks that are amusing but helpful with vegetables I have never seen before. Crew make excellent guinea pigs to try all my dishes. The skipper is happy because he had Yorkshire pudding for the first time in ages. Florence won't make them for him, as they are not French.

I've begun to enjoy the climate out here now, the heat is not as oppressive as in the Med and there is always a predictable sailing breeze. It is hot in the galley but the air conditioning works well.

I saw a pelican today, unbelievable the way they throw themselves at the water – the birds out here are so amazing and I feel lucky to have seen a hummingbird.

I must get this ready to post today as I rarely step ashore whilst on charter.

Lots of love…

Write to me,

Elle

The season rushed on in a blur for Elle, cooking sailing, shopping and planning menus. Down to the Grenadines, St Vincent, Bequia, Mustique, the latter a lonely jetty with a busy bar set in glorious isolation, and on then to the Southern Grenadines, revisiting Tabago Cays, Palm Island, Union Island, Petit St Vincent and Carriacou where she saw a turtle killed for the meat. The sight made her sad.

Sometimes she saw a yacht she knew but there was never a chance to talk to other crew in the evening. She was far too tired to venture out to the "jump up" on the nearest beach. She saw *Solstice* sail by resplendent under full canvas but did not dare to ask Chris if she could make radio contact. The VHF was abuzz night and day with channel 14 reserved for inter yacht communication. The chat made Elle laugh, desperate cooks summoning their crew who appeared to be late for dinner, or furious skippers who appeared to have mislaid their crew completely. It was all so intimate and friendly, as if all were one big family across the expanse of the islands. She had to admit, although worn out, she was enjoying life and steadily improving and gaining confidence in the galley.

At night she fell asleep to Gray's loud whispered complaints and moans about the skipper, concerning his bad planning and general laziness, but she tried not to join him in this mutinous vein, as it served for little and the season would soon be gone.

They raced with other Ocean 71s and struck a reef off Petit Martinique which although it brought them to a dramatic halt, the boat sustained no damage. From that day on whenever they passed through narrow reef passages, Elle was asked to stand in the bow to keep watch for the helmsman.

Life had changed so much for her, all the happenings on the other side of the Atlantic were disconnected from this new world; a far off distant grey mass of cloud on the dim, misty horizon of the past. Life was full of sunshine and fair winds.

One afternoon Freddie came out of the blue, roaring across the anchorage in a smart Boston Whaler, 'Tender to Fandango', she read on the stern as he came alongside, smiling his ever-awkward smile. 'Well hello Elle,' he called, are you working right now or could I take you for a swim or drink or something?'

'My goodness, is there no end to your admirers?' Chris was always hovering. 'Go on disappear for an hour then, if you must.'

A trifle grumpy Elle thought, but thanked him and gathered a towel, from where it hung on the rail. She climbed into the whaler and they hugged briefly and sped away. Sometimes there was an overwhelming sense of freedom to be found in being whizzed helplessly away from one's place of work and confinement and Elle most certainly welcomed the chance to escape.

'Thanks Fred,' she shouted over the engine noise, 'I needed a break.'

'He did seem a bit put out.'

'Oh don't worry about him. He'll get over it.'

The "incident" back on her first night aboard had given her a secret hold over him. At times like this she relished the power, and her improving prowess in the galley left him no room for manoeuvre. She had overheard his chats with Florence about retiring to grow coffee on an island somewhere and she could so easily blow that idea right out of the water. What an apt expression!

'Where have you been then Freddie?'

'Oh here and there. We have had the owner on board for a fair stretch, now we have a couple of days break before we pick up some of his family. Joe's note reached you then?'

'Yes, did you have a hand in that delivery?'

'Just made sure it was passed to a boat coming your way that's all. I have some post for you too on *Fandango* but I wanted to give you it personally.'

'How exciting, that's so kind of you.'

They dropped a small anchor from the whaler and swam in the shallow, bath temperature water near the beach, lazily chatting and laughing. For the first time in ages Elle finally relaxed. Afterwards they sat and drank Earl Grey tea in the canvas-shaded grandeur of the cockpit aboard *Fandango*. She decided to keep her letters for later as to sit and read in Freddie's company would be rude.

'I wish I could work on a boat like one this next but I can only dream,' mused Elle.

'Well maybe you will, I am only sad our skipper has this fixed rule never to hire female crew.'

'He's probably incredibly sensible, he knows what trouble we are! But then a woman's touch is never a bad thing,' she said looking around and noticing the lack of flowers and pictures, in fact from her view of the deck saloon all looked spartan, tidy and exceedingly batchelor-ish. She imagined all the cabins to be the same.

'Well soon I shall be back in Antigua and looking for work again. I don't know where life will take me, back to the Med or maybe to the States, now that would be exciting.'

'Yes, we shall be heading north as *Fandango* is booked for some sprucing up in a shipyard in Fort Lauderdale. I hope we do catch up with each other again, that's the problem with this business, one makes a friend and then we go in separate directions.'

'Yes, I agree but the world suddenly becomes much smaller when you bump into them again, don't you think? Like now for instance, I had no idea *Fandango* was here.'

'You're right, and now I must take you back as our hour is up and I shall be in trouble for kidnapping the cook.'

Elle looked at him carefully and thought how handsome he was with his shiny, clean black hair, a contrast to the bright whiteness of his uniform. I could do a lot worse than Freddie, she thought as they bounced back across the dividing waters between *Fandango* and *Ocean Sun*.

'Til we meet again my Princess,' he said with a silly bow which he executed with such a typical Freddie like flourish, that he almost fell over board.'

'Don't call me that,' Elle said, more crossly then she intended.

'Why's that?'

'Someone else did that's all, an old man, a skipper I sailed with on the crossing. Don't worry it doesn't matter, you just gave me a start.'

'I shall never do it again,' so saying he kissed her on both cheeks and hugged her hard. 'Until soon then.'

'Yes, soon.'

Back on board she nipped below to have a quick look at her mail in the half-hour she had before she needed to start the dinner preparations. All was quiet with everyone ashore.

A letter from the States, from Geoff. Elle skimmed through the type written missive quickly. His letter was full of affection and inquisitive to know how she was getting on and what friends she had made. He has absolutely know idea how little time I have for socializing, she thought, even if I am in paradise I am still at work. She stopped reading to try and visualise his face, but it was hard to see him clearly. The brief time that they had spent together seemed like a long time ago. She set his letter aside and took one she knew was from her father. He always wrote those blue airmail letters that she had to open carefully for fear of tearing his precious words. His scrawly pale blue fountain pen writing made her eyes prick. She missed him. She was glad he found time to reply to her letters.

Darling Elle, – your letter came at the end of last week – glad you got there okay, but what a way to spend Christmas Day!! Well I am snowed in and have been unable to work for a week, and am running out of food and fuel – never mind help is at hand in the form of a bulldozer digging it's way up the drive so with any luck we shall soon be able to get out. Bogey (the dog) had a terrible adventure, as he was lost in the cold for 24 hours, there were some, I hasten to add, who hoped he would never come back. But he was found and I had to bail him out of police custody.

And so it went on the whole page full of the escapades of the dog with the following page about the family, and at the bottom strangely he had written – "I wish sometimes I could leave it all," which made her wonder if he was indeed happy and her tears brimmed again.

Next she took a look at her mother's letters of which there were two. She always had been a prolific letter writer, Elle receiving more than any of her friends when she was away at school, mostly nonsense but in her mother's individual chatty way, it was comforting nonsense.

Darling, It was so cold yesterday I've put my winter vest on again and David Rook (Elle had absolutely no idea who he was) says he's still got his long johns on. But there is plenty to do here thank heaven, otherwise life becomes boring and depressing and everyone gets cross, miserable and nasty. Beastly weather and high wind and your step-father is listening to the news as we have those blasted hippies camping in the village again…

More tales of village life and animals, mostly sheep this time, a glimpse of another world, so far away and left behind. Hmm, no letter from Ben although she had written twice. Hearing voices Elle stashed them away and forced herself back to the reality of making tea and preparing dinner.

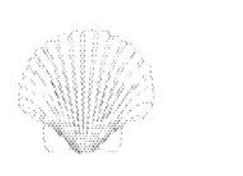 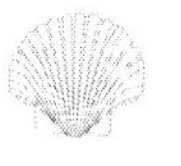 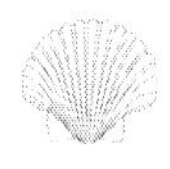

English Harbour … Only a few months had passed since her arrival on *El Guero* but to Elle it seemed far longer. She was stronger and hopefully wiser, having learnt from all her experiences both bad and good. Time to look for another job, another home and another crew. She had a couple of weeks grace before *Ocean Sun* was hauled out for maintenance. Some thinking time. The first evening in the Inn she recognised the back of a head across the crowded bar area and she pushed her way through eagerly to surprise him but when he turned, oh the embarrassment, for it was not Geoff as she had thought.

'Sorry, sorry,' she stammered awkwardly, 'I thought you were someone else.'

'Interesting,' the golden-bearded gent replied, 'and who pray did you think I was?'

'No one really, a guy called Geoff who I met at Christmas.'

'He is certainly not no one, if you don't mind, he's my cousin. Ralphie, pleased to meet you, you must be Elle and every bit as pretty as Geoff told me.'

Relieved at the excuse for her mistake, Elle shook his hand and he pulled her closer and kissed her mouth firmly. She pulled away confused by his intimacy.

'Are you staying at your Aunt's house where Geoff was?'

'Yes except she's not my Aunt, she's my mother.'

'Oh yes, of course I see, how slow of me. Have a good evening, Ralphie, nice to have met you,' so saying Elle wandered away to find people she knew a little better. To her joy she found the crew of *Bonaire* sitting quietly outside and they were pleased to see her too, greeting her fondly.

So much news to relate on both sides but the main revelation of the night came from Ted.

'Your Peter was here.'

'Here, in Antigua, in English Harbour?' The whiteness of her pallor silenced all conversation amongst the group.

'Yes he was, for a couple of days but they pressed on up to the Bahamas I think.'

'Who is they, did he sail over in his own boat?' Elle was shaking and flushed.

'Yes with his girlfriend and her brother.'

'Did he ask if I was in the islands, did you tell him I was on the Ocean Fleet?'

'Yes I told him how well you were doing since you arrived.'

Elle just could not cope with the idea of him having been there with his girl friend, and so recently that she had missed him by only a few days. Maybe that was for the best. It felt almost as if he was in some way intruding on her life by being in the islands. She could hardly bear to think of him perhaps sitting with 'her' in the Inn.

Ted broke into her thoughts, 'Did you see your grandfather yet?'

'No, I know exactly where he is, but I need time in St Lucia when I am not working to hire a car and find him. I will get the opportunity, it's just I don't know when.

Elle was grumpy, preoccupied and unable to continue with sociable conversation. She made her excuses and returned to *Ocean Sun*. So Peter was sailing the world with this other girl, they must be happy and she was probably never thought of or mentioned. She knew she had lost him but the confirmation of that fact was hard to stomach, in fact she felt sick. Why could she not forget about him, and move on with a clear mind, no dreams, and no haunting memories? He was always in her thoughts and it was as if in everything she did she was setting out to try to impress him and regain his favour, which was ridiculous as he didn't even know or probably care where she was or what she was doing. She slept fitfully, her outlook on life shaken by the knowledge of his arrival in the West Indies and the company he kept.

Elle spent most of her time after her return, sitting on her own, watching the comings and goings of English Harbour. She was resting from the cooking, but she had also found the cramped living quarters, and forced intimacy with people she did not know at all well on *Ocean Sun*, claustrophobic, even more than the Atlantic crossing itself. She had always had trouble feeling at ease with people and some situations were more difficult than others. She had never been one for bosom-buddies... even at school when everyone was firmly inseparable from a chosen friend, Elle stood alone. Amiable but never close to anyone in particular. All her friendships waned in the end and left her, set apart keeping her own company.

She sat at the small cafe bar on the quay sucking a banana pineapple milkshake through a straw. It was so thick she worked out that it was easier to scoop the shake up and use the straws sort of like chopsticks. She knew they used tinned evaporated milk as there was no fresh, but she had become accustomed to the flavour and mistakenly supposed that it was fairly nutritious as a lunch choice combined with the roasted monkey nuts. In short, as far as cooks go, her own chosen diet was disastrous.

It had just stopped raining. One of those marvelous Atlantic, tropical squalls breaking from just a few dark clouds gliding prominently to the forefront of a fierce blue background. Elle loved the freshness after a storm, the hibiscus shone an even brighter red and all the floral scents were exaggerated as the sun fell on puddles with such heat that stones began to steam. English rain falling from a solid grey sky, had never given her a feeling of exhilaration or wonder. She watched the deckhands rush out with their chammy leathers to dry the varnish and replace the cushions, hurriedly stashed at the threat of rain. A blue hull she recognised at once was skimming through flat water to make her approach to the wall. *Pandora's Box*.

Almost before the lines were secure, James had spotted her. Too late to hide, nowhere to escape, she saw him nod in her direction to Lara as she bent to attach the fenders. She was wearing a T-shirt today, Elle noted, to protect her modesty. Another man, who she did not recognise, had obviously been watching for their arrival as he stood anxiously, impatiently waiting for the gangplank to go down. Judging by the grin spreading across Lara's elfin face, this must be the French lover, come to whisk his bride away. He was handsome in a Latin sort of way and Elle felt a small knife of jealousy that wounded. Where was her Lancelot? There was of course James, bounding across the stubbly grass to her seat outside the café, enthusiastic yes, but unfortunately not the knight of her choice.

'Elle, it's so great to see you, are you on a bit of a break from the galley now?'

'Yes, of course, good to see you too,' and she rose reluctantly to fill his embrace.

'Will you have supper with me tonight, Lara's leaving me, packing and running off with her man so I shall be so lonely. I'll cook, please come.'

Enticed by his enthusiasm she agreed to eat with him on *Pandora's Box* and made her way back to *Ocean Sun* to write letters home, long overdue. What was she to write when her immediate future felt so uncertain?

Later, before they had even sat down to dinner Elle quickly understood the presumptuous plans that James had made, as he wasted no time in speaking out. 'Have you done any racing Elle?'

'No, well only dinghy sailing, I'm not sure it would be my thing, it's not what I'm used to, that's for sure.'

'It's an extreme challenge and being part of a team makes it all the more enjoyable. With Lara gone I have no cook for the transatlantic race. Give it some serious thought, for me, please? You could move aboard as soon as you are free from *Ocean Sun*.'

Elle was not expecting such a direct approach before she had even tasted her drink. She was rendered somewhat speechless, biding for time and looking for excuses.

'I'm not sure what I want to do yet, just enjoy a few days off with some money in my pocket, I think.'

The corners of his mouth dropped, the persuasive smile gone. 'Well think hard and sleep on it and come back to me with an answer as soon as you can, okay?'

The dinner passed amiably with her tales of the Grunt antics to amuse him. She declined to mention the discord amongst the others aboard *Ocean Sun* having decided that a mutinous crew was probably quite a common problem. She wondered about him and Lara, sure that they must have previously been a couple. It did look as though her departure with the Frenchman was causing him pain, but she refrained from prying. Lara had returned noisily during their meal to collect more baggage and she could read the sadness in James's face as he watched her coming and going. Elle lay awake for hours trying to decide whether to accept and take to the high seas with a crew of thirteen men to race back to home waters again, or to wait and see what other opportunities might arise.

Ted told her she should go. 'T'would be a fantastic experience,' he said, but Robin said she would be mad, 'Little you squashed in with thirteen racing men, I think not, they are all brawn no brain, you know,' was his comment.

As nothing else was appearing on the horizon, after a few days of deliberation she decided she would accept. Almost as soon as she had told James she regretted it, especially when he told her that space was limited and she would have to share a cabin with him. However she moved aboard with new resolve, glad to be away from Gray and his moaning and at least James was too much of a gentleman to repeat the antics of her previous skipper.

Darling Daddy,

I am back in Antigua again so I got your last letter. I have finished the charter season on Ocean Sun and have made the decision to join Pandora's Box, a racing boat, which doesn't really sound like my style at all I know. I shall probably be doing the race to Bermuda and the Transatlantic so pray for me!! Anyway I am beginning a trial period for Antigua Race Week, so wish me luck. This week I am having a much needed rest out of the galley, keeping my hands well away from the sink! I sort of know my new skipper James having met him in Lymington some time ago. If we do the Transatlantic we will be cruising Norway afterwards. Anyway it all depends on whether I can cope with the racing or not.

Well I have visited all the islands now from Antigua to Grenada but really seen so little of them being always stuck in the galley.

My brother ACTUALLY wrote to me, unbelievable, first one since he left prep school. I wonder if he wrote it in the bath as it seemed a little soggy.

Snow sounds great, I have had a streaming cold all week, a Caribbean cold feels twenty times worse than a cold weather one, possibly because of the heat, but the rum makes the best hot toddy I have ever tasted.

Now I must write to Mummy...write to me soon I get quite homesick,

My love to all

Elle

So the next few days she was to be found polishing the hull of *Pandora's Box*, back on a payroll again, but still with nagging doubts about her future as a race cook. A young man from Harrisons hailed her from the quayside.

'Hey there.'

'Yes, can I help?'

'Are you Elle?'

'Yes, that's me.'

'Thank goodness, I found you, I've been chasing round English Harbour looking for you.'

'Why, what did I do?'

'No silly, you didn't do anything, there's a call coming for you at noon on the Harrison flagship anchored round in the bay and as it's already eleven thirty, we should hurry.'

'Who would call me? From where?'

'From Fort Lauderdale I think.'

'But I don't know anyone in Fort Lauderdale. They must have the wrong Elle.'

'No time to worry about it, come on we have to go, I shall be in trouble if I don't get you there.'

'James!' No response, 'JAMES!' She shouted louder this time and he appeared from below.

'Got to go with this guy, to receive a radio call at twelve, I'll be back as soon as possible okay?'

'What's that all about Elle?' he looked concerned.

'Not a clue, tell you when I get back,' and attaching the dingy firmly to the stern she jumped ashore and ran after the man who was already disappearing up the road. That is how surprises happen sometimes, like a rock tossed into a peaceful lake.

The pair half walked, half ran down the track leading to the jetty in the bay. A small motor launch was there, the engine idling.

'That's for us come on,' grabbing Elle's hand he ran dragging her along behind him. 'Quick, quick on you jump.'

They were in the launch for a mere second before the uniformed driver cast off and accelerated away in a wide arc of spray, which knocked them laughing off their feet and onto the cushioned bench at the rear of the cockpit.

'What's your name anyway?' shouted Elle, 'you definitely already know mine.'

'Mark,' her chaperone replied turning his gaze to their destination, the solitary yacht, at anchor far out in the bay.

The flagship belonging to the Harrison family was a resplendent old motorboat. A wooden ship from a past era, Elle adored such vessels, all polished brass and shining varnish, so stately and important. The smell of wood polish as they climbed aboard, transported her back to *Talisman* in an instant. She certainly felt special. Everyone seemed to be making an effort to get her to the right place at the right time.

A small group of people were huddled around the SSB radio and the call for her came through immediately. Elle felt incredibly nervous, too flustered to think straight, she was terrified in case it could be bad news from home, which of course it could not be as the call was from Fort Lauderdale.

A feminine voice came from the radio addressing her directly by name.

'Hello, am I speaking to Elle?' The words were pronounced so carefully that Elle knew instinctively that the caller was not speaking in her own language.

'Yes hello that's me.'

'My name is Cajsa, and I work for a company based in Oklahoma. My partner Charles and I look after a large motor sailing yacht that belongs to them. The boat is currently undergoing a refit in the shipyard in Fort Lauderdale.'

Elle realised she was stupidly nodding her head as if the caller could see her.

'We have heard from several sources that you are the best cook in the Caribbean this season and we would like you to fly up and join our crew. I will call again tomorrow to hear your decision, as I understand you will probably want to think this over. Do you have any questions you would like to ask me, before you decide?'

Elle felt stunned and tongue tied but she knew one thing, any allegiance to *Pandora's Box* and Nigel had vanished in a few short seconds. Questions? She had so many she was bewildered. Her mind a blur, she looked briefly to the faces around her as if they should advise what she should ask, but no one spoke.

'What is the boat like, what sort of design so I may picture it please?'

'The yacht is one hundred and three feet long, a ketch, designed by Philip Rhodes and built by Abeking and Rasmussen in Germany. She is very comfortable and luxurious and you would share a cabin with a stewardess.' Phillip Rhodes, Elle had heard that name recently and as well as thinking what to ask next she was struggling to place the design to the yacht.

'How many crew will there be?'

'There is the skipper and myself, an engineer, a bosun and a stewardess, so with you that will make six. We don't normally charter, the boat is kept exclusively for the owners and their families. So I will call again tomorrow Elle for your decision and we can proceed from there.'

'Thank you so much for your offer, if I accept how soon would I come?'

'As soon as we can sort out your travel arrangements, we need you right away.'

Elle could sense a smile behind the voice now.

'Until tomorrow then. Goodbye,' and the connection was gone.

All present were looking at Elle, she was wobbly, excited, confused and emotional all at once.

'Well done Elle,' said Mark. 'Amazing news, come on I will take you back to the harbour, you've certainly got some thinking to do.'

James was sitting in the cockpit waiting for her, his face a picture of concern, expecting some bad news maybe, but totally unaware of Elle's predicament and the choice she faced. She had to tell him straight away and she knew already which path she would take.

She sat beside him and took his hand affectionately. 'James I am really grateful for everything you have done and I know working with you would have been fun but I have been offered another job which I know is more suitable, as I am a charter cook, not really a racing cook at all. If I am honest I like tables laid, napkins folded and pretty china to serve my food, rather than struggling with bowls and stormy waves. I hope you will understand and not be angry.'

'No Elle, not angry exactly, just sad, I sort of thought we might have something, you and I, with time, not just skipper and cook. Having said that I suppose I am on the rebound from Lara and I am vulnerable to your charms,' he smiled with his eyes at her now, little wrinkles appearing in his deeply tanned face and she understood that it would be alright and she could go with a light heart.

PART THREE

Florida

14

Casja…

"I met Charles in Greece and having suffered a traumatic marriage breakdown first time around I was nervous of a new relationship, but I fell for him, he was just irresistible. Funny, kind and clever, he had all the qualities I admired in a man, and he was handsome too. He had recently left his life as a pilot in the Royal Navy to 'go yachting' when we met and we set up an agency together in Greece. My fluency in many languages combined with Charles's sound business sense made us a formidable team. Charles had an obsessive enthusiasm both for work and for play, and it was this that attracted me to him right from the moment we met. Our wanderlust drew us towards the idea of driving super-yachts and we were lucky enough to be hired to look after *Sea Princess* for her American owners.

After our first season in the Mediterranean, it became apparent that the yacht needed a major refit, and as we had become accustomed to her we knew exactly what she needed. So we took her to Florida with a skeleton crew but we had found Tony, a marvelously conscientious engineer in the Balearics so we took him too, although we knew he could not stay for the whole refit in Fort Lauderdale. He told us of a girl who had gone back to England to learn how to cook, and although he chose not to reveal the depth of their relationship, we guessed that he had been fond of her. Her name was Elle, and when our newly hired stewardess spoke of an outstanding cook of the same name down in the islands, we quizzed both Tony and Lulu and after piecing the two stories together, we knew it had to be the same girl.

So there we were that humid Florida day, standing at the airport with a placard waiting for Elle, our new cook, to join us. We could not believe how thin and small she was as she walked nervously towards us and Charles made an unfortunate remark about her not being strong enough to lift a pan of any size but we were to be proved quite wrong."

  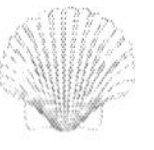

Phillip Rhodes ... of course, she had it now. The boat was just a bigger version of *Fandango*! Elle was bursting to tell Freddie but of course she had no idea where he was, perhaps she could contact him by radio, but then again no time for that, she had to pack and sort herself out. Her stomach churned with nervous excitement for her ticket was already on its way to the office and tomorrow she would fly to Fort Lauderdale. Of course she had never been to America, she had no idea how it would be at all, looking at herself in the mirror all white hair and brown skin, she accused her reflection of being unkempt and inadequate. Grabbing her hairbrush she scrapped wildly and fiercely to tidy herself and to her dismay her hair was leaving her head in clumps and clogging her brush with golden strands. I must eat properly, she resolved, new job, new healthy me.

She tried to say goodbye to people but no one seemed to be around. Lulu and *Solstice* she supposed were still down islands somewhere, even *Bonaire* had vanished with her owners aboard, so there was only James, sweet bereft James who carried her bags and loaded them into a taxi on the quay.

'Take care Elle,' he said, as with a solemn kiss he stood and watched her drive away and whilst a small stab of guilt touched her for a second, it was quickly banished away by the thrill of overwhelming excitement.

Flying through blue skies and layers of fairy tale clouds, glimpses of turquoise water, reefs and islands far below. Was that the Bahamas? Was Peter down there in his perfect life with his perfect girl who wasn't her? It all seemed so unreal and far away now, the experiences of another life the other side of an ocean. She was at the beginning of a new adventure and she would embrace it firmly. Her thoughts rearranged themselves and she closed her eyes and slept and dreamt in vivid waves of colour ... *she was naked in a pool where no one else was naked and so she became aware of her own smooth, daisy white, rounded body. Someone handed her a costume, frilly, spotted and softly pink such as she had worn as a child. She tried to put it on in the water with the awkwardness of straps. Then a bus, crowded, hot and airless where her seat was not her own, a friend pushing an infant wearing a hat with a long braided nose* ... Elle awoke with a wriggle and glanced directly at the man beside her, blushing as if he too had seen her dream.

The captain of the plane was announcing their descent and looking out of the window she saw what looked like skyscrapers on the beach and she realised that it must be Miami. As they came lower she could see the landscape of the Everglades and Fort Lauderdale which looked like a metropolis without end, a world marked into tidy squares with roads and houses, and a predominance of waterways making all the rest seem as though it was probably floating. Where did Miami end and Fort Lauderdale begin exactly? Patches of green and then large stretches of water followed by a spaghetti of roads interwoven, orderly and planned, not at all like flying into England or any European country for that matter. This was surely a world such as she had never seen, and so amazingly flat. Suddenly the ground looked like heath land, another lake or two where she could see ripples on dark water and then the airport runway as the plane turned for the final descent.

Elle walked in a daze across to the airport buildings. She was increasingly aware of looking like some refugee rescued from a desert island, the dress she had chosen to wear which had seemed totally appropriate in the islands, now struck her as vastly out of place. It was a shift of sky blue, the colour of a summer day, with a gradual darkening of the hue until it became the shade of the ocean at the hem. Her hair, bleached white by the ravages of sun, sea and salt, lacked condition and hung in tangles down her back. The young around her in the airport, bristled about their business in crispy shorts and startling white sneakers, and she was a conspicuous ocean gypsy with heavy bags and a fish smoker strapped to the top, the paint peeling from salt and use.

A couple caught her eye, they were holding a sign, which as they turned towards her revealed her name, ELLE in thick black letters. Should she run back and never reveal herself? Too late they were walking quickly towards her, smiling.

'You must be Elle.' The lady, with shiny black hair in stark contrast to her fair complexion, took her hand and then hurriedly embraced her as an afterthought.

'I am Cajsa, and this is my partner, Charles, we are so glad you decided to come, we have heard so much about you.'

Elle immediately liked Charles, his face so open and friendly, he held her worried gaze and calmed her, dispelling all her nervous inclination.

'You look so dainty,' he said, 'are you sure you can manage saucepans and things.'

'I am stronger than I look,' she said although at that moment she did actually feel rather frail, with all the excitement of her journey.

'The boat is in dry dock in the shipyard right now, so we are living in apartments, one for crew and one close by for Charles and I,' Cajsa explained. 'So we will take you to the apartment where there might be a few surprises, and then we will show you the boat tomorrow, when you are settled and have had a chance to unpack and acclimatize.'

'Thank you,' Elle replied, trying to take in her new city surroundings, everything was so different from the islands. As they drove along, there was a supermarket and a burger joint on every block. All the streets were identical with repetitive landmarks around every corner. If she were to be set down, she would be lost in this land of Macdonalds and frozen yogurt kiosks. Small shopping malls were duplicated every mile or so with large parking areas.

Charles and Cajsa were heatedly discussing some aspect of the refit, so Elle allowed herself to relax and adsorb the view from the back of the car. It was probably the largest car she had ever ridden in, she understood everything in America had a reputation for being large but this was surely ridiculous. The air conditioning worked so well that for the first time in many months, she was rather cold. They turned off into some apartment blocks with numbered parking spaces and Charles slid the car into a space near the entrance to Block 11.

Up they went in a lift, with Elle mildly embarrassed about her goods and chattels. Her companions did not seem in the slightest concerned about the weight of her luggage, continuing their chat all the way, now and again asking Elle her preferences for fine china and all sorts of other things as they made their way down and around the corridors until they finally stopped at No. 71 and tapped loudly upon the door.

'Coming …' a bright cheery voice, the door flew open and there stood Lulu.

Elle had never been so pleased to see anyone in her entire life. 'How did you get here?' she stammered.

'Same way you did I guess,' laughed her friend. It was me that told Charles and Casja about you!'

'Well we shall leave you girls,' Charles butted in, 'and catch up with you tomorrow at the shipyard for a crew meeting, nine o'clock sharp.'

'Perfect,' said Lulu who seemed to have her wits about her, unlike Elle who was still in shock. 'See you tomorrow.'

With the skipper and his lady gone, Elle, still mystified about how everything had come about, quizzed her friend. 'I still don't quite believe all this, so how did you find out about the stewardess job?'

'The skipper of *Solstice* recommended me, so I found myself here and then Cajsa and Charles asked me if there was a good cook in the islands who was due to be finishing the season, so I told them about you. The engineer who is leaving the crew here knows you as well so one thing led to another.'

'The engineer knows me? Who for goodness sake might that be?'

'A guy called Tony, apparently you had a brief something with him whilst you were crew on *Talisman*, I know it didn't work out for you, but he never forgot you and he is still fond of you I reckon. Anyway he's been working for Charles for eighteen months but he's going to New Zealand for a job, so there's a new engineer coming. Tony is hanging around for a month to show him the ropes.'

'So is he here now, Tony, I mean?' Elle looked around her worriedly.

'No, he has a separate apartment just down the way, I expect we will meet up for supper with him later. Don't look so scared, whatever happened between the two of you, he has nothing but good to say about you. The new guy, Mark is coming out from England tomorrow, he's never worked on a boat before so heaven help us, or him!' Lulu laughed her joyful, happy laugh, which splashed over Elle and made her laugh too.

'So who else then, are there any more shocks in store for me?'

'Well there's this chap, Jamie, who is first mate, bosun,

deckhand sort of thing and he's staying here too. He and I hit it off rather well so we are sort of sharing a room already.'

'But you only arrived a few days ago, Lu, you really are impossible.'

'Doesn't take me long to have what I want does it?' They laughed again collapsing on the sofa with mirth.

'Well where is he now this Jamie?'

'Down at the yard sorting part of the rigging or something, totally too complicated for a mere stewardess to comprehend.'

'Oh you,' said Elle, 'I am so happy to see you. Never for a moment did I guess you would be here.' She studied Lulu who looked so smart and beautiful in her new shorts and polo shirt, twisting the stud in her ear lobe as she always did, completely unaware of her own bewitching little mannerisms that held such power over the opposite sex.

'Tomorrow we are to be measured for new uniforms, polo shirts, with the name of the boat of course and shorts, all in white,' she chattered on …

'Well I don't even know the name of the boat, no one has even mentioned that to me yet,' Elle interrupted.

'Oh gosh its *Sea Princess*, you silly duck, I thought you knew!'

'How could I unless someone told me. I do have an idea that she might look a lot like *Fandango*, did you see *Fandango* in Antigua?'

'Not sure I noticed her to be honest.'

'No I suppose you were too wrapped up in some Rastafarian or other,' said Elle playfully whacking her friend with a cushion.

'Shhh, shhh, less of that, I have moved on anyway,' Lulu said firmly.

'This or should I say HE remains to be seen,' replied Elle.

A tap at the door ended the conversation.

'Who is that going to be?' she asked nervously.

Lulu made for the door, 'Not Jamie home yet because he has a key. Lets find out shall we.'

She peeped through the tiny spy hole in the front door. 'Its Tony,' she said with a giggle.

Elle visibly blanched even under her tan 'What now already? Must I see him like this? I feel such a mess.'

Too late the door was open. There he stood an image from her past, but no, his soft blue eyes, immaculately trimmed beard, and his droll solemn mouth, with little humour lying within unless you sought it out ... all of this was most assuredly real. Elle recalled all of their time together within a moment, those lazy weekends in Mallorca when they had travelled around the island in his old car, sampling the gourmet peasant delights of remote restaurants far from the tourist areas. Sopas Mallorquinas, a traditional dish, washed down with Hierbas, the sweet aniseed flavoured liquor steeped in herbs, sleepy drives in the sunshine, followed by comforting, gentle love making. But one day he had looked at her and said it was over. She had been devastated, by the loss maybe not, but by the rejection with no explanation. She had foolishly imagined they would return to England and build a future together. How could she face him bravely when he had never said why ... was she not pretty, nor clever enough? Or had he just become bored with her and seeing no future for them, had he decided to draw the line cruelly and quickly to save her further pain? After all, he could not think badly of her as he had obviously not offered any negative advice when questioned about her suitability by her new employers. Elle wished she was not driven to have these stabs at love, it was all so painful, tiring and distracting.

He gave her a quick hug, 'You look well, and so slim and brown, glowing in fact, the Caribbean has clearly suited you.'

'Yes I suppose it has, it's been an exciting time for me.'

Still a man of a few words she noticed, as he turned to Lulu, 'I won't be around this evening so you guys carry on and eat or whatever okay?'

'Message understood,' she replied with a mock salute.

When he was gone and the door safely closed behind him, Lulu looked at Elle and the latter could feel the questions building behind the glance so she spoke quickly, ‘I think I will unpack and have a lie down before we go to eat, it’s been an exhausting day full of surprises.’

‘Yes, you must be tired,’ replied her friend, ‘I will give you a shout when Jamie gets in so we can go and find some food. We have a busy day tomorrow, I think we have a crew meeting at nine before we go down to the shipyard to see what’s going on.’

Elle took her things gratefully into her new, small room. How strange, she thought, to be sleeping in a real bed on dry land after all this time. Exhaustion overwhelmed her almost immediately and she slept.

15

"Love is like a grain of sand,
Slowly slipping though my hand..."

Fleetwood Mac

Lulu left her, not liking to disturb someone who seemed to need her sleep so badly, so she slept right around the clock, waking at seven, starving hungry and desperate for a cup of tea. She busied herself as quietly as she could in the tiny kitchen and found both toast and tea. A sleepy boy appeared, with the curly golden locks of an angel and the face of a choirboy just woken.

'You must be Jamie,' she said.

'Yes how are you Elle, refreshed I hope? You slept so well.' As he stood there barefooted in a hugely over-sized toweling gown swamping his slight frame, he could have passed for twelve years old. The difference between him and Lulu's last beau, the Antiguan native was extraordinary. His complexion was fair, his mouth with the full-lipped pout of a cherub, hung a little open even when he was silent.

'Lu will be up in a minute, would you like to have first shower?'

'Yes, thank you, I would.'

Elle followed the newly formed couple down under the apartments to a garage where an electric door rose obediently to reveal four push bikes. They each selected one.

'Tony has a hire car, but this is how us mere mortals get about,' said Jamie, 'Just follow us, we ride on the sidewalks it's far too dangerous on the road.' Off they set, Elle a bit wobbly at first, for it was a long time since she had ridden a bike. She was glad she had chosen to wear shorts and not one of her island dresses. She guessed they must have cycled for more than a mile when they arrived at a huge gate displaying a sign which read, "Bradford's Marine Shipyard. Authorised Personnel Only." Jamie stepped off his bike and pressing a button beside the gate announced to the wall, '*Sea Princess* crew.' The gates swung open and they peddled on through.

They left the bikes in some racks outside a group of porta-cabin type offices. 'We have one of these for crew meetings and stuff, like a *Sea Princess* office during the refit, if you like,' said Jamie and knocking on the door first to announce their arrival, he opened it and the others followed him inside. Charles and Cajsa were already there, pouring over plans of the interior of the yacht with steaming coffees.

'Ah, brilliant, you are all here,' said Charles rising from his chair, 'Did you have a good night Elle? I trust your flat mates made you welcome.'

'Yes, thank you, I slept for over twelve hours I think.'

'You must have needed the rest,' returned Cajsa with a smile.

During this meeting Elle learnt that the refit was expected to last six weeks and that after initial sea trials they would set out across the Atlantic via Bermuda and the Azores to the Mediterranean where the owners would join them to cruise the Greek Islands, Turkey, Southern Italy, and possibly Yugoslavia as well. Elle was to prepare meals to fill the freezer for the crossing with Lulu to help her, as for the time being there was nothing they could do on board whilst the yacht was full of carpenters, plumbers and electricians. They were also to help Cajsa with her selection of galley equipment, and tableware and linen, which sounded like the best job to Elle, who liked nothing more than a food orientated shopping spree. She was given details of her salary and invited to open an account with the company bank into which her wages could be paid if she did not require the cash. Elle felt so important. There would also be air tickets home for holidays when appropriate.

'*Sea Princess*,' there she was, with her name barely legible on the stern where busy sanders had been working on the paint. She was every bit as stunning as Elle knew she would be, tucked away in the bowels of Bradford Marine shipyard, the inner sanctum, in a dry dock safely undercover. Her masts lay beside her, riggers already at work with a spaghetti of new stainless steel stays, which would anchor them to the deck. Blocks and shackles, half opened packages of creamy white rope, some shot through with red for sheets, lazy jacks, all new to replace the old. The proud, round stately stern of her was being prepared for the paint job of her life, the newest toughest spray, a mirror hard finish to cover the solid steel of her belly ready to slice through the storms of the Atlantic and beyond. Elle rode on a buoyant wave, she was so happy to be a part of it all.

Cabinet makers were working in all of the cabins and the deck saloon and there seemed to be an argument going on as a side-board had been installed in the bar area before the plumber had been able to place a pipe for the sink and ice maker beneath. There was much shouting and swearing and Charles was faced with placating two or three angry men, so the girls passed quickly down to the galley. Two electric ovens were already half fitted, the fridges, being the original ones, were in situ already. They opened the long horizontal deep freeze and peeped inside. 'Built to take a body I believe, in case anyone died at sea,' remarked Cajsa. A dishwasher was sitting in the middle of the floor waiting for installation. She explained the layout to Elle. 'We will have one side for myself and Lulu with a sink, draining board and dishwasher underneath, so we won't get in your way when we are clearing away. The other side is your sink and draining board, with work surface and the ovens and gas hob behind you there. I know it's a small space so we will all have to be well organised and extremely tidy. Oh, and of course we will have air conditioning. The little cabin behind the galley is for myself and Charles, the crew quarters are up forward but it's a big mess up there for the moment. I am sure it will be cosy with a big shower for us all right up in the bow.'

She showed them the dining room below the deck saloon, with a fine table safely wrapped in dust sheets, and then on down aft to the guest cabins and bathrooms, one with a hip bath where the owner could sit and bathe in luxury. Elle thought the accommodation fairly limited but then the layout was not designed for charter, just for the owners and their guests, a maximum of six in total.

They were measured for their uniforms and that first day passed in a blur of new experiences, culminating in her first visit to an American supermarket as they cycled home. She wandered up and down the aisles in a total daze, never having seen so many varieties of bread, muffins, milks, yogurts, in fact every product seemed have a multitude of guises, how did anybody possibly choose? This was going to take some getting used to for sure. Everyone was enchanted and amused when they spoke finding their English accents quirky and funny, pressing them to say more. They were wished a nice day so many times that by the end of the day, Elle found that the repetitiveness had destroyed the sincerity of the good wishes.

The new engineer arrived, but no one saw him the first few days as he slept his way through jet lag. When he did appear he was whisked off to the engine room aboard *Sea Princess*, and returned with them exhausted in the evening. Mark was an engineer from Bristol following a romantic notion. He had never travelled before in his twenty-four years. To Elle he looked baffled and lost in his new surroundings, and she wondered how he would fare at sea, with all magnitude of problems an engineer has to face on a yacht such as *Sea Princess*. His duties would not just be confined to the engine room but to everything mechanical and electrical on board. Still he was friendly and pleasant and could put his feet behind his head when sitting cross-legged on the floor in a most alarming, bendy manner which made them all laugh.

The crew was complete, all six selected and present, plus Tony, of course, who was soon to leave them. He appeared one evening when she had spent the day making and freezing meals for the crossing. Finding her alone in the apartment he asked her if she would like to go and see a film. Elle was hesitant, not sure if it was wise, but it was a tempting offer as she had not been to the cinema since she left England. At his request she left a simple note to say she had gone out, not revealing any details, which she knew they would find a bit strange, but Tony stated their case firmly. 'We are grown ups aren't we and can do as we please. I am sure they will guess anyway but I don't see why we should announce to them all that we have gone somewhere together.' Feeling ill at ease, she followed him out of the door.

The awkwardness hung over her in the cinema. She was uncomfortable about her disappearance knowing her crew mates would be discussing their 'date' at length when they got home. Her mind drifted to her grandfather too, given that she had travelled in completely the wrong direction. Charles had hinted that a Caribbean winter might be on the cards so she tried to hope for the best. Following a dream was difficult. She had to work as well.

Tony whispered. 'Are you enjoying it?'

She was glad he refrained from any further enquiry because she really had no idea what was happening on the screen. Sliding down in her seat she tried to concentrate but her mind was everywhere. When Elle was preoccupied in thought the world could end around her and she probably wouldn't notice.

The film over she politely agreed to a drink at his apartment, as it was, after all, in the same block as her own and they made their way fairly silently on the short walk home. He poured her a glass of rosé and she could not help but notice the open, neatly packed suitcases on the floor in one corner.

Elle took a deep breath. 'You are all packed and ready I see.'

'Yes I'm flying back to England the day after tomorrow to see my Mum and sister, and then I'm off to New Zealand within a week or so.'

Elle knew Tony's sister from Spain in fact she had introduced them. 'How is Suzanne, we had a night out together in London when I was doing my diploma, did she tell you that?'

'Yes, she did mention something I remember she told me how stupid I was to break up with someone as lovely as you.' Elle blushed and looked away from him.

'Just not the right time I suppose, for something to grow serious,' he said.

'Oh,' she said, which came out more like a grunt than a word.

'Come to bed with me Elle, just one night before I go and then you can forget all about me again, as I shall be the other side of the world.'

'It was hard to forget about you before and now you would put me through it all again?'

'Just tonight please so we can part on happier terms this time.'

'We shan't tell anyone shall we?'she asked.

'Why would we? Our private secret I promise.'

So he held her and made love to her tenderly that night just as she had remembered him to be, gentle and loving, a different person to the somewhat serious, mirthless Tony that others saw, a contrast indeed to the cruel person who had dismissed her from his life in Spain.

She dressed quickly in the dark so as not to wake him, and crept along corridors letting herself quietly back into the apartment she shared with the others and safely to her own bed. She lay there and wondered if she would ever know what love was all about.

  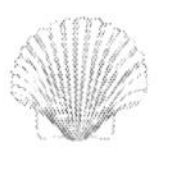

Almost 2 months later the day of the relaunch dawned and *Sea Princess* made a smooth decent into the water and wound her way back to the marina with full crew and a dozen men from the yard. Some were still finishing off with their heads in cupboards and others were checking the systems and engines. Elle was fascinated on the trip through the inland waterways, edged with luxurious properties with their own moorings and boats literally at the foot of their gardens.

The crew moved all their belongings out of the apartments and happily installed themselves on board. Lulu and Jamie took the cabin on the starboard side of the galley, equal in size to that of Charles and Casja on the port side. This cabin was traditionally for the engineer, but as they were a couple they pleaded the need for privacy, Charles muttering all the while that normally he disapproved of relationships amongst newly hired crew. Lulu successfully won him over, and so Elle was left to share the accommodation forward with Mark. Their areas were separated not only by the crew dining table, but also by concertina doors which pulled across at night to create two cabins, small but adequate. Elle had two bunks in hers and Mark had a small double with limited standing room when the doors were shut at night. Casja said it reminded her of two eggs cracking when they opened their respective doors each morning.

Elle adored working with Charles and Casja. Charles had the traits she admired in a man, charisma, logic, humour, and an adventurous fun loving spirit. He was marvelous at handling people and had a rock solid view of life. He was quick to bring out the best in his crew by working hard alongside them, full of sound advice on every level. A skipper upon whose decisions Elle would trust her life. He recognised her strengths and her weaknesses and drew the best from her. She learnt quickly never to argue with him, as he had studied law and would always put across his side of an argument with no room for doubt, or even discussion.

There could, in Elle's opinion, be no couple better suited than Charles and Casja. Opposites had most certainly attracted an Egyptian girl to a Cornish man. They had met several years before joining *Sea Princess* and since then they had, as far as Elle knew, barely been apart even for a day.

Casja was a classic Egyptian beauty with the palest complexion and the blackest hair of any Cleopatra. She quickly began to advise Lulu and Elle how to safe guard their youthful looks with lotions and potions and they began to spend time pampering themselves, even visiting a Vidal Sassoon hair and beauty parlour in Miami.

Elle thrived in this safe, almost family environment, with contentment beginning to envelop her like a secure, warm blanket. She settled into her job and her galley, looking forward to each new day with enthusiasm, as they prepared to leave for Europe. On receipt of her first batch of mail from her new address which was now care of the company in Tolsa, she felt even more well travelled than she actually was, for of course she had never been to Oklahoma. In the marina bar one evening she stumbled across Geoff's lookalike cousin who greeted her with open arms although their first encounter had been a brief one, down in the islands.

'Come round,' he said. 'I work on a boat just on the next quay, we could have a game of backgammon and a drink on Sunday afternoon.'

So, not having anything planned, Elle agreed and wandered around to his boat at the arranged hour. Why she went she did not know, she did not even like the guy. His similarity to his cousin perhaps, physically if nothing else, tempted her. She was not sure she trusted him, but maybe she went because she felt like some company other than the crew mates with whom she spent all her time. Anyway the die was cast and it was a bad decision. After several drinks and games of backgammon he lunged and tried to kiss her, boldly grabbing her and placing a hand firmly on her breast. She shoved him away as hard as she could, disgusted and betrayed.

'Oh come on, you gave my cousin Geoff what he wanted pretty easily so don't come all innocent with me.'

'Geoff and I built a relationship together, based on mutual feelings, he wasn't a rude bully like you!' He wouldn't be at all happy that you tried to force yourself on me either. Thank you for your hospitality but I'm going home now, before I get really angry,' Elle said, but she was already furious and could feel her colour rising. She was close to striking him. She stopped herself in time. If she slapped his face she sensed she could be letting herself in for real trouble. She wanted to be away from him as soon as possible back in her safe haven. Why had she come? How could she have been so stupid?

'I think we should talk about this Elle.'

His use of her name seemed at once both sly and patronising.

'Nothing to talk about.' She rose and taking their glasses to the sink started to mount the stairs of the companionway.

'Oh I think there is,' he continued in the same brutish, confident tone. 'If you don't let me have my wicked way with you like a good girl then I will tell Geoff you did anyway, so it's a win win situation from where I am standing.'

'Get lost you ignorant pig, he would never believe you, and I will write to him and tell him exactly how you behaved. Do you really think he will take your word against mine?'

'Yes I do actually, blood is thicker and all that, Madame. We shall see won't we?'

She swallowed her reply and turned, running back down the pontoon, feeling the tickle of tears through her furious anger, desperate that he should not follow or see her distress.

Elle never heard from Geoff ever again, so his treacherous cousin had been right, his story had been believed and he had broken Geoff's heart. Hers was luckily still intact but she was greatly saddened that he must now think so badly of her. She was powerless to plead her case, except by letter which she wrote immediately. There was no reply. The blackmailer had won his game.

Elle threw herself back into her work, shopping carefully to stock the larder with all the dried goods for the crossing. The freezer was already full of prepared meals with just enough room left for her to freeze some dairy produce, and a space for fish in case they should be lucky enough to catch some on the long trip ahead. The supermarket loved her as she wandered round filling four or five trolleys at each visit. She was amazed how kind and helpful the staff were with packing and delivering her purchases in large brown paper bags down to the boat and helping her to load everything on board.

New sails were bent on, protected by sail covers, crisp and gleaming, Elle loved the feel, touch and smell of their virgin condition, untouched as yet by salt and wind. Varnish shone against perfect paintwork and smooth, bright teak decks. *Sea Princess* was born again defying her years, ready to face oceans and storms and to protect her crew and guests alike. Elle liked best to sit in a corner she had found resting her back against the wheelhouse, and listen to the comments of admiration from passers by. She was a part of it all, and she feared someone might wake her from what appeared to be an impossible dream.

16

"You can go to heaven if you want, I would rather stay in Bermuda"

Mark Twain

After four or five sea trials with engineers from the yard aboard, the day finally arrived for all of those who had worked on *Sea Princess* those long months, to stand on the quayside and watch her set sail for Bermuda with only her crew. Elle requested to stand a night watch with the others although she was cooking, as otherwise she felt left out of the action. She chose the early morning watch with the skipper so that he could teach her some navigational skills, and also because none of the others were keen early birds, whereas for Elle it was the best time of the day, fresh and exciting.

All the frantic days of preparation ashore behind them, they set the sails, *Sea Princess* finding her pace in the light, steady breeze and sunshine. Elle experienced again the wonderful feeling of calm that always fell upon her when she left the land and the hustle bustle behind. She had prepared a great many meals so all she had to do was to plan the vegetables to accompany the dish she chose to defrost and to experiment and play baking cakes in her new ovens.

Jamie and Lulu, Charles and Cajsa, Mark and … Elle, how ever many jokes the rest of the crew might choose to make, the latter would never be a couple. She suspected they all were aware of the unsettling effect that Tony had had upon her, although no one had said anything. She and Mark were friends but that was all and he was not settling in at all well with life aboard ship. Elle suspected that when he had considered how life would be on a yacht whilst in his home in Bristol, he had probably envisaged a glamorous stress free existence with more play than work. But the reality was that as the engineer he was responsible for all manner of things all with a tendency to malfunction. Toilets, air-conditioning, pumps a plenty, refrigeration, and a water heater, to name just a few, never mind the main engines themselves and generators. The engine room became a stifling hot, noisy environment that accelerated the seasickness that gripped them all in varying degrees those first few days. Elle shook hers aside and undertook her engine checks on watch with the enthusiasm that learning something new can bring. Charles had rigged up safety grab lines so that they might find their way comfortably from the wheelhouse to the engine room hatch, and of course *Sea Princess* had huge, mast mounted flood lights at the flick of a switch.

The wheelhouse. How she grew to adore perching high on the bench seat with the view of the ocean all around her listening to the small background noises that serenaded the wind and the sails. The tick, tick tick, of the gyro compass as it righted their course after the surge of a wave, the screw that someone had left trapped in the woodwork so it rolled endlessly from side to side under her seat, and the hum of the radar screen, into which she would peep at regular intervals. Elle was fascinated to be able to detect other vessels, rain showers, even rubbish bags as they floated on the surface, such sophistication after the long nights straining her eyes to watch the horizon on *El Guero*.

Peter was climbing on the boom trying to reattach a stray piece of lazy jack, stretching, reaching just that bit higher until he tumbled between, as if falling through a frame and he fell more helplessly than would seem normal to the topside, and then to the deck below. She cradled his dear face, some small blood on his forehead but when he spoke his jaw seemed misshapen and wrong ...

Elle woke abruptly her automatic alarm in her head telling her it was 3.45am and time to get up for her watch at 4. Where did the dreams come from for she only occasionally thought of Peter now? Her subconscious must still be full of him, shelved memories and thoughts waiting to be triggered whilst she slept, enveloping her in their false reality for one fragmented moment, so perplexing! She crept on to the bridge, silent slippered feet on thick carpet. Charles visibly jumped.

'I simply cannot get used to a watch partner who needs no call,' he said.

'Oh don't mind me,' replied Elle, 'I have always been the same, never late for anything, always early. Trains, buses, watches, I will never change.'

Charles laughed and they settled into their routine of checks and recalculation of their position. Elle felt proud of her ever-increasing knowledge of stars and sextant, although she found it difficult to grasp the mathematics involved in the calculation to finally plot their position, and she admired Charles for his endless patience. She hoped that by the time they reached Bermuda she would have begun to understand the method.

A few days out there were some grumblings from the main engine, all was not well, faces were tense. After many hours in the engine room, Mark was doubly disgruntled having come upon Lulu and Jamie in a compromising position in the wheel-house during their watch. Charles changed the watches so he had to stand vigil with Lulu, and Jamie was partnered with Casja in order to guarantee the safety of them all. He did not particularly see eye to eye with the domineering way of the stewardess, being oblivious to her good looks, which usually put her in control of all male crew members. So a small discord began to weave amongst them, although Elle could not help but be privately amused that Lulu should be taken thus upon the radar when she should have been looking into the screen.

She was busy cooking supper when the call came summoning all the crew to the bridge, where they found an unusually serious Charles. 'Sorry kids,' he began, 'we have lost engine power, we still have generators to run everything crucial and to charge the batteries, but we are reliant on the wind now. Casja and I have talked at length and as we are well over half way to Bermuda we shall carry on and arrange for the necessary parts for the engine to meet us there.'

'Won't it be difficult coming alongside with no engine?' Jamie asked. (Elle felt tempted to say she knew all about that, she'd done it before.)

'We'll drop anchor to begin with in Hamilton harbour, plenty of room for us there while we make a game plan. At least it means the visit from the members of the owner's company for their scheduled meeting can go ahead as planned.'

'How long do you think we will stay in Bermuda,' piped up Lulu.

'However long it takes for them to ship the parts to us and for us to fit them, could be several weeks even a month.'

As they all absorbed the information and the possible delay in their departure for Europe, a smoke alarm went off. 'Oh bloody hell the beans,' mumbled Elle leaping down the stairs, towards the galley.

'Well at least something's working,' remarked Mark, a frustrated edge to his tone.

The pan was black and the beans unrecognisable. Elle filled it with cold water making more smoke and returned to the bridge.

'I burnt the beans,' she announced by way of explanation.

'And so one disaster leads to another,' said Charles, 'luckily a lot less serious and less costly than an engine.'

They continued to maintain a good speed under sail and were due to make landfall on Elle's watch. She was so busy calculating their position by the stars that when Charles gave her a nudge and pointed through the windscreen at the feint loom of Bermuda, she felt stupid not to have noticed first.

'Sometimes observation coupled with navigation is a good idea,' said Charles with a broadening smile. 'We still need our exact position though so carry on.'

Sea Princess came to rest at anchor in the middle of Hamilton harbour, and they were a huge point of interest for those in the Royal Yacht Club who saw many cruise ships come and go, but few large sailing yachts of her type. A launch came alongside inviting them to use the Yacht Club facilities should they wish, but Charles, although polite, was faintly dismissive. His main concern was to make everything perfect for the company meeting to be held on board just a few days after their arrival.

They all fell in love with the quaint feel of a British island with policeman in helmets and Bermudan shorts, Marks and Spencer, and to Elle's glee digestive biscuits, which she had not seen since Gibraltar. There was live music in almost every pub they found, singers at pianos playing Carole King, small bands professionally rendering tunes from Marshall Tucker and the Eagles. Such a friendly, old fashioned and sort of cosy island in the middle of wind swept seas with tales of the triangle and ships prone to vanishing without trace. They entertained the company with great success and then moved round quayside in the harbour of St Georges to await spares for the engine.

Such was their delay that Charles suggested holidays be taken. Elle had no wish to go anywhere, least of all England so said she was quite happy to remain to care take while everyone else went home. Cajsa was keen to return to Egypt to see her father and the other three crew were excited to have the opportunity for an unexpected break to see their families. Charles was to remain with Elle.

He proved to be quite a handful without Casja to restrain him, often drinking late in the bar they found, with Elle struggling to guide his path carefully back on board without incident. One particular evening he launched himself merrily off a wall, but luckily no harm came, bar a few bruises.

On a Saturday night after listening to their favourite band for several hours, Charles invited the whole group to go sailing the following day. Elle was horrified, the boat maimed as she was, and with just the two of them! The whole idea was preposterous but as she had been engaging in a mild flirtation with one of band she hoped it would just turn into a picnic or something, without them leaving the dock.

Charles was stubborn as usual and determined to prove that it could be done, and the two of them managed to navigate *Sea Princess* around the length of the harbour as if she were a dinghy, and place her safely alongside again much to Elle's relief. After an excess of beer the band stayed aboard and Elle slept fully clothed alongside her new friend, ironically enough another Peter, in one of the guest cabins. She could not help thinking that none of this would have occurred if Casja had been there to maintain normality, but their day had been exciting and she felt proud of their team work.

After supper the following night when Charles and Elle found themselves alone again he had taken her hand and led her to the cabin he shared with Casja. 'I'm lonely,' he said slightly the worse for a bottle of wine. 'Come and give me a hug, Elle please?' She knew it was wrong but she lay down beside him and they embraced, kissing each other deeply. He fell asleep before any more damage could be done and she quietly returned to her own bunk, feeling guilty and confused. She resolved to tell Casja on her return. To live with such a secret would be impossible.

Darling Daddy,

The crew have all gone home for a break excepting Charles and myself, as I have not been aboard long I thought I would save my holiday flights for later on. We are on holiday too though, the pair of us, and on board Sea Princess we have two Topper dinghies, so we spend 90% of our time chasing each other around the harbour playing tag and tipping each other over ... childish but fun. They are super boats made of plastic dustbin material so completely indestructible. Charles said I disappear so far that he shall fit a chart table to mine.

The weather is wonderful and I swim a lot at night as the phosphorescence in the water is the most remarkable I have ever seen. Today I can't sail out and around as I planned because the wind is picking up and a hurricane is due to pass close to the island ...

The crew flew in bar one. Jamie stayed in England, Elle did not delve into what had happened with Lulu, just consoled her, but Charles and Casja seemed relieved that the issues created by having a volatile couple on board had been so easily resolved. The rows had been audible from the galley causing an uncomfortable atmosphere and Jamie's bottom lip had fallen almost to his brand new deck shoes for days on end, with everyone creeping around him too scared to say a word.

A new bosun was on his way from England, already organised through an agency. Lulu was to move into the other bunk in Elle's corner and so the new guy could have the small cabin starboard of the galley to himself.

'Well,' Casja began, 'I haven't had a chance to ask you since I got back, did you manage to keep Charles under control, and what about this story I heard of taking a whole jazz band out sailing?'

'Well there were only four of them.'

'And you quite sweet on one of them I believe?'

'Sort of, yes, I suppose so,' said Elle cagily. 'Charles was a handful sometimes though.'

'I can imagine, thank you for keeping watch over him and making sure he didn't make a total fool of himself.'

'He was a little affectionate one night and we had a kiss and cuddle before we went to bed,' Elle offered the information carefully, a great weight off her heart.

'Oh, I see,' said Casja, 'Thank you for telling me that.' With her comment revealing nothing concerning her feelings on the matter, she passed through into her cabin and firmly closed the door. Elle saw nothing of her for about three days after this, and her anxiety that she might be the cause welled in her head until she could stand it no longer.

'Charles, is Casja alright?' she asked, as he was busy boiling eggs for his lady in the galley.

'Yes Elle,' he replied, without really meeting her eye, 'Just a bit jet lagged and unsettled, she will be fine.'

A couple of days later Charles and Casja sneaked off the boat and were married without saying a word to anyone. When they returned and announced their sudden news it was back to business as usual, with no talk of a celebration.

Cajsa, catching Elle alone in the galley said, 'It is okay to be a little in love with Charles you know, I understand. He is extremely lovable although exasperating at times.'

Elle was not at all sure how to respond, 'Of course I am equally fond of both of you, not just Charles.'

'I brought you something from Egypt,' Casja continued, 'just a small thing.'

She presented Elle with a silver twisted bangle.

'Wear it for fertility.' she said seriously.

'Well I'm not sure that's such a good idea,' said Elle her voice shaking.

'I brought more Henna for our hair so we could do that tomorrow together couldn't we? It's supposed to help protect against sun and wind if we do it regularly. 'Fantastic,' said Elle slowly exhaling with relief for the return of the friend she thought she might have lost.

Tomasz arrived, the new bosun … luckily this time not Lulu's cup of tea at all. Of Polish descent, with a great smile and firm views on how things would be above decks, to Elle he seemed like a ready-made pirate sort of character. He walked the decks with a strange gait, heavy on his heels, as Casja was quick to remark. With his music firmly in his ears as he worked on the varnish, Tomasz or just plain Tom as he liked to be known was king in his own world.

While they waited for news of engine spares little work was done, although Elle still cooked of course, and the others cleaned and polished. They continuously played their silly games with the two sailing dinghies chucking cushions around and capsizing willy-nilly. They met a young man who taught Charles and Tom to windsurf but Elle was hopeless and spent all her time in the water. Charles taught them to drive the Boston whalers in formation around the still waters of the harbour, like aeroplanes in the sky, leaving perfect trails of white spray. It was strange how the removal of one character that did not quite fit changed the whole atmosphere on board for the better. Lulu was happier, proving Charles right about the whole couples thing, excepting him and Casja of course.

So many tourists stopped and asked the same questions about the boat that Charles made a board and set it in the rigging answering the most obvious. The parts eventually arrived and repairs were satisfactorily made, but Charles called a crew meeting and informed them sadly that they were too late to pursue the season in the Mediterranean and *Sea Princess* would return to Fort Lauderdale briefly and then down to the islands for the whole winter season.

'We shall be heavily reliant on Elle to show us the way with her experience,' he finished causing Elle to blush.

'Mine too remember,' said Lulu, 'I was there!'

'Yes, but were you paying attention to the navigation of the islands? I doubt it,' said Charles coiffing her affectionately on her curly head. Sad to leave their island bliss, they motor-sailed back to Fort Lauderdale.

Charles found it was hard to install discipline again after all the fun and games in Bermuda. He shouted at Lulu and Elle to go below and put on their uniform as they were clambering around on the upper deck removing sail ties in skimpy pareos and bare feet. That was the first time Elle had heard him sound angry and it would not be the last. It was just as well he pulled them into line, as the journey back to Florida was a rough one. She resumed her watches with Charles and her navigation lessons for the return trip. Again the landfall was scheduled on their early morning watch. Charles went down to his cabin to have some shuteye, leaving her instructions to wake him as soon as she could see the loom of Miami Beach. Elle was content, proud to be left in charge. After an hour had passed she saw the lights and busily carried on plotting and altering their course to take them through the harbour entrance.

Maybe I will let him sleep just a few more minutes, she thought, and when they were just three miles out by her calculations she went and tapped on his door. A sleepy skipper came up the companion way to the wheelhouse, rubbed his eyes and let out a shriek.

'Good God Elle, that's the hotel on the corner of Miami Beach!' The lights were towering above them, illuminated giants in the night sky.

'Yes I know,' said Elle smugly, 'but we are on a perfect course for the entrance.'

'I don't bloody care what course we are on you silly girl, I asked you to wake me when you saw the loom, did you not listen?'

'Yes Charles, I am sorry, but I though you needed the rest and we are okay on this course aren't we?'

'I will say this only once Elle, please follow my orders so that if something does go wrong, it's my fault not yours! Now go and call everyone to make ready shore lines and fenders.'

Charles was to tell this story many times and in the telling his anger towards her softened by degrees.

Back in Fort Lauderdale with the engineers aboard again, it hardly felt as though they had been away. Now it was Elle who decided to have a bit of a break. Peter from the band in Bermuda had returned to Maine and wrote inviting her to go there for a few days and see a bit more of America. The others all encouraged her to go. Tom said, 'It's a long way to go for a bonk, I could oblige and save you all that trouble!' She both loved and hated him for his comical observations.

With a flight booked to Boston she arranged a hire car so she could drive to meet Peter and then they would go together to see the rest of the band in the White Mountains.

Maine in the fall. Everyone had told her it was beautiful and so it was. The leaves were turning in the crisp autumn sunshine as they drove to small fishing harbours with a pleasant absence of burger joints. The roads actually bent into corners unlike the straight lines of Florida. Elle had not bargained on Peter's constant craving for fast food, wanting to sit up all night munching and watching television in some small, cheap, motel. Admiring him singing with the band in Bermuda was one thing, but the day to day reality of spending time with him was depressing. It is extraordinary how seeing someone in a different situation can change how you first perceived them to be, exposing the gritty reality of how in truth, they live and think. In her mind Elle quickly replaced interest with indifference. Sex she told him, was not on the cards, as she preferred to safe guard their friendship, for what it was, in her mind, superficial and new. An almost tangible strength had lifted her opinion of herself, she had a good job and a small family behind her on *Sea Princess*. She knew her own mind and could recognise her past errors of judgement only too painfully. Her striving, endless search for a meaningful relationship had previously been driven, not by suitability or affection for a possible partner but by her own insecurities. She could not wait for her short holiday to be over and to fly back to *Sea Princess*. Of course she would tell them all she did have a fantastic time, which in a way she had, the scenery in the White Mountains had been breathtaking.

Darling Daddy,

So glad to hear that the little owl from Bermuda arrived safely and that you liked him.

We are now back in Fort Lauderdale after an exceedingly rough ride. We were steaming along at fourteen knots one night and I regret to state that everyone was sick except for myself and the mate, which didn't make us very popular. We are now delaying a while longer than expected here (don't we always?) in order to have a new radar installed as the other one has finally died. Charles is also toying with the idea of a scanner soon, which means we would virtually never have to navigate at all ... bit of a shame really.

The British navy ship Blake has been here with some Fleet Air Arm pilots that Charles used to fly with. One of them knew your friend very well ... a big coincidence. I went with Charles and Casja to an official dinner on their ship, Casja and I being the only two women there it was a bit like being thrown to the lions.

I am still baking Christmas cakes for the boss to be sent north. The sixth came out of the oven today. We've had our accountant from Oklahoma staying as well so I've been quite busy.

I have seen two films this week, Death on the Nile and Who's killing the Great Chefs. Both were really good. Halloween was an unbelievable occasion with the most bizarre costumes everywhere but November 5th passed by without even a pop, which felt a bit sad.

Our last March charter in the islands has just been cancelled so we shall be heading back to Europe sooner than expected – I am homesick for European waters now.

Charles is busy phoning our December guests, frantically quizzing me, I am his Caribbean pilot apparently as he has never been down there before.

A week has slipped away in the middle of this letter while I flew to Boston, hired a car and drove through Maine into New Hampshire, up into the White Mountains. I stayed with a band we listened to night after night in Bermuda.

There was no snow but it was excruciatingly cold with everyone poised for the skiing season to begin. It has improved my opinion of America; they actually do have something other than hamburger shops and drive-in movies. The White Mountains are impressive, so called because they are covered in silver birch trees. I arrived back yesterday to find the new radar installed and our departure date set for 21st November.

The Christmas cakes that went to the boss were accompanied by explicit instructions for storage for December but some have been eaten for BREAKFAST, and needless to say, found to be perfection. Americans are heathens. Nothing is sacred.

I did bring an Advent calendar and a few bits back from Boston to try and make Christmas feel a bit more Christmassy this time around in the islands.

I ordered all the meat for the Caribbean today. I am much

better at stocking up than I used to be ... still a bit of worry about whether I have bought enough. Another thousand dollars spent.

We have the world's greatest maker of model ships arriving tonight from New York to stay on board and study the boat in preparation for a miniature replica. A man drew a picture of Sea Princess in Bermuda and he said he thought it was no good so he gave it me and I shall treasure it forever.

I have promised to jog with Lulu tomorrow at 6.30am followed by my cholera shot – a good start to the day don't you think?

I miss you so much

All my love

Elle

Charles found an old friend on the navy ship, a kind man who came from the same part of the world in Cornwall as he, and subsequently they had worked together too, forming a strong bond. He confided in Charles and Casja that his absence from home was causing him some marital problems and he feared he had lost his wife to another man. His sadness affected Charles and he asked Elle if she would partner his old friend to the events on the ship and join them in taking him for a picnic on Miami Beach. So Elle found herself, walking hand in hand on the Florida sands with a total stranger, and sitting at his table for dinner on HMS Blake. A somewhat bizarre and uncomfortable situation for them both, Elle was glad when the favour came to an end and her duty was done.

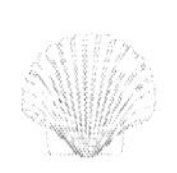 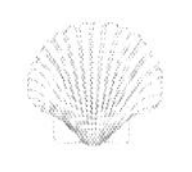 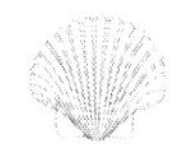

Sitting in the sun on the top deck with Casja and Lulu, their hair covered in green henna to make them beautiful, Elle felt completely relaxed.

'Someone to see you Elle,' Charles shouted up.

'Who is it,' she asked 'I don't want to see anyone I have green hair for goodness sake.'

Casja and Lulu thought this situation hilarious.

'Old friend of yours apparently, Freddie, Freddie Cooke, ring any bells?'

'Oh my God, quick what can I do,' she implored of the others.

'Here,' said Casja, 'make a turban with this towel and just go on down and tell him we are in the middle of a pamper session and to come back later.'

'Good plan,' she agreed and down she went with a face as red as her hair was green.

'So wonderful to see you Elle,' he said throwing his arms wide and ending up with green on his face as well, 'I knew I could track you down, we have so much catching up to do.'

'Can you come back in a bit, when I have got this stuff off my head.'

'Yes of course we can go and have a drink at the marina or something.'

Such genuinely understanding friend, Elle was so glad to see his grin again and although their time together was brief she knew she had special feelings for this slightly awkward and hopelessly polite young man. Casja had liked him immediately and did not hesitate to say that he was probably a much safer bet than the band member from Bermuda who she felt had led both Elle and Charles astray during her absence.

Plans were laid that this time Elle would definitely be able to finally see her grandfather John in St Lucia. Elle was so excited in the knowledge that the meeting between them would finally happen at last.

PART FOUR

Revisiting the Islands

17

"Life is made up of so many partings welded together."
Charles Dickens

Freddie…

"Elle was like a butterfly flying from island to island, and from boat to boat, whilst I trailed behind forever hoping to catch a glimpse of her before she darted on again, restlessly pursuing her work. At least I knew that she would be safe for a while on *Sea Princess* and that they would take to find her grandfather John.

I planned everything I would say to her each time I caught up with her but I could never quite manage to tell her how I felt and I knew there were others braver, more outspoken than me. I just hoped they would treat her kindly, for once she had set sail for Europe again I knew I would have lost her forever.

I had the same intentions as the old sea captain who brought her to the Caribbean, I wanted to confine and imprison her so that she could not meet or become involved with anyone who might not appreciate her, or worse defile her in some way.

How young and carefree we all were, out there. We thought we knew it all but we knew nothing. Nothing but the sunshine and the breezes chasing us around the islands, playing with our lives, free of responsibility and the normal land locked anxieties of ordinary people. But where would we fit in when we grew old?"

Impatient for the islands, they set sail for the Grenadines; their course took them first to the Bahamas, where Elle discovered another unspoilt utopia of windswept white sands and picture-perfect anchorages. Such a blue and turquoise heaven. The Caribbean Sea was responsible for the green shoots of the new life that grew around her feet, a chance to leave all the dead vegetation of her past behind, not forgotten entirely but the bitter hurt and confusion was fading. Alice had climbed out of the rabbit hole, to blink in the tropical sunshine, a different girl to the one who had fallen to the depths. In her head she had metamorphosed, shed her skin, a new Elle.

Charles and Casja laughed and covered each other in oil in the fierce sun, Tom sat under a palm tree offering her his undying love, whilst trying to persuade her that to fall for him would surely be the easiest and most convenient way of securing the happiness she sought. Charles explained to her that this solution would be the result of propinquity and therefore not a good or strong basis for a relationship. 'What does that mean?' she asked him. 'It means that you would have fallen into each others arms because of the close vicinity you found yourselves in and not because of a genuine attraction.' This she knew and Elle began to express her fears aloud to Casja of ever being attractive to the right sort of man. She had little faith that her love life could ever be anything but a disaster.

They sailed south finding themselves anchored in a grey bay in the proximity of the island of St Kitts which looked to Elle like a slate coloured mountain, not beautiful at all and surrounded by windy, intimidating dark waves. The atmosphere of this island made her feel strangely uncomfortable ... maybe it was just due to the turn of the weather.

An aircraft carrier, the Arc Royal, held a commanding presence far out in the bay. Charles and Casja were invited for drinks, and Elle too which made the rest of the crew envious to a degree. There was to be high jinks on a training exercise involving a giant can of baked beans being lowered from a helicopter into a Boston whaler belonging to *Sea Princess*; this fun healed the wound with Tom and Mark. Elle was fascinated by the regimented orderliness of the carrier and crew and also by the huge elastic bands to catch the planes as they landed. This was the navy at its most exciting. The size of the galley was so intimidating, and the mountains of potatoes to be peeled even more so. She was glad to return to her own, snug place of work in her tidy small galley.

Their stay in St Kitts ended badly ... Tom and Mark went ashore for a few drinks and on their return one of them must have sloppily tied the whaler (one glass too many perhaps) for in the morning it was gone. Charles was tight lipped and furious that such carelessness could occur and called all hands on deck to head out into the stormy, uninviting seas to look for the boat. They could see it in the distance for a moment, rising to the top of a wave and then gone from sight into the trough that followed each swell. Charles realised straight away that they would be risking life to attempt to secure a line on the erratic whaler so *Sea Princess* turned around with a heavy heart. They all shared in the misery of having let the owners down, the responsibility and blame could not be placed on one crew member alone. They continued their journey south shortly after the whaler incident, in order to be in English Harbour in time for the agent's week. *Sea Princess* was to be an "open house" to show her level of excellence and suitability for the charter season in the islands.

Elle was excited, almost a homecoming feeling with the chance of seeing friends, Freddie perhaps and the crew of *Bonaire* at least. There was much talk of finding her grandfather as soon as they sailed to St Lucia and she had posted him a letter from St Kitts, care of the customs at Le Vieux Fort where she believed him to be, attaching her address in Antigua. She was wild with the hope that he might reply.

It seemed such a long time since her first arrival there with John and *El Guero*. So much had happened in a year, so many paths crossed and sea miles sailed.

Sea Princess rested at anchor in the bay while they scrubbed and polished ready for the show, but needless to say there was much partying at *The Admiral's Inn*. Tom seemed to be a little too jovial and his eyes were always red. Elle guessed this had something to do with his frequent 'row boat rides' as he aptly named his trips into the mangroves with his new found Antiguan friends. Luckily he managed to pull himself together to get the job done as did Lulu who was a little that way inclined as well.

Elle for her part found herself newly enjoying the company of the crew of *Bonaire*, Robin in particular. He was always quietly there, at her side, making sure she had a lift back out to *Sea Princess* at a reasonable hour. One night he climbed aboard with her and they made love softly on the cushions of the aft deck, hoping that they would not wake Charles and Casja nor be discovered by any returning crew. Elle knew they would soon be parted probably for the rest of the season but she became fond of him and hoped they might see one another again somewhere. She never knew if her secret romance was common knowledge amongst the others for if it was, nothing was said.

Darling Daddy,

We have just had packets of mail, long awaited, including a lovely long letter from you.

We have been in Antigua for the last few days for agent's week and were voted easily the most beautiful yacht here, which has made us very conceited! We are now in St Maartins for just one day to pick up a new Boston Whaler as we lost one in St Kitts, a big disaster as they are not cheap, but accidents happen. Tomorrow we go to St Barths for a quick overnight visit and then straight to Martinique to pick up our first group of guests. I wrote to John to warn him of my imminent arrival in St Lucia and he wrote back immediately, VERY EXCITED! We will probably pick him up for a few days in-between charters- I think he will love it on board although I fear he will be most scathing about the grandeur of it all.

I have been doing loads of small boat sailing and yesterday I navigated one of our sailing dinghies out to sea around Antigua but the seas got bigger and bigger on the way home and I was glad to arrive safe and sound. It's great to be back in the West Indies after America and soon we will be back in Europe.

I have just finished icing the Christmas cake but as usual I can't quite get into the spirit when it's so hot and tropical.

Mother tells me my brother has become involved, I don't believe it!

O yes, John said in his letter that your half-brother Willy might be in St Lucia for Christmas. I do hope I meet him ... another missing piece of the puzzle that is my family.

I met up with a fair few of my old yachting friends in Antigua and was chuffed by the number of jobs I have been offered. Charles and Casja have my feet firmly nailed to the deck and I am not complaining. I met a boy too, someone I knew from last winter but in this profession relationships are ripped to pieces by constant traveling. It's hard not to get mopey when you keep sailing off in opposite directions.

Our new whaler has been christened Humphrey of all things. The weather here is even hotter than ever with huge sea swells apparently caused by a tidal wave, which passed

1000 miles away. We are off again in an hour so I must get changed and finish stowing the galley.

Miss you all

Love

Elle

  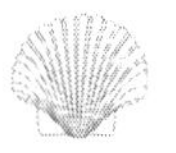

Elle was never to cross paths with Robin ever again, nor did she see Chris and Florence, who had left the Ocean charter fleet behind them, married and gone to grow coffee in the Azores, or so the English Harbour grapevine whispered. Such was her life, the people who seemed so important for a short moment in time, always disappeared over the horizon and were blown away, like clouds in a gusty sky. What must an existence be like where one saw the same people in the same environment everyday? There were so many questions that Elle could not answer. Was life always such a lonely place even when you stood amongst a crowd? She would hold on to *Sea Princess*, Charles and Casja for as long as she possibly could because they were her world and her home, in whatever waters they found themselves.

They sailed down through the islands Elle reveling in her knowledge of the area, spending hours advising Charles of the best places and anchorages. They collected their first guests as well as a whaler full of French delicacies in Martinique and then headed on stopping for a couple of nights in Marigot Bay before heading to the Piton anchorage that she knew so well from *Ocean Sun*.

The bay, with such a narrow entrance and opulent vegetation growing out across the water on all sides, was a real hurricane hole in every sense of the word. There were buoys for visiting yachts and work had begun to place pontoons in one section.

They spotted a small shack that was obviously the local bar, betrayed by the assortment of small craft tied higgledy-piggledy alongside a ramshackle jetty. The water was a still lagoon in contrast to the windy ocean they had left outside the bay. Elle knew from experience that the mosquitoes would be hungry on their night time sortie from the mangroves so she smothered herself in repellent. There was much activity on the hillsides around the anchorage, cranes and scaffolding, diggers and builders, and on the small quayside there seemed to be men with cameras on poles and other such paraphernalia.

'What do you think is happening over there?' Elle inquired generally of everyone on the bridge, crew and guests alike.

Casja was the first to raise a pair of binoculars, 'A film, I think they must be making a film,' she said excitedly, handing the glasses to one of the guests, 'I could see someone holding a parasol over a lady in period dress.'

'I'll send Tom to ask shortly,' said Charles. 'He can find out if we can see the set, if it is a film.'

The guests invited all the crew to join them for dinner at the only hotel that appeared to be open, and as the sun dropped lower behind the hill they all went ashore together.

The hotel felt old and colonial, with palms and hibiscus in reception that one had to weave through to find the desk where a sleepy receptionist sat, her face transformed into a visage full of worry at the size of the hungry party. 'May we eat?' asked Charles politely.

'Just wait a minute and I will ask in the restaurant,' she said and vanished through a small door behind the counter.

Eventually, when crew and guests had almost given up and Elle was beginning to wonder what could she dream up on the spur of the moment back on board ship, she reappeared.

'Chef says it will be okay but all we have is fish tonight,' she announced firmly in case anyone should argue.

'Fish and bananas I shouldn't wonder,' muttered Tom, whereupon Elle trod on his toe to silence him.

'I think if you are not careful we won't be offered anything at all,' she whispered.

Seating themselves in the large, dining room, a smart, local waiter in a suit with tails and bow tie attended them, his attire was, in itself, rather surprising. They were all happy to order the local fish and fresh vegetables, including the plantains that Tom had predicted.

'You see,' he said smugly to Elle for her ears alone, 'I told you so.'

'Of course, bananas are the main crop that's grown here, what do you expect, broccoli and carrots?

Charles asked for a wine list and was presented with one bottle of red wine which seemed to be the only choice on offer. The waiter disappeared in search of a corkscrew that they might taste the wine before ordering more. When he returned with the bottle and tool, he proceeded to attempt to open it at the table. Elle felt for him as all eyes were watching as he struggled awkwardly with the cork holding stubbornly to the bottle, no matter how hard he tugged. Red seeped through the coal blackness of his skin; a visible blush.

He wound the corkscrew back out of the cork and turning his back to the thirsty diners retreated to the bar area. On his return he placed the bottle onto the table in front of Charles with a flourish. The cork was floating in the wine. A titter was heard from Lulu but Charles, determined not to embarrass the poor waiter any further poured the wine around several glasses and after a quick taste ordered a further two bottles and so the incident was dismissed entirely.

'Do you know what they are filming in the bay?' asked Casja, a quick thinking attempt to draw the attention away from a potentially disastrous meal.

'Yes, it's Dr Dolittle Madame, Rex Harrison is here I believe,' and having disclosed this interesting titbit of news, he went in search of the fish and bananas.

How wonderful it was to sit with Tom in the small bar late in the evening in Marigot Bay. Elle began to have a soft spot for the Pole that grew and spread slowly. When would she see Robin again, she was glad that Tom (as far as she knew) had not noticed their secret liaison. And where was Freddie, life was indeed complicated. Plans changed again and *Sea Princess* was bound for Tobago Cays and St Vincent so the guests could dive, snorkel and windsurf. Every time Elle was within a few miles of her grandfather, their route was altered, but such was life when it was governed by those determined to make the best of their special holiday. Sometimes it was as though the guests could never be satisfied, always pushing on in search of something better, a calmer anchorage, a more beautiful bay, a superior reef with more fish.

A Polish flag was spotted in one of the spots they chose to anchor, Tom could not wait for the day to be done so he could go and greet his comrades in true Polish fashion with a bottle of vodka, especially saved for occasions such as this. Luckily they did not occur often. Sure enough with Charles's permission he disappeared after a stern warning not to disgrace himself or *Sea Princess* and to remember the influential guests aboard.

His stumbling return woke Elle with a start, she was accustomed to the mate having one too many but the stagger of his footsteps sounded ominous and unwillingly she rose to go and try to shovel him, somehow, into his bunk. He was lying close to the forward hatch, singing and talking, to himself. He was, she noticed, drenched, reeking of booze and something rather fishy.

'Elle, Elle, I am so pleased to see you,' he slurred merrily.

'Yes, well, I can't really say I feel the same, I am going to check you tied the whaler up properly. 'Why are you wet, did you fall in?'

'Think so, my mate, he saved me from drowning, mished my footing …'

The boat safely tied with a double knot, Elle went to wake Mark, she couldn't move him on her own.

The engineer was not amused but between them they pushed him down the steps, crashing and bumping.

'He'll have a few bruises tomorrow,' observed Mark.

'Serve him bloody right, idiot.'

In the crew quarter he made a dive for Elle's bunk waking Lulu as he landed face down.

'For goodness sake, that's my bunk and he's soaking wet!'

'Well we will never move him now, he's unconscious.'

'Ugh and he stinks, where am I supposed to sleep?'

'In his bunk I'm afraid, you will just have to hope he doesn't climb in with you in the night,' Mark was now beginning to see the funny side which Elle was most definitely not.

The night passed without further disturbance and Tom was suitably sorry for himself in the morning. Having been awoken in the middle of the night, Charles summoned him early to the bridge.

A reprimand was not forthcoming for the skipper had a more subtle punishment in mind. He made no reference at all to the night time antics, 'There is to be a diving party this morning Tom, and I would like you to be in charge. What's the matter? You look pale are you under the weather?'

'No, I'll be fine, what time are we to go?'

'10 o'clock, so you have an hour to prepare the equipment.'

'Nothing else?'

'No, nothing else, have a good dive.'

With the size of his hangover, the crew all understood this

must have been an awful undertaking for the poor Pole, with his bloodshot eyes and terrible breath, they all kept their distance.

A relentless succession of guests followed one party after another. Elle resented somewhat that when they did have a few days off she still had to cook for the crew, so she would disappear in the sailing dinghy for hours on end in-between meals, to have some time alone, to return refreshed and burnt to a crisp, the salt spray and perpetual sun leaving her sore. She adored Mustique, it was always the crew's favourite choice for a few days of rest. Basil's bar was a wooden square set right on the water, with a long pontoon reaching far out into the shallows. Clear water of the palest blue reflected the light sand beneath. Elle often swam ashore after dinner; the warm sea having a luxurious feel cushioning her tired limbs. Only a few of the guest groups were in fact paying charterers, most were part owners, or guests and family, so the atmosphere on board was always formal and yet relaxed, with an easy relationship between visitors and crew.

Lulu left them, quite suddenly, well maybe the drama only appeared to be sudden to Elle as she had not foreseen the problem nor the outcome. There had been some upset over a box of homeopathic medicine being mistaken for drugs. Elle was ignorant of what had happened concerning this mysterious box. Anyway another stewardess came to join them and so the family unit altered again, with Charles, Casja and Elle the only original solid core remaining. She missed her friend acutely and found she had little in common with Lulu's replacement. She was a large girl who seemed to spend all her time flirting with Mark, the two of them constantly guffawing over nothing. Tom continued with his persistent wooing, taking advantage of her loneliness after her friend's departure but Elle remained aloof, tossing her blond hair in defiance of his efforts.

Darling Daddy,

Thank you so much for the super pinny, which I have hardly taken off for the last 3 weeks while have had people on board. Charles and Casja love it, Charles saying that PVC turns him on and all I need is little wellies to match (he's not really that kinky!).

What's been happening ... we've been shooting up and down islands thro' gales and calm. We've rescued 3 boats in distress none of which had an insurance policy or 2 pennies to rub together, but still the feeling is good and one hopes that other people would do the same for us.

We blew out our mainsail and No1 jib, quite exciting but a little hard on the owner's pocket. The bosses have just left and I must say they kept us all on our toes. I haven't been ashore for 2 weeks. They didn't take one single meal ashore which is, I suppose a compliment, tho' exhausting. We have a new stewardess ... there is rather a lot of her but she is industrious and fun loving.

I had a quiet birthday this time on charter although a fair amount of alcohol was consumed on my behalf!

We haven't been to find John yet as we are still busy but with luck we will be there the last week in March, a plan has been made for this. Do write to him, I am sure he would like that, c/o Barclays Bank, Castries, St Lucia.

We now have 2 whole weeks rest but with a lot to fill our time. 4 days playing in Mustique where we are expecting a visit from the Jaggers, (we are of course sworn to secrecy) and a week in Martinique shopping for the crossing. Europe here we come! I may try to come back to visit before we start our season but knowing our bosses as I do, our time schedule may again be tight.

I am glad to hear that you may buy another boat, shall it be fiberglass or wood? So many lovely boats out here, only a few more years and I shall be buying mine!

The first year has gone quickly and the feeling of having a secure job that I love is the best.

I am trying to make a collection of model boats of the islands for my sister – latest acquisition is a sugar cane boat, a schooner intricately made – I have it hanging in a plastic bag pinned to the wall for fear of it being smashed in rough weather.

Must stop and sleep

Love Elle

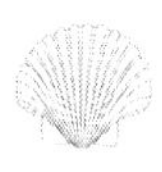 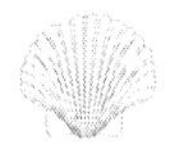 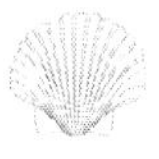

The end of March came at last, although Elle had been too busy to count the days. As promised *Sea Princess* lay moored in the Pitons and Casja went with her, both dressed smartly in their uniforms, to collect a hire car that they had booked to be delivered to a nearby hotel. Their destination, Vieux Fort was more of a fishing port than a tourist haven. Elle knew that her grandfather used to have a fishing boat or two, so it would have been an ideal choice for him on his arrival in St Lucia all those years ago.

He had written to her that after a recent illness he had gone to live with the customs officer and his wife. She had an address so she was confident they would find him.

They arrived at dusk and after stopping and asking a few workers who were on their way home they were advised to leave the car and continue the short distance to his village on foot.

So they pressed on, walking against a steady flow of banana plantation workers carrying machetes. Two girls in shorts, who were reminded of their vulnerability with every stare. The realisation of how these islanders lived was humbling, while they sailed by in the opulent world of private yachting and corporate business. Elle wondered how safe they were in truth, as the long knives around them glinted in the setting sun. Intruders walking on bravely through a plantation of jealous hearts, their heads bowed as they passed, then they turned to take a long look at the girls slight receding figures as they walked on. The village was not at all how Elle had imagined and Casja too looked shocked, for the street they were searching for was nothing more than a row of dilapidated shacks set close together with earthen paths between leaning fences. They asked again of some children if they knew of John, and were shown the way to the last hut.

Elle looked in vain for something to knock on to announce their arrival. Timidly she pushed her way through the colourful bead curtain with Casja at her heals.

'Hello, anyone home?'

The first thing she saw was a large pot of Marmite on the table with the lid off, with flies buzzing all around what looked like the remains of a meal, so she did not immediately take in the figure laid behind on a sort of day bed. They calmly looked at one another for a few silent moments when the lady of the 'house' bustled in from behind another fly curtain, ineffective in its purpose, for there was an abundance of the biggest blue-bottles that had Elle had ever seen in the stifling, dirty place.

John pulled himself to his feet and introduced her, 'This is my son's daughter, and her friend, I am sorry I don't know your name.'

'Casja,' said Elle quickly, 'Her name is Casja and she is my captain's wife.'

John shook their hands and held onto Elle's as he spoke.

'I always walk down for a swim and a rum at this hour of the day, you would be welcome to join me, for the walk anyway if not for the swim,' and he smiled softly at his own humour.

Elle was muted momentarily by the overwhelming realisation that she was actually there, after all the anxious hoping, and more importantly this was her grandfather leaning heavily on his stick beside her.

'Yes,' she mumbled throwing a questioning glance at Casja, who nodded her agreement for she too was spellbound.

The three of them walked together at John's slow pace for he strolled with the aid of two sticks, down the path to the waters edge, where abandoning his shawl he swam a fair way out to sea before he turned and made his way back to the shore. After solemnly rubbing himself down with the old towel he had tied around his waist for the journey down, they set off again, the strange threesome, the two girls still attracting many a glance. John was obviously not accustomed to company during this evening ritual for he spoke little, concentrating on the uphill path before him. Stopping at the tiny bar with a couple of chairs outside, the proprietor served him a rum with no communication with his customer at all, such was their daily pattern, the niceties worn silent with time. His companions asked for water and they sat together making idle chatter about the port, the fishing and the sea.

Elle studied her grandfather, he was stooped with age and pain but she saw a tall, proud figure within this old man with determined, strong eyes the colour of the Caribbean sea. He had sparse hair, almost bald, and his colour had turned to a dark mahogany, but not as wrinkled or lizard like as he should have been after the weather had taken it's toll on his once fair skin. She wished she had known him when he was younger. He enquired kindly after her grandmother, but showed little interest when she began to tell him of other family members. She guessed he had left all that behind and would prefer to keep his mind in his present reality. In a way she understood. This was his chosen life, there was no other. He had left his family forever finding peace in his solitude.

She had come with the intention to reveal all to this absent head of her fragmented family, to tell him the of the anguish and misery behind her leaving, on her arrival there she had stepped into a new place, a different room, as if on closing a door, she had discovered him waiting. Their meeting was a step forward not a falling back. After all he had his secrets too, and she thought about her grandmother working in her cottage garden, lost in her memories of their past, a box without a key. But to move on Elle too had to set the past to one side, and guarding it closely, only return awhile for answers. She could take control as he had done, and forge new memories, kinder ones, as she twisted along her path of choices, but sadly she was still free to make mistakes that could put her future happiness at risk. She acknowledged her intrusion into John's chosen haven, his private place to reach the end, which was plainly drawing closer hastened by the disease that ravaged him, but he appeared comfortable with her company nonetheless.

They continued on their way and Casja asked him kindly if he would like to join them for a few days on *Sea Princess*, as this had always been their plan. But the sad shake of his head told them the answer, this was his world and he wished for no other.

Elle promised to write and they left him dozing on his bed. They walked back to the car, Elle silent and tearful for she understood she would probably never see him again.

Their backs to a palm tree, Tom and Elle sat under the Pitons as he debriefed her of her day with his willing ear. She wept in the telling, and as he slipped his arms around her, the tears fell for everything, the distance between her and her family, both in miles and emotions, John's estrangement for all the long years and for the loss of her first love who clung to her heart.

He kissed her gently, smoothing her wet cheeks.

'Propinquity,' she muttered, but he had no idea what she meant.

The season in the islands came to an end and *Sea Princess* headed north again for a quick visit to Fort Lauderdale for engine servicing, then they followed the northern route across the Atlantic, taking them back through the Bermuda triangle. On leaving Florida they were notified of a drugs haul that had been dumped in the ocean in black bin bags, so Charles obliged by wasting a few hours searching for them, but nothing was to be seen so they pressed on. It was a fairly common occurrence apparently for smugglers who feared they had been detected to dump their cargo and then return later to try to retrieve it, hoping the coastguards had not been successful in a search. But aided by all available vessels in the area, the drugs were most often impounded.

The Bemuda Triangle was eerie, quiet and foggy, the water almost devoid of waves but swirling with mysterious eddies and currents in the expanse of oily murk around them. Charles told them stories of all the vessels that had supposedly vanished there and the atmosphere succeeded in striking a chill around *Sea Princess*. They left this uncomfortable zone as quickly as they had entered and found themselves facing a choppy sea with the wind forward of the beam. They began a fierce beat to windward with an unpredictable jerky motion.

Charles had teamed Tom with Elle for watches, noticing their strong friendship and perhaps encouraging them a little; the new arrangement certainly meant they had to spend more time together. How they enjoyed standing on the bridge in control of everything but the sea and weather, smashing through the waves, listening to their favourite music, similar souls, restless and adventurous.

The wind strengthened and the guys reduced the canvas until

they were rigged with small, well-reefed storm sails and the engines ticked over to help them make progress against mounting seas.

Elle loved the sea for the varying moods of the weather, no two days were ever alike, and obviously one Atlantic crossing could be totally different to another. It was clear to her that this one was not going to be anything like the last when the wind had been more agreeably behind them. They had been in the storm for a day and a half, cooking was almost impossible with Elle struggling to serve bowls of stew with hunks of bread and butter. She was glad she had baked fruit cakes whist in Florida, and the carpet in the wheelhouse was littered with crumbs and raisins. With no cleaning up possible until the weather calmed, the passage felt like a survival course. No one had seen Casja since the storm began, sea sickness kept her to her cabin, although Elle was sure she would feel better if she surfaced for some fresh air in the sheltered corner under the roof on the aft deck. This was her place for hours on end. She sat and watched the sea, huddled in waterproof layers, lost in dreams and waves.

The worst thought was that they were not managing to cover much ground, one wave to carry them forward and two to carry them back. They were a long way from the other side and making hardly any progress. Tom found her there brooding away the afternoon dozing behind a book, until it was time for her to brave the turbulent galley again, quite the worst place to be in a head sea.

'There you are, what you up to?' Tom was always infuriatingly cheerful unless of course he was having a moan about something specific.

'Just reading, sort of.' Elle sighed. She looked up into his bearded smiley face with his earring in one ear which always put her off slightly, a snobby thing, she had always considered piercings on a man slightly lower-class, but he was a Pole so maybe the same rule didn't apply. Would she, could she have an affair or serious relationship with him? She was fond of him she knew that, but there was no heart fluttering or awakening of passion. Should she wait until she found that feeling again or slip into the easy going cosy relationship that was on offer?

'Well we are all wanted in the wheelhouse, Charles has heard a May Day call and there is talk of us turning around.'

Sure enough they were to retrace their path in the hope of finding the stricken yacht behind them.

Turning around in one sense was bliss. The epiphany of how life would be if they were travelling in the opposite direction even brought Casja from her cabin, her white face seeking answers for the relief found in the new motion. Although the seas were still mountainous they were venting their wrath aft of the beam which made all the difference. Settled on a reach they scanned radar and horizon for a glimpse of the vessel who had issued such a serious call. The progress they had made was lost in a few hours of running back with the wind and sea. The men managed to attach the storm boards so that when *Sea Princess* resumed her course, the glass windows of the deck saloon would be protected should the storm take further hold. The barometer was falling.

For twelve hours they headed back until Charles received word that a ship had reached the mayday caller and was offering assistance. He spun the wheel and resumed course for Europe, the guys winching the storm sails hard against the wind again. For four days and nights they battled on, with morale slipping a little more each hour as fatigue took hold of each of the crew. On the fifth day as Elle sat listlessly propped on the wheelhouse seat listening to the spin and tick of the gyro as it worked ceaselessly to correct their course after every wave, the heavy rain gave her the impression of flattening the sea and her spirits rose with the optimism of calm.

PART FIVE

Europe

18

"And remember this, that if you've been hated, you've also been loved."

Henry James, *Portrait of a Lady*

Tom...

"If a were to make a list of the things I liked about Elle and another of the things I disliked about her, the first would be longer than the second, so I could possibly conclude that I was in love with her (whatever that means).

I admired the way she stuck like a stubborn limpet to her work and routines, such a good influence, for I was renowned for being distracted by the possibility of a few bevies (or other inappropriate substances) and a good time. That would always be my downfall, but then life is for having fun as well isn't it? She successfully turned all my pleasures into guilty ones, looking scornfully at me and I knew I would never be good enough for her, but I had to keep trying.

She even implied that she knew more about varnishing and deck-cleaning than me! Well she probably knew quite a bit for a girl but for goodness sakes, not more than me. Tomasz Kawasaki, king of the varnish brush! On the other hand she needed to realise that as a team we would have been perfect, we could have run a boat like *Sea Princess* together and she would have kept me on the straight and narrow.

In truth, I would have laid down my life for her, but I how

could I have kept her? I wish I had been there in Bermuda, to prevent her from falling in with that folk singer (or whatever he was). And she told me that she had a few cuddles and kisses with Charles whilst Casja was away ... I would never have let that happen. I saw the way she looked at Charles and I knew that he was her dream man. She hid secrets from me about her past, or preferred not to talk about it, but then I wasn't keen on telling her about my life up to that point either, not much to be proud of there.

Charles was never keen on our friendship turning into something more serious ... told me that we would not look twice at each other if we were not closeted together twenty four hours a day, but who knows?"

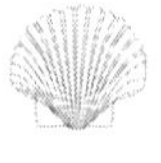 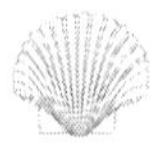 

Sea Princess made her way into the Straits of Gibraltar on a bright April day amongst more shipping traffic than they had encountered in days. Elle was relieved they had not entered these busy waters in the middle of the night. Eighteen months had passed since she had left the destroyer pens. Dozens of questions ran through her mind. Maybe she would see Ben? He had never answered her letters. Did she really believe he would? He would be a father by now, and would Peter be there in Gibraltar as well? He could be, how would she handle seeing him with his partner? Don and Janie too, how she longed to see them and tell them all her news.

They coasted in gracefully alongside, Elle and Casja arranging the fenders as they always did when entering port. There was a figure astride a monkey bike on the quay but Elle did not really look at him properly until the ropes were all secure and then she glanced up the wall into the somber face of Ben. He was not smiling, just waiting quietly to speak to her and her stomach churned, with awkward nervousness. Why was he there? How could he possibly know she was back?

She walked quickly to the wheelhouse resisting the temptation to run. 'May I step onto the quay for a few moments, there is someone I know,' she said struggling to address Charles calmly but she knew he would detect her excitement.

'Yes but we have to wait for customs so stay close to the boat where we can see you please.'

'Thank you, I will only be a few moments I promise.'

She pulled herself up the metal rungs of the ladder to the top of the wall where Ben was seated on a bollard. Tom was watching and muttering. To hell with that, she thought, he knows nothing about anything. Ben shook her hand in the strangest way, she thought she might have merited a hug or even a kiss.

'How did you know?' was the best she could manage, feeling her colour rise.

'Of course I knew that you were on *Sea Princess* because you wrote to me, and I heard your skipper making radio contact in the office yesterday with your estimated arrival time.'

'Oh, I see, it wasn't such a miracle then, you sitting here waiting.'

'No, and I know this doesn't sound friendly, but I didn't want to risk you coming looking for me as Marianne is very touchy these days and she thought something happened between you and I before you left.'

'But it didn't!' Elle was outraged.

'Try telling her that, I have but she doesn't believe me. Peter must have said something to her about your track record.'

'Peter? Is he here then?'

'Not now no, but he passed through not long after you did on his way across. He went in convoy with the Belgian couple from Ibiza, remember them?'

‘Yes, Peter bought a boat from them there.’ Elle did not particularly want to talk about Ibiza.

‘Did you not hear what happened, did you not bump into them?’

‘No I think I just missed Peter a few times.’

‘The Belgian girl, I don’t remember her name, they took a cat on the boat and she fell over the side trying to save it in the night, as far as I know, but no one is quite sure exactly what happened. Her husband was asleep, he searched for her for days but there was no trace.’

Elle struggled to comprehend the news he was relating to her, horrified to imagine the grief and terror of such a tragedy.

‘So did he come back, Phillipe I mean, where is he now?’

‘In Spain somewhere I think, I don’t know. I am sorry I thought you would have heard from someone, on your travels. Anyway I have to go back to work, I am sorry,’ he said again and Elle wished he would stop apologising. She turned away and stepped back on to the ladder trying not to cry, it was certainly a long time since she had felt so disturbed, both by his news and by the personal condemnation from his girlfriend. A few hours in Europe and her confidence was on the dung heap.

Tom was waiting on the deck. ‘What’s up?’ he said taking in her distressed face.

‘Nothing, leave it okay, right now I wish we had stayed in the Caribbean,’ she stomped away from him and went below before he could interrogate her further.

Elle found *Talisman* in the marina on her trip to the supermarket. She ran joyously down the pontoon her heart lifted by the sight of that familiar black hull and monkey bike askew as if thrown carelessly on the deck.

She knocked cautiously on the cockpit combing as she took off her shoes, Don’s head popped out.

‘Stupid girl! It’s you, you look wonderful! Come down but quietly, Janie and baby are sleeping.’

'Baby!' Elle was astonished, how could such a huge event have occurred in such a short time without her knowledge.

'Yes, she's just a few weeks old. Janie had a difficult birth and we haven't had much sleep since.'

Elle looked at him properly now taking in the dark shadows under his eyes, and the worry. 'Where's Dammit?' The question hung between them for a few timeless moments before he spoke.

' He ate some poisonous berries just before the baby came, I can barely talk about it, just feels like a bad dream.'

Elle looked away, things were not the same, one baby replacing the other, he was more than a dog, he was a family member. She stammered for the right words to say and decided that a change of tack was better. 'The baby, what's her name? May I come back and see her if I have time before we leave? I have so much to tell you, I have a fabulous job now, so much has happened since you left me here.'

'April, her name is April, give us a call hey, we have the phone on board, let us know when you can come and hopefully they will be awake.'

A quick hug, she left him then, sensing unannounced visitors were not ideal for them right now. Their lives had obviously been turned topsy-turvy by the new arrival, she was sure they would find normality again given time.

Sea Princess set sail next day for Antibes in the South of France so Elle was not to see them again for quite awhile.

Whether she was destabilised by their arrival in Europe, or just feeling woebegone, below ebb and in need of comfort, Elle was not sure but she joined Tom in his bed during the last part of the journey. Certainly for her part, their union was not blessed by overpowering passion or true love. His practice of casting sheep's eyes at her, and offering praise and reassurance at her every turn finally broke her resolve to keep him at a distance. With his strong Polish arms engulfing her, she was safe and protected and he was devoted and amorous. His sword was drawn to slay all her dragons.

Charles and Casja were silent on the matter, but she knew they must have discussed the mismatched couple when in the privacy of their tiny cabin. She imagined their disapproval and suspicion of her motives for bewitching the mate, whom Charles had always seen as vulnerable in love. He described Tom as not wearing his heart just upon his sleeve, but in fact blazoned across the front of his T-shirt. If any one was to be wounded within this liaison, it certainly would not be Elle. Why was she always the bad guy? For her part she was genuinely fond of him, he was such a manly man, so caring and kind, but there was one trait that bothered her. When he had a few drinks, he had to have a few more until totally inebriated and then another Tom came to the surface and this other person she found difficult to deal with for he was the opposite of his sober self. He became stubborn, unreasonable and unbearably pigheaded. She assured herself she would be able to change this, to keep him away from the devil drink and temptation, and by nurturing him and using her womanly wiles, she could keep him forever as the Tom she respected and admired, gradually ridding him of his bad side.

They arrived in Antibes with the dynamics of the crew altered again, no longer Charles, Casja and Elle, but Tom and Elle, Charles and Casja. A new couple, engineer and stewardess were to join them shortly as Mark had finally requested to go home and the stewardess had never suited. They would set out for the Greek Islands as three couples, although Charles had always maintained that twosomes amongst a small crew were not a good idea, he now had a complete crew of exactly that.

The South of France, the mountainous backdrop still topped with snow, the bright blue days when the mistral blew, the hot chocolate in the Bar du Port and the windows steamed with the garlic laden breath of local chatter. 'Monsieurdame.' What a smooth way to greet two people with one word that simply rolled off the tongue. Elle would not have cared were she to have been marooned there forever.

Charles suggested she should go home for a short break and although she was not particularly keen, she decided to take Tom with her. If she could keep him away from alcohol, or at least ration him to drink a moderate amount, they would be fine.

Of course nothing went her way. Plenty of drinks were had at every possible opportunity, increased by their holiday situation. On the drive down to her mother's he actually demanded that she stop the car so he could get out. 'No, no I don't want a leak I just want to go for a walk for a bit.' By the time they arrived Elle was tired, forlorn and embarrassed. Not the homecoming she had foreseen for everything was awkward. Going back to *Sea Princess*, the work, the routine and normality, was joyous in all respects.

A ladies lunch planned for the day after the Monaco Grand Prix, turned out to be a false start to their season. Not only was Monaco a desolate sight of empty stalls and litter, but the swell was so wide coming in at the harbour mouth, that the yachts moored on the T quay were lifted up and down like toys. Elle having laid a fabulous cold buffet out on the aft deck, observed the gangway to be rising some five or six feet off the quayside with every bulge of water that passed beneath. The ladies came, they looked and they went. Game over.

They left Antibes on a windy May, almost June day, fully laden with food ready for a carefully planned timetable for a succession of guests, filling the summer months until they would return in the fall to winter in the shipyard berth they had just left behind. Elle was to miss the yard over the summer. A comfortable sense of wellbeing had fallen over her there with the habitual sounds and smells of the '*chantier*', surely annoying to some, soothed and calmed her anxiety concerning life in general.

The two brothers who owned the yard, drove their cranes around endlessly lifting boats onto to the hard standing, jet washing, painting and placing them back in the water sometimes all within one day. Their rugged features charmed her as did their broad Antiboise accents, although it was hard to decipher their words sometimes as they shouted a greeting to her as she came and went. The blond one, whose eyes she could hardly bear to meet for such a thrill went through her, always seemed to be watching her and she was sure he looked for her attention. He was, without a doubt married, and she was sharing Tom's bed. No crime in looking though was there? She had felt his gaze resting on her continuously these past weeks. He would miss her surely.

Off they went to be at the bidding of their owner and his guests all summer long. A wonderful sojourn in Venice, how could the Adriatic be so rough? Down the Yugoslavian coast, on into Turkey to anchor in her magnificent coves with fir trees and wasps, and to walk the streets of the carpet sellers. Across to Rhodes to begin to circumnavigate the islands of Greece, tzatziki, olives, retsina and the best yoghurt and feta cheese from barrels in the market. Tuna fish, swordfish, baklava oozing with local honey, octopus and olives ... Elle gathered it all into her mind and her fridge, charming the guests again with her menus. Life was about Meltemi winds and Mistrals and the sleepy blue day when they were rammed by a Turkish freighter whose crew had abandoned the watch. (Luckily no one was hurt.)

She danced the night away with Tom on a makeshift dance

floor out on the water in Sardinia, and was happy, his sobriety whilst working, keeping her safely in his grasp. Charles with his inexhaustible sense of fun, leapt out of the whaler dressed in tails with a silver salver and champagne, as they sat on a millionaire's beach, imposters amongst the idle rich, laughing loudly and digging castles in the hot sand. If only life could have stayed the same for them forever, but the winter inevitably arrived, with a rest period that would always spell disaster for the union of bosun and cook.

Charles had devised a new system for arriving stern to the quay, which involved a navy-like professional operation as from the wheelhouse he was unable to see how close the stern was to dry land. Elle had been chosen to wear headphones, (what are we doing here, flying an aeroplane?) and to stand on the aft deck, relating to the skipper exactly how close they were with every thrust of the propellers. 'Ten feet, five feet, a foot ... stop now!' Five feet was perfect, ideal for lowering the gangway. Of course on the day they docked back in the ship yard, HE was there watching with a rye smile from his crane, and Elle's colour maddeningly, uncontrollably rose to her sun brown cheeks.

'What are you blushing about?' Tom observed, amused as he secured the stern lines.

'I always feel embarrassed when I have to wear this stupid headset,' and in so saying she stuffed the offending article firmly back in the aft locker.

'Should be used to it by now,' he glanced up clocking the face in the crane, shaking his head as if in disbelief. 'Anyway we are here now, time to party!' His words filled her with dread.

They had holiday leave to take and Elle certainly did not want to go home again after the shambles of their last visit, so as Tom had some friends who had recently bought a house in Malta, they chose to go there in search of some rest and winter sun.

They managed to have a reasonably enjoyable time, although Elle found the island old fashioned and lacking in countryside, (rocky hillsides with stony tracks) and little in the way of amusement, apart from cheap liquor of course. The films at the cinema were centuries old, and the shops were uninteresting and shabby. There were signs of the ruins that the army had left behind, as though the island had stood still the day they left their camps. She found horses to ride but the terrain was unsuitable with no soft grass to canter anywhere. Malta was not a place to which she would ever be inclined to return and her disposition for the whole holiday was on average, taciturn and bad tempered, only lifting when the day for their return to France due near.

'Well we had to give Charles and Casja some peace,' shrugged Tom, by way of explanation as to why he had suggested the island in the first place. They went for two days to Gozo to find some coves for Tom to dive and Elle had an asthma attack induced by a damp blanket on the hotel bed. A drama in the night was followed by a swift boat trip back to Malta.

19

"It may be observed that there is no regular path for getting out of love as there is for getting in. Some look upon marriage as a short cut that way but it has been known to fail."

Thomas Hardy, *Far from the Madding Crowd*

Elle was happy to return, throwing herself back into cleaning her galley, and preparing for spring and the season ahead. She spent much of her leisure time reading and dreaming, hardly noticing Tom's frequent absences to the Yacht Hotel or the Bar du Port. They fell into an easy way of life together again on *Sea Princess*, both having the space to do as they pleased with their differences becoming less obvious whilst cocooned in the familiar situation at work. They were so much at ease, going about their habitual duties with a mutual, unchallenged affection for each other that Tom asked Elle if she might marry him and she surprised herself by saying yes. Charles and Casja, although visibly shocked, after a period of silence and reflection, decked their bunk with ribbons and messages of a congratulatory nature.

Throughout the long summer, the varnish flowed smoothly for Tom, and Elle's word was law within her busy galley. (Charles had a plaque made for the oven engraved "The Cook's Word is Law" lest anyone should challenge her which they frequently did.)

Elle had a solid dream now, well as real as a dream could be, to save enough to buy a little house somewhere or maybe a boat, something she could call her own home at last. Strangely enough she was not at all sure where Tom fitted in this reverie, if at all, but she hoped the mist that hung over their future would clear in the end. On their return in the autumn, as she trudged her familiar route from the shipyard towards the town for groceries she spied a small wooden boat with '*A Vendre*' written on a wooden board attached between the backstays. This was love. She could think or talk with Tom of little else. He seemed more than a touch bemused.

'What would happen while we are away half the year?'

'I will find someone to keep an eye on her I suppose.' Elle had not even begun to think about the details of ownership at all. 'Anyway I am going to have a look at her, you coming?'

'Yeah okay.' Not much enthusiasm there, she thought, maybe he sensed it was all for her rather than for them. Could he sense her inability to reconcile herself to sharing her life? Elle was not fond of loneliness, she liked to have a confidante in times of worry but she was an isolated, independent soul who had always stood alone, pushing her own path through the heavy gravel of her life. Their 'engagement' was just a word to her, she had not accepted that it might infer a long term commitment.

She phoned the number and they went together to meet the small (they were often not tall) Frenchman who was keen to part with the old boat that had belonged to his père, recently deceased.

'What does the name mean?' Elle inquired gently, '*Acheron*' she could barely pronounce it correctly.

'*C'etait le nom du soumarine de mon père.*' She considered that owning a boat named after a submarine was not a favourable omen, so made a mental note to think of a new name, or to find out the original one, which was an even better plan as she knew it was bad luck to change the build name of a boat.

Inside she was instantly disappointed, for all the original fittings were gone, in short there was nothing, an old sea toilet at least, some spare sails and a sculling oar for propulsion should the engine fail.

Tom saw the shock on her face. 'We could find a carpenter to fit out the inside I expect.'

Elle studied the space, imagining the task of making the inside how she wanted, a cooker, a sink, a fridge under a small work surface and a double bunk in the forepeak. In the naivety of her youth, the construction of her cosy home on board seemed a small hurdle. She had money saved, hers to spend.

She walked around the deck, the varnished combing enchanted her as did the thinly laid strip planking and the brass portholes she could polish. Never did the thought enter her positive, optimistic mind that the deck might leak, the fore hatch too, that the engine was old, petrol and probably not properly mounted or secured within the hull, she just simply fell for the boat's charming double ended lines and the way her proud bow rose above the water.

'I want it,' she announced.

Tom shrugged, 'Buy it then.'

'I will.'

Elle shook the Frenchman's hand and the deal was done.

That was a turning point in her life. Every possible moment when work was done she could be found busy in her own heaven, painting, polishing, scraping or just simply sitting thinking, both proud and ecstatic with her purchase. Her admirer in the shipyard watched her progress with a grin, she peeped out of her hatch and frequently caught him observing her. Tom tried to persuade her to come to the hotel as she used to sometimes in the evening, but socialisation was out of the question now. She was simply too busy, so he would go alone, exasperated by her relentless purpose.

Galuette. That was the original name bestowed on her vessel when she had been built in Brittany in the 1950s, meaning a small seabird, so it was, without question, the name she should have.

Elle set about ordering a cooker, a caravan fridge, lights, a new hatch, a sink and tap and cushions for the bunk that was not yet built. She bought a bright yellow kettle to sit upon the stove and a couple of saucepans too although she did not yet have cupboards.

Two friends of theirs who sought carpentry work, having recently arrived from the UK agreed to undertake the job and began immediately sawing and assembling the interior from sheets of marine ply. Elle could not wait for it all to be finished and as soon as it was she began varnishing all the new wood to perfection. Putting some clothes away in her tiny new cupboards, at last she had found a home, one that belonged to her, the most precious possession in all the world.

Tom and she invited some friends and sailed to St Tropez, a lazy calm sail on the way there, but a punishing tack to windward on the return. Elle realised the inefficiency of a small petrol engine, which hardly helped their speed under sail, and how long it took to beat a few miles against a head wind in her small craft. 'Let me helm a while,' Tom implored, as she sat struggling to maintain their course against wind and waves. She ignored him and remained firmly on the tiller for the whole journey.

The case against her hasty engagement to Tom developed in Elle's mind until it filled every space and finally her thoughts escaped, flying like a missile to strike him one evening when he had, as he habitually did, saturated himself with alcohol. She told him it was over.

Charles and Casja were sad. Their immediate unanimous decision shocked Elle. As it was her choice to end the relationship, she must be the one to leave *Sea Princess*. 'After all, you have your own boat now, somewhere to go until you find another position, which we are sure you will.'

Her reference was penned, signed and delivered along with her final pay slips with little ado, almost as if the moment had been foreseen. "Quiet and unflappable, a valuable member of the crew with sailing and navigational skills, in addition to her excellence in the galley," Charles had undeniably written some complimentary words. But words they were and nothing could ease her discomfort and sadness at their choice to keep the drunken Pole and let her leave. Regret swamped her as she packed all her possessions and crammed them in to her new cabin, just a stone's throw away at the end of the quay.

20

"In Baffin Bay where the whale fish blow,
The fate of Franklin no man may know..."

J.P. Faulkner, *Lady Franklin's Lament*, 1850

Elle sat on the bow of *Galuette* mulling over her life having suddenly found more than enough time to ponder. So many meetings and partings, the key figures in her days at sea changed with such rapidity, all equally important for a time and then carried away, as if on a passing wave. Where were they all? How did they feel about her? Peter, Ben, Don and Janie, John from Nantucket, Mac the Smuggler, Geoff, Freddie, Robin ... and finally now Tom. They were all out of sight. Were other people's lives like hers? As if she was sitting in a train, hurtling on, watching people and places flash by, while she voyaged on alone, as free as a swimming fish. She was more than a little perturbed, watching life continuing on *Sea Princess* without her. Charles and Casja waving to her as they passed was just not the same. She had been cut out, abandoned, and isolated.

She settled down to having a few days off before hunting for work, she deserved a holiday and decided she might go sailing, on her own. Be foolhardy, be brave ... she told herself firmly.

The security guard for the marina, a dark, latin type with twinkling eyes and an extremely accurate beard, chatted to Elle before he went off duty in the early mornings. '*En vacances, jeune fille?*' he enquired, the familiarity of his tone was not lost on Elle, out of place yet strangely comforting in her new independent circumstances. '*Mais oui, bien sur, la vie est belle, merci.*' She would work hard at her French now, make new friends.

She sorted out charts and provisions, Charles had given her life jackets, one decent one anyway, and flares, all that she needed and she set out early one calm morning intent on reaching Corsica late in the evening. There was little wind so she was forced to motor sail with the genoa flapping around in the gentle following breeze. The sun was fierce, and with the boat holding her course, and the new automatic pilot successfully attached to the tiller, Elle went below and closed her eyes. She lay there for only few moments but it must have been longer, for she awoke with a burning headache and when she looked out at the water there were horizontal wavy lines in front of her eyes and she was at once both dizzy and sick. 'What's the matter with me?' She spoke aloud in her sudden fear with no one to hear.

The breeze had become more reliable so she shut down the engine and looking over the side where the water-cooling sputtered out she understood what had happened. The slight wind behind had been blowing the exhaust fumes directly back into the boat, and what she was experiencing was carbon monoxide poisoning. If she had slept on she would, without a doubt, have been dead. 'Bloody hell!' she exclaimed.

She found a bay just south of Calvi, where they had anchored with *Sea Princess* so she knew the holding to be good. She tucked *Galuette* in as close to the shore as she dared and dropped anchor. After watching for an hour or so to make sure she was secure, she ate a lonely dinner and slept, undisturbed, with not a single boat for company.

A bright, calm beautiful day greeted her when she awoke. All traces of her headache were gone, along with her insecurities of the previous day. It was easy to sail the world with a professional crew beside you, but on your own, quite a different story. 'Nearly killed myself yesterday, but here's hoping I do better today,' she toasted herself with her mug of tea, and lay in her cockpit in the caress of the early sun, listening to the nibbling waves lapping the hull. The redolence of the thyme on the hillsides, floated around the bay, carried on the wind. Such languor and such liberty!

A benevolent breeze chased the boat on down the Corsican coast and through the Straits of Bonifacio. Life began to be bumpier, with the wind turning so that when she made a course to head back north up the other side of the island the breeze was on the nose. A different day, like the turn of a page, the sky became grey, and the sea menacing. Elle was forced to tack making small progress on each diagonal.

After a long, exhausting sail she finally took refuge in the port of Bastia, which offered little solace as she found it to be almost as windy and desolate as the open sea. She motored around considering trying to go stern to a wall where there were a couple of other yachts, but they seemed under threat of being blown on to the quay, their anchors barely holding.

'Galuette, Galuette ... Sunrider.'

Someone was calling her on Channel 16.

'Sunrider ... Galuette.'

'Galuette ... Sunrider, Channel 14 going down.'

'Galuette ... Sunrider ... why not come alongside us for the night? We are firmly tied to a deep mooring that won't shift. It's blowing up nasty.'

'Thank you so much, I'll just get some fenders out and a line ready and I will try and come alongside.'

Saved by strangers, after one failed attempt to throw a rope she circled again and second time around she was secure, with bowline, stern and springs and another line looped through the mooring buoy, all thanks to her neighbour in his wobbly dingy. Elle had a drink with the couple who seemed like old hippies of the sea, and then gratefully she retired to sleep, overcome by ineffable fatigue.

Three days she remained lashed there, until the wind lost its grip and pleasant conditions returned. She had seriously diminished her food supplies with this unexpected confinement and knew she must ready herself for a dash to the mainland. The wind was favourable for St Remo, the first port over the Italian border and from there home was only a day away. She set off, bravery overridden now by a fierce desire to be home, back in her berth in the marina.

About five miles out from the Corsican coast the sea changed colour. Elle glanced over the port side and to her horror she thought she was seeing the seabed, or worse still rocks, just below the surface. There was nothing on the chart, she had begun to shake uncontrollably. Mottled brown and green, she yanked the tiller over to avoid collision, and as she looked harder and harder at this surface below the waves she realised it was moving, shifting slowly alongside and in that instant she knew. 'For God's sake it's a bloody flipping whale,' she shouted in terror and comprehension.

Grabbing the VHF receiver she tried to control the panic. 'Monaco Radio, Monaco Radio, this is Yacht Galuette, do you read?

Yacht Galuette ... Monaco Radio loud and clear, position please.

'Monaco Radio ... about five miles from the Northern tip of Corsica and I have a whale alongside, please stay in radio contact.'

'Yacht Galuette, do you have a life jacket?'

Could she detect a smile in his tone, she thought so, well it might be hilarious to him but it certainly wasn't from where she was sitting.

'Yes I am wearing it, anymore suggestions?'

'Yacht Galuette ... Monaco Radio we will keep watch for you on Channel 14, over and out.'

For the next two hours or so Elle sat nervously gripping the tiller, too scared to attach the pilot, peering into the water around her until her eyes ached from the glare of the sun and the sea.

Whales apart, an easy sail took her swiftly back to familiar territory and as she motored slowly into San Remo she was overjoyed to see the familiar bowsprit belonging to *Talisman* poking out from the yachts on one of the central pontoons. There was a convenient *Galuette*-sized space right alongside so she carefully maneuvered in reaching over and tying herself on firmly to the cleats inside the gunwales, calling out as she arrived. *Talisman* appeared however to be locked up and deserted.

Somewhat disappointed but not too disheartened, Elle strolled up to the restaurant she knew well on the quayside, and sitting outside she ordered herself a bowl of *spaghetti vongole* and a glass of Orvieto. She was starving and from the balcony she had an advantageous view of the pontoon should her friends return.

She finished her meal and there was still no sign of them at all. She climbed back on board and fell immediately asleep on her cosy bunk, only to be awoken by stomach cramps forecasting imminent sickness. She just managed to reach her heads before she vomited until she could retch no more, slipping in and out of a delirious sleep, managing to raise herself to pump her small toilet, which seemed to need every ounce of strength she could muster.

'Stupid girl, are you there?' It was Don.

'I think I have food poisoning,' she whimpered.

'Well do you think you could come and have whatever it is over here, your toilet makes such a racket each time you pump the blasted thing, its keeping us all awake!'

She took a towel and on unsteady legs climbed thankfully onto the deck of *Talisman* where Don helped her below to her old cabin.

'Now settle down and try and sleep a bit, you look dreadful. What on earth did you eat?'

'I don't really want to talk about that right now, just thank goodness you are here and thank you, I am so sorry I kept you awake.'

'Get some rest, Elle.'

Elle was ill for two days, and on the third day she showered and felt almost normal. April their daughter, who was almost two now (where did that time go?) delighted in having a surprise guest, taking Elle by the hand to look for the "crocodilios" (lizards to call them by their correct name), that sunbathed in the tall grasses surrounding the marina path ways.

'You be alright to sail home?'

'Yes I will be fine, and I shall drive back down in my new car with some fizzy wine and we will celebrate whatever springs to mind.'

They waved her off and in six or seven hours with a kind breeze she was nosing the bow of *Galuette* back into her berth with relief.

He was there, right there, how could he have known she would arrive or was it just a coincidence. Elle didn't really feel like mustering up her french to talk to him right now. She was tired, close to grumpy probably. There was no escaping his open-topped moke parked right by her electric and water box on the quay. Antoine, the security guard was waiting to take her line.

'*Bonsoir Mademoiselle, donnez moi ça.*' He pointed towards the rope in her hand.

'*Je peux le faire,*' she said stubbornly stepping ashore and attaching her own bow.

He stood so close to her now, she could smell the *Chanel Pour Homme*, which was not too disagreeable, she would remember to buy some for her father.

'*Merci quand-même,*' she smiled realising how terse she must have seemed. '*Je suis desolé, très fatigué.*'

He nodded, appearing to understand the situation and she scurried below, hoping he would go, which thankfully he did.

A visit to the crew/yacht agency in the town to collect her mail proved beneficial. The perfect job to tide her over for the summer months fell into her lap. *Cardigrae V1*, a glorious, stylish old motor boat moored on the main jetty was looking for a cook to prepare luxurious lunches for day excursions only. Also to sleep on board for a couple of nights a week on a rota with the other crew to caretake the vessel. Elle was so excited, primarily because this would mean she could spend the summer near her boat, and secondly because she might be able to arrange for her father to join her for a few days holiday together. She had never been able to invite him since she left home. She had in her mind that he could sleep on *Galuette* (he loved small wooden boats) and she would stay on *Cardigrae*, appearing each morning to breakfast with him and plan their day.

She secured the position easily, and found herself in a wonderful old galley, preparing dressed crab and poached salmon on a daily basis. There was a stewardess, Frankie, a sassy, fetching, excitable, lively brunette with a steady boyfriend and some wild ideas. Elle discovered her stash of *Penthouse* magazines in the cabin they shared on her first night. She had never met anyone quiet like Frankie. 'Have you ever been with a girl?' she demanded of Elle whilst she carefully wiped away her makeup before bed. 'I might ask my boyfriend to buy me one for a night for my birthday, just to see.'

'Just to see what?' said Elle visibly horrified.

'Well to see if I like to be with a girl stupid, why else?'

She made Elle feel inadequate and unworldly, she didn't even possess any makeup never mind the wherewithal to remove it, and as for the girl thing, she was both fascinated and disgusted all at once.

'I am sure it wouldn't be for me,' she said finally watching

Frankie sort through her drawers of the laciest, most provocative underwear she had ever seen.

'Oh no, I can tell you are not the type,' declared Frankie, which left Elle embarrassed and wondering what on earth type she could be exactly.

Everything was arranged for her father to come for a whole week and Elle was beside herself with excitement. Having booked a few days off so they could sail somewhere together, she scrubbed and polished *Galuette*, a chance to make her father proud at last.

He had arrived. Grumpy, hot and disorientated at first, inappropriately dressed for the weather as if straight from the office, but once he had settled in the cockpit, glass of wine in hand it was as if he had been there forever. In the evening she took him to *Cardigrae* where he sat lordly in a deckchair on the foredeck, a gin and tonic by his side. They sailed *Galuette* to Villefranche where they swam and laughed and she thought she had never been so close to him and wondered if she ever would have the chance to have him to herself again.

He wandered off a few times but she always found him sitting on a wall somewhere watching the activity in the busy French port. Sometimes early in the morning or late into the night he would stray following his own dreams to forget about life at home. Things had not gone well in his marriage; the blame (this time) could not entirely be laid at his feet. It was a sad, sad, affair.

Sometimes Elle would write poetry, which she scribbled and squirreled in a small ring bound book. Seeing the words there soothed somehow the deep, dark rough patches in her own private sea where she feared she might drown. She and her father had thrown each other a line those few days and pulling hard they had both floated back to the surface and the sun ready to carry on with bright faces, and their hopes for a steady life rekindled.

21

"The heart was made to be broken."

Oscar Wilde

'*Il y a quel qu'un sur ton bateau?*' Was this really a question or a statement and the intimate use of the pronoun did not go unnoticed, "ton bateau" when he should more correctly and politely have said, "votre bateau".

'*C'est mon père,*' she replied wondering why on earth she needed to reveal anything at all to this over inquisitive but not totally displeasing Frenchman.

'*Excusez-moi, il faut que je te demande, c'est mon travaille après tout.*'

Again the use of the intimate pronoun. 'Ah yes, *mais oui, securité, ça va, ne s'inquiete pas, c'est mon père*, not a pirate!' Elle laughed and Antoine seemed to acknowledge the joke for he laughed too, his smile more beguiling than she had previously noticed.

'You take a coffee wiz me, one day soon?' So he would have a bash at English now for her, she knew he was making a tremendous effort because she had heard him a few days before assuring a boat owner just up the quay that he spoke not a word, "pas un mot," he had said, closed shop, typical Frenchman.

'*Peut-etre,*' she replied leaving him satisfactorily hanging on her word.

Their relationship developed faster than Elle would have wished. Considerably older than her (she wouldn't hazard a guess by how much) he mesmerised her just by being French. He epitomised every detail of her life there that she had come to adore, from the food and wine to the romanticism. His attention to detail in the presentation of every aspect of his culture, seduced her. And of course the language, she was learning fast, her mistakes causing him a fair amount of mirth, but she knew she was making progress with her endeavours, facilitated of course by his almost total lack of English. Either she spoke French or there was silence.

Antoine was so sexually verbal, there was no other way to describe his constant whisperings of admiration for every part of her physique, right from the first time he pushed her against the sink on *Cardigrae*, his hands on her breasts, murmuring '*Tes seins, tes seins, je t'adore, J'ai envie de toi.*' At first she thought this latter comment meant he was envious of her but when she looked it up the light dawned, he desired her. Well, she knew that by his behaviour there was no need to keep on saying it surely?

Whether she liked it or not, (she was really not quite sure) she was smitten. She liked the way he would not shorten her name but called her Ele-a-nor, dragging out the syllables in the most charming way, and his gallant gentlemanly ways, opening doors, being protective and kind, and the flowers? His generosity knew no bounds; he would rarely arrive without a gigantic bunch. There was no doubt about it, he was the most wildly romantic man she had ever met. "*Je suis à toi, je suis à toi*," he would cry out at the culmination of their ferocious love making within the confines of her forward bunk. He taught her that to say "*je t'aime*" meant nothing but to say "*je vous aime*" was a genuine declaration of love. He repeated the words over and over.

Antoine was possessive and jealous. A passionate Latin lover in every sense of the word, he wanted to know where she was while he was working at night or sleeping during the day. He would look for her in the evening, persuade her into the moke and taking her into the old part of the port he would make love to her against the wall in the shadowy darkness, until she cried for him to stop and let her go. But she always went with him. He was like a drug possessing her, stifling her independence. He hated to see her go to the bar with her friends, told her she stank of smoke and beer, and she fell more and more under his control, for fear of his displeasure.

One evening while leaning down on her small gangway to release the electricity connection before she went to meet her friends, she slipped and fell awkwardly into the dirty water of the port directly behind *Galuette*. Luckily she missed banging her head and escaped with grazes. She clambered up the iron-rung ladder in the wall nearby. He must have seen her or been watching for her to start the long walk into town because he was instantly there and shaken as she was, she fell thankfully into his arms, tears welling from shock and humiliation at her own stupidity.

'*Viens, je t'emene chez moi, d'acord, et tu va prendre un bain.*' Elle was soaking and shaking with cold so was not in a position to argue with his firm hand. She had never been to Antoine's apartment before and it seemed as good a time as any, especially with the prospect of a hot bath and some loving care and attention.

A short drive and a small brass plaque by the door, that was all it took to shatter the faith she had placed in him. "Antoine et Sabine Massen."

She stared at it transfixed as he fumbled with the key.

'*Tu es marieé?*' she said.

He did not meet her demanding gaze but led her inside and closed the door.

'*Oui mais elle n' habite plus chez moi.*'

'Where does she live then?' Elle raised her voice now in English the tension mounting.

'*Paris.*'

'Separated then, *dites moi que tu es separé au moins.*'

'*Si tu veux.*' This was all he said while he set about running her a bath and fetching her a dressing gown.

He washed her tenderly, dried her hair, made her hot chocolate and smoked salmon on toast, and placing her carefully in his bed he had left her there and returned to work his night shift. She rose early before he returned and exploring cupboards and drawers she found enough evidence to realise that there were two people who shared a life together there and she wept for her own naivety. Elle was in too deep now to walk away although she knew she should.

She slowly worked out that when with total regularity she saw nothing of him for one whole weekend each month, that his wife must be there with him at the apartment.(His excuses were as dubious as they were numerous.) She managed to wheedle some information out of some mutual French friends of theirs, that although not formally separated they spent practically no time together, with Sabine following her life in Paris and holidaying in the Caribbean alone every year. The small red car he drove she realised belonged to his wife as did the dog VIP (very important person). Elle had looked after the dog sometimes for Antoine while he was working and had a special bond with the little spaniel who spent so much time locked in the apartment alone. What had she done? Surely she could not be so much to blame as he had never disclosed his marital status at all. In fact he had openly encouraged her to believe he lived alone.

Elle saw the car come around the port one Saturday morning and park up at the end of the pontoon next to her own. Strange that he should park there she thought, and sat waiting and watching in her cockpit. It was not Antoine, of course not, he would never park there. It was Sabine who walked down the next quay with a picnic basket with Veep (this was how Antoine pronounced the name) trotting happily at her heels. She stopped at a small wooden fishing boat and pulling back the cover stepped on board. Elle could feel her heart in her mouth as she slowly grasped the circumstances unfolding in front of her. Sabine owned a boat opposite hers, with not more than a few metres separating them. She stared openly, taking in her lustrous, curly, auburn hair that fell almost her waist. She was obviously a good bit older than Elle, but stunning nonetheless. She felt sick. Sabine was clearly going fishing, on her own, a solitary picnic while Antoine was sleeping at home.

She wanted to drive to the apartment, right that minute, for a confrontation, and tell him that whatever was between them was finished, but what if Sabine came back unexpectedly. Too risky. She vowed she would tell him as soon as she could, her stomach was tied in knots, with nervous anguish. This could not go on.

The disaster for them all occurred on the Sunday morning, the next day after Sabine's lonely picnic. Elle was just having an early cup of tea in her cockpit when Sabine, Antoine and Veep walked past *Galuette*. What did the dog do? Well, he did what he always did of course, jumped on her gangway and ran down the deck to leap contentedly onto the seat beside her. 'Talk yourself out of this one, why don't you' she muttered under her breath. Antoine certainly did try, introducing her as his English friend who sometimes looked after the dog, and shaking hands with Sabine she felt like a heinous criminal. Elle could instinctively tell the sharp French woman wasn't convinced by the story and Antoine was to be seriously interrogated behind closed doors.

She saw nothing of him for a few days, not a sign, and during this time she managed to secure herself a cooking job on a new motor boat in San Remo, not a full time position but enough to take her away, for a few days a week, thus to widen the gap between her and her amorous, deceitful lover.

Finally he appeared the night before she was to leave. The small bag he was carrying alarmed her.

'*Qu'es que tu as dans ton sac?*', she demanded without even greeting him.

'*Une chemise propre et mon rasoir, elle ma mis à la porte pour le temps qu'elle reste.*'

Elle was stupefied, 'But she can't, you can't stay here, *je m'en vais demian pour le travail.*'

'*Pour un nuit seulement et demain elle s'en va à Paris.*'

She explained to him kindly, although she felt angry and tired from worry, that she was going to go away, for short periods at first and then she would try to find a boat and leave for the whole impending season. He had to accept this decision, it was for the best. He wept, his head buried in her lap like a child.

Elle drove away, flying down the auto route to the Italian border, grateful to secure distance between her and Antoine. Strangely betrayed, and disillusioned by the man he had turned out to be, she grieved for the the one she had fallen for, she had to come to terms with him not being that person at all. He was someone else entirely.

22

> "When love flies it is remembered not as love but as something else."
>
> E.M. Forster, *Maurice*

Once she parked up and walked down the quay to *Talisman* she felt so much better, Italy was another world, fresh and calm.

'Hi everyone,' she called gaily as she took off her shoes.

'Fizzy wine as I promised,' she pressed the bottles into Janie's outstretched arms and then laughingly accepted the hug, the bottles pressed awkwardly between them.

'How's it going, 'Stupid Girl'? Don stood beside them. 'You recovered from your intrepid madden voyage yet?'

'Yeah, just about, I'm working down here on and off for a few weeks. New motor boat the other side of the marina, *Mary 2* it's called, you seen it?'

'Yes,' replied Don, but you know how much notice I take of boats like that!'

'Me too, but they pay well. I had better get on round there and see what's happening I suppose. I need to introduce myself, I have only spoken to the skipper on the phone.'

'Come back later for a drink if you can, we need to know all your news.'

'I don't think you do really,' Elle shook her head, grinned and headed off to meet her new crew.

The skipper was one of those, 'warf, warf, warf' ex-navy types who would obviously try to skipper a yacht following the same disciplines as a naval destroyer or similar. She couldn't help but take an instant dislike, her hackles rising with his every word. Charles had been such an admirable skipper but this man she regarded with disdain. She resolved to just do what she must and keep her eyes open for something better.

Adam, the deckhand also arrived that day. A year younger than herself, they were allies right from the start. Blue eyed with a mop of straw blond hair, he sauntered aboard fresh faced from Lowestoft, and owing to his never having been on a private yacht before, every single aspect of the life was new to him. With his quirky, dry sense of humour, they were inseparable right from the start, not romantically so to begin with, but playing with each other through their working day as siblings would. They even looked alike, and were enchanted to discover their birthdays to be but one day apart, fellow Aquarians, making a harmonious combination.

Everyone noticed their similarities until Elle remarked one day, 'You could even be my cousin Adam,' and there the simple lie began. Their intimacy at this stage was restricted to a kiss and a cuddle before they went to separate cabins, away from watching eyes, for she had told him she was coming to the end of a sensitive relationship in France. 'He's still in my mind, it's messy,' was all she would say.

Elle was not enjoying the position as cook, there were too many restrictions preventing her from excelling in the galley. Insufficient equipment, and a lack of forward planning by the skipper, made the provisioning haphazard. She handed in her notice, wanting to go home, back to *Galuette*. To her joy and huge surprise Adam followed suit, immediately asking her if he could catch a lift with her to France to try his luck there.

'Of course, how exciting, you can stay with me on *Galuette* for a while, I can fit you on my spare bunk,' she laughed. 'After all you are not very big.'

'And what, exactly, to you propose to tell your boyfriend, or ex-boyfriend or whatever he is?'

'I shall say you are my cousin.'

Of course, Antoine did not believe for one instant that they were cousins, but he had to accept the story, being terse and unfriendly with Adam at every encounter. This suited Elle perfectly for Adam's presence kept him away, sulking and moody as he followed his well trodden route around the marina at night. He observed their comings and goings, looking for signs of the intimacy he suspected, often unnoticed by Elle and her 'cousin'. Once she was sure she saw a shadow move aboard Sabine's boat as they climbed onto *Galuette*, not a care in the world. She knew he carried a weapon as did all the security guards and she was unnerved and shaky, pushing Adam below quickly.

Adam found a deckhand position, and moved to Cannes. Elle was both sad and happy. She missed him but the pressure of Antoine's anger was lifted and although the Frenchman passed by a little too often, he left her alone, except for placing flowers on her car sometimes, which was a little creepy. Anyway she became a frequent visitor to Cannes marina, distracting Adam from his work, the two of them scurrying off to watch the world go by in one of the quayside cafe bars.

'When you arrive like that all dressed up wearing your sun glasses, you look like Jackie Onassis!' Adam bowed as she jumped out of her car, and she was flattered and happy and they grew ever closer. Another job came along for Elle, surprisingly aboard a Phillip Rhodes again, a miniature *Sea Princess*. There was a fair amount of maintenance to be done to prepare for the summer, then they would cruise to Greece for a couple of months. She was well acquainted with the deck hand and engineer so there were no problems there, and the skipper was an elderly gent who was a personal friend of the owners. Also it meant she could stay on *Galuette* until they set sail, and to be far away from Antoine for the bulk of the summer would surely calm him down. She told him she was going away at the first opportunity and he was grief stricken again.

'*Mais Antoine, s'est finis entre nous,*' she implored him to let her go but he held fast, hanging around to way lay her at every possible opportunity.

Adam returned to Suffolk to collect his car, a small stylish soft top. At weekends Elle would pack a picnic and they would disappear into the hills and sit with a bottle of rosé, laughing on the sun-baked earth between the olive trees. There it was that they began to touch and kiss, lulled by the wine and the sunshine, Elle believed this look alike cousin to be stealing her heart, they were lost in each other. When they returned to the coast they kept up the pretence of a family connection, although some had begun to have their suspicions.

Elle organised to lift *Galuette* out of the water, to clean and paint the underneath and topsides before she went away for the summer. This would mean a week of work in the shipyard at least. Her friend and admirer who owned the Chantier Naval, jumped her boat to the front of the queue of local boats awaiting his services, slotting her into a space that was almost directly behind the gangway of *Sea Princess* which was somewhat strange, but she had to focus on the task in hand. She sanded and scraped until her fingers were bleeding. She ground off the old layers of antifouling below the waterline and prepared the topsides for paint. She filled every tiny blemish and crack, and smoothed it down determined to have as near to a perfect finish as an old boat could possibly have. Casja came and gave her some protective cream for her face, concerned about all the chemicals she was using. She arranged some painters to apply the top coat not trusting her own skills.

Each evening, too tired to go and see Adam she would go to the swimming pool at the top of the town, have a quick swim and benefit from their shower facilities. She discouraged him from coming near as Antoine was always hovering somewhere around. The confrontation was best avoided as it would have been stressful and heated.

One evening the work almost done, she snuggled down in her bunk completely exhausted and began to drift into a deep sleep, lulled by the clinking of halyards on aluminium masts (the French were hopeless at restraining them). She adsorbed the occasional rhythmic sound of the trains as they passed on their way along the coastal track. Awoken abruptly by the noise of someone on board, in fact inside her small cabin, she spoke from her sleep without opening her eyes, so sure of the identity of her intruder. 'Adam, I told you not to come here,' and with her arms stretched out towards him, she continued softly, her tone full of affection, 'Antoine works at night all around the …' she took a fierce blow to the side of the head and then another the brute force of which seemed to land somewhere in the region of her neck, crying out she fell back.

'*Adam, tu as dit, Adam, c'est lui alors que tu attends dans le milieu de la nuit. Ton cousin, quelle blague, je te tue et lui aussi je te jure,*' and he left, he just climbed out again and stamped across the yard back to the car, she saw the glow of his lights as he turned the vehicle around.

Elle was crying quietly with shock and pain. What was the point in swearing he would kill her when she felt he had nearly succeeded in that already. She saw the blood smeared on her hand from the side of her face and she could barely swallow. She barricaded the doors on the inside as best she could and went back to her bunk nursing her throbbing head. How could she have been so stupid? Of course Adam would not have come to her in the night he was wary enough of Antoine to know better. And yet she had said his name and reached for him, it was her own fault, she had brought this entirely on herself.

As she crawled around finishing under the boat the next day, Alain from the yard was visibly concerned.

'*Ne s'inquiète pas,*' she assured him, '*C'est rien, je me suis tombé pendant la nuit sur l'eschelle, ma faulte, je suis bête.'* She didn't suppose for one moment he believed her, but it sounded plausible, she could have easily slipped on the ladder, tired as she was.

Her shining clean boat dropped safely back in the water, she drove off to find Adam and tell him what had occurred and that she had a plan. When he looked at her poor bruised face, he was naturally both horrified and frightened. So when she suggested that while Antoine was at home asleep during the day, he should help her move *Galuette* to Baie des Anges the next marina down the coast, he happily agreed. 'In fact we could go further,' she said, 'Beaulieu even, its lovely there.'

'Well why don't we go as soon as possible then as I have next week off and then we can sail back to Baie des Anges and leave the boat safely out of the way when we go back to work.'

So the plan was fixed. She had seen no sign of Antoine and they left mid morning on a sunny, rather windy day and had a hectic sail down the coast to Beaulieu.

How could things have come to this? He was so unfair, he did happen to have a wife after all, one that he had just not happened to mention when they had first became entangled? Elle spread all the facts in front of Adam again and again, looking for his support, desperate for someone to reassure her that she was not the guilty one. Of course he calmed her and did his best to soothe but they fell to bickering a little, life seemed so tenuous and uncertain.

The port of Beaulieu worked magic upon them. Far from the rush and tumble of Antibes and the threat of Antoine, the high cliffs around the marina blinked in the clarity of light brought by the air off the mountains. The wind was still and the harbour quiet, the surface of the water broken only by the greedy mouths of the mullet as they fed on the crumbs that Elle idly tossed over the side.

This was the first time Elle and Adam had spent time together away from the pressures of friends, work and the person they had sworn not to mention lest he should spoil their time alone. They shopped in Les Halles, the undercover market brimming with good things to eat as only a French market can do, bought new bedding for *Galuette*, and some more saucepans as though they were moving in, a couple, nesting and choosing. Elle felt almost ready to share, but she was still holding back deep inside her and carrying the knowledge that this dream was only a brief reality. They would soon awaken and have to resume their work, separately.

He made her so happy, that was the craziest part, she should commit to him forever and forget the single life. They sat for hours just touching hands, gazing with blue eyes into blue eyes. He appeared such a boy, an angelic youth, with his blond locks and fair skin, but yet a changeling gifted with the ardour and sexual prowess of a man. He was not like Peter though, he had no maturity of thought, and he lacked dependability, maybe he would grow alongside her. They chaffed like sister and brother, he would sulk if she turned her attention away, or spoke of a single life.

Adam caught the train to collect her mail; she stayed behind, fearing the places where Antoine knew she had to go since the terrible night in the shipyard.

A letter from her father brought sadness.

Darling Elle,

Thank you for your last letter. I too, treasure those few days larking about on your lovely little boat.

Some news now, your grandfather passed away peacefully in hospital this week. You probably don't know but the customs family who were kind enough to care for him, used the last of his money to fly him home to London, in order to maximise his care in the last few weeks when the cancer overcame his will to live.

He behaved as though he had never been away at all, when of course forty years had passed, sitting in his bed demanding a copy of Horse and Hound to catch up with the life he had long since left behind. Needless to say Granny had no wish to visit him, but I believe he wrote to her. Your sister went and they shared his poems, and of course I went too, dressed in my suit for work and he said, 'What are you now, some sort of footman?' dismissing me as he always did throughout my childhood. So there ends his story, he is gone, but I am glad you had a chance to meet him in the end.

He does not really merit our grief, but I am sure you will be sad as I am, when all is said and done.

Much love

Daddy

 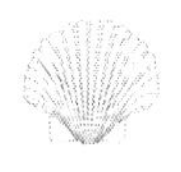 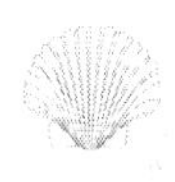

The Caribbean was a far away world when they sailed back to Baie des Anges and Elle began her preparations for her summer departure to Greece. She had a cover made to protect Galuette from stem to stern, and Alain from the shipyard promised to check on her from time to time, when the weather was bad, in return for a bottle of good Irish whisky. She rented an underground garage for the car and the precious possessions that she was reluctant to leave on board.

Adam was cruising to Spain ... the opposite direction so they would not see each other for two months at least.

The few days before they left Antoine would drive past Voyager, her new home, as many times as he possibly could and when she peeped out from behind the aft cabin curtains, she could see he was unshaven and drawn. She would not allow herself to feel responsible for his miserable state. One day she saw him peering into her car, and realised to her terror that he was looking for a marina entry sticker to reveal where her boat was safely hidden. Luckily the only one visible was the one from Beaulieu. He would be disappointed if he drove all the way down there, but she doubted he would. Antoine, like many local men, barely ever left his own town. Beaulieu would be foreign territory for him.

Elle went to the agent's office to collect her mail on the day before she left, and to her horror they told her that someone else had collected on her behalf, a Frenchman, a friend they said.

'Don't ever give my post to anyone one again, whoever they say they are, please, please understand that he is not my friend and I have lost my letters.'

'We will make a note on your file,' they said, apologetically and Elle thought she might cry.

Adam followed Voyager the first few nights after they left, sleeping in his car in order that he might spend the evening with her in San Remo and then again the following night in their next port of call. They made love tearfully in a sheltered corner on the beach far into the night for they had finally to say goodbye for the summer. Next morning when Adam awoke scrunched in his car Voyager was gone.

The cruise was long and hard, Elle did not particularly warm to the owners of the boat nor they to her. The owner's wife called her Miss Muffet, when she believed Elle to be out of earshot, in fact she heard her perfectly clearly, chanting the nursery rhyme.

'Why does she not like me, I am doing my best?' Elle enquired of the skipper.

'That's why she doesn't like you,' he replied, 'because you are young, pretty and extremely capable, its a jealous reaction, I have seen it before.'

'Well it's extremely unfair.' Elle was tired, disgruntled and hot.

'She was the same with the last girl.'

'Oh and you didn't think it a good idea to give me some of warning, some sort of inkling that the owner's wife would treat me like something nasty she has trodden in?'

'Come on Elle you are over reacting and I will make everything right by you in the end.'

The promise of a financial bonus convinced her to carry on, do her best and ignore the snide remarks of the embittered elderly lady, for she was old, seventy at least, lamenting her lost youth possibly every time she looked at Elle.

The weather was as hot as the tropics in the Greek islands. Elle was stung by a wasp on the back of the leg, which swelled to such a gigantic size she could not bend her leg at all, so she limped around for want of antihistamine which further annoyed her patron, through, as usual, no fault of her own.

A package of mail was collected from an office in Piraeus and there were half a dozen letters for Elle all in the same hand. 'But who had this address?' she demanded of the captain forgetting her manners in her distress, as the skipper sat having a drink with her lady highness.

'A man asked me before we left, you know that nice security chap who is always hanging about.'

How was he supposed to know the sordid details, she couldn't blame him really. 'Sorry, it's not your fault, but he has been bothering me, that's all.' She went below to open her mail and the two carried on conversing without a second thought for Elle's insignificant drama.

She tore the first letter open and to her dismay the envelope held several pages of Antoine's almost illegible, scrawly handwriting. Glancing through she was quick to grasp that the content was of an extremely sexual nature, and she blushed as she read. These were not love letters although he swore to love her forever, they were pornography from a crazed mind, and she should not read further. Her grasp of written French was not proficient enough to understand half of the manuscripts but she certainly followed the drift. The descriptions of her body and his actions upon her were easy to decipher. She tore them all into pieces and stuffed them in the galley rubbish bin.

The engineer who was well aware of the situation, remarked, 'Well that's dealt with him then. Good show.'

'You didn't see what he had written,' she said as if in her own defense.

'I can imagine,' he said sympathetically.

So much for the expectation of an extra month's pay as was normal at the end of working seven days a week for three months. Nothing was forth coming. The skipper told her she could stay on and do some maintenance thereby bolstering her earnings but no, she decided she would rather look for something else. As they tied Voyager back up to the town quay in Antibes she could see Antoine's red car coming through the old stone archway in their direction. Her heart flipped with terror as it had once done with joy at the expectation of seeing the man she believed to be hers alone. She moved towards the car to tell him politely to depart, as she hardly wanted an emotional scene at the end of the gangway. As she reached the door she realised too late who it was driving to meet her. Sabine, her face twisted with disgust as she rolled the window down. '*Regard,*' she spat the words, '*C'est la pute des bateaux Anglais qui rentre.*' With a sneer she drove on and disappeared.

Elle was shaking. Her work mate put his arm around her and led her back on board. 'Don't take it to heart,' he said, 'we all know how it really was and you are not a whore. Let us hope he stays away and does not upset either of you further.'

Elle phoned Adam and was so excited at the prospect of seeing him none of the rest mattered.

Someone said Antoine was renting a studio at the back of town, near the swimming pool, so that was one place she would not be going. Adam had left the boat in Cannes and was staying in a hotel belonging to some English friends in return for helping them a bit behind the bar in the evenings, but she found him depressed and hankering to go home. She took some time off in the peace and serenity of Baie des Anges, reveling in being on her own on *Galuette*, waking late and wandering around the marina to buy a few groceries, and then returning to her home to continue making her ship shape. She loved to just sit on the opposite quay and admire her graceful yet somehow stubby and quaint lines upon the water. In the evening Elle would go to the hotel and spend a couple of hours with Adam if he was not busy, retiring to his attic bedroom to make love but somehow they lacked the passion they had captured before, they had become used to each other, a habit.

One evening Antoine's familiar red *Renault* had loomed behind her, whether he had been waiting, having had some intelligence about her movements, or if his appearance was a merely a coincidence Elle never knew, but he followed her. She had been too terrified to go to the hotel, so she led him a merry dance through the back streets, driving like an idiot possessed for the fear of him had exploded into a monstrous threat to her and Adam's well being. With one reckless jumping of lights and a tight swerve round a sharp bend into a one-way street, she stopped and took breath, and looking in her mirror she saw him continue on, the other way. She sat there some ten minutes before she was calm enough to turn around and make her way to the hotel.

The incident provoked a row between them.

'But Elle,' Adam remonstrated, 'We can't live like this, scared to be seen in town separately let alone together, with you jumpy as a rabbit when you see a car like his in Baie des Anges. Well you might like the situation but I certainly don't.'

'Of course I don't like it, what a stupid, immature comment to make. I just don't see how we can change anything, he will calm down in the end, he will lose interest, and move on.'

'And how long do you think that might take exactly, come on, you know the guy, a week, months, years?'

'There you go again, I can't talk to you reasonably when you are in this mood, and lately you seem unable to snap out of your grumpy face.' With that comment she had walked out and driven home where she could shut herself away from men and all the troubles and worry they caused her.

Adam went to his family for Christmas and as soon as he had gone illogically she pined for him. She placed her car on the train in Nice, and followed him, contracting a stomach bug or food poisoning on the journey and arriving in Kent weak from loss of fluids and exhaustion. He had taken a coach to meet her and they booked into a bed and breakfast with Elle too weak to travel further on that day.

They spent the festive few days with their respective parents, Elle having lunch with her father in a seaside pub as he had found himself sadly alone on Christmas day. Adam came back down to join her again but she found him still moody and depressed even though they found themselves in completely different surroundings. He seemed to want to watch television under a duvet, day in and day out.

A job came up for her, cooking on a motor yacht returning from Florida to Via Reggio in Italy and without any hesitation she accepted. Adam was taciturn and awkward.

'You do what you want,' he shrugged, 'You usually do.'

Elle drove away, sadly wondering how they had reached this sorrowful position, and blaming his frame of mind, that had failed to find hope in any aspect of their life together. Infuriated, and frustrated, she left him sitting on his mother's settee, gloomy, dejected, and abandoned.

23

"Beyond myself again I ranged;
And saw the free
Life by the sea,
And folk indifferent to me."

Thomas Hardy, *Young Lovers Reverie*

Elle's journey to Fort Lauderdale turned out to be complicated. She drove back to Antibes, placed the car in the garage, swapped some clothes, checked *Galuette* and boarded a plane. She had to change in Paris and again in New York in order to arrive as quickly as possible for the boat was waiting, urgently for a cook. Already tired from the drive, it was a further thirty-six hours before she finally touched down at her destination. She did not look or feel her best when she walked across the tarmac at seven o'clock in the evening, overcome by the humidity and glaring heat of the day in Florida.

Holding a placard aloft, two members of the crew were there to meet her. Ted and Lottie, both Welsh with broad accents, which Elle found enchanting.

Lottie's chatter was irrepressible, 'We are not a couple, you know, you have to realise this straight away,'

'Okay, Lottie,' said Ted, 'Spare the poor girl all the gory details, she's only just landed.'

Ignoring him, the petite, blonde hairdresser chatted on regardless, 'I used to be in a relationship with the deckhand but we are just friends now, and our last cook is leaving to marry the engineer, so he's leaving too.'

Elle's head span with all this information, she felt displaced and decidedly peculiar.

'You do have lovely hair, can I cut some layers for you? I think layers would be stunning.'

'I have never really had any layers,' she replied but Lottie was off on another tack now.

'We have all been waiting for you so we can go have a meal and then show you some of the best bars around here.'

'I have been here before, so I know some places, but I have to admit I am completely worn out, and may just have to go to bed.'

Lottie looked crest fallen, 'Oh I suppose we shall have to tuck you up in bed then and leave you to sleep, you will feel better tomorrow.'

The boat, *Lucky Blue*, was the biggest motor boat Elle had ever been aboard, built in a shipyard on the Italian coast, not far from Pisa, their ultimate destination.

She met all her new crew, Ted and Lottie she sensed instantly would be her friends but she felt awkward under the critical gaze of the others. They were a team, and not ready to welcome a newcomer. The cook who was leaving still buzzed about well in control of them all, stunningly beautiful she had their hearts as well as their loyalty. Elle felt misplaced, an outsider who had been dropped into the wrong camp. Even her shoes embarrassed her, and she had lost her tan at Christmas leaving her white and pasty amongst these god-like beings.

The other thing was she had gradually begun to accept that she was not like normal twenty somethings, she found being one of the girls and having "a good fun time" neigh on impossible. Maybe she had Asperges or some other complicated condition with symptoms beyond her control which left her happiest reading a book, scraping and varnishing, sailing or some other equally lonely pursuit. Trying to be jolly in a crowd was not her concept of leisure, and for that reason she was not only in the minority, but also she was yet to meet any one person who felt the same.

She did manage to buy some shoes which bizarrely improved her frame of mind over the following days. The model-like cook flew away, and Elle took over her duties in the vast stainless steel galley of *Lucky Blue*. They were to take the owner to the Bahamas for a few days before they headed back to Europe so she was to be tossed in in at the deep end. The crew were as fussy as the owners and the atmosphere certainly bore no resemblance to the cosiness and amiability aboard *Sea Princess*. The skipper was yet another ex navy type, not the sort of person with whom one could make normal conversation at all, and the owner was on board with his mistress. Elle felt uncomfortable with all of them except for her two Welsh friends. She missed Adam and forgave him everything, she longed to be back on *Galuette*, out of work perhaps, but at that moment she simply would not have cared.

A barbecue was planned in the Bahamas, on one of the many paradise beaches. This entailed a huge amount of preparation for Elle, and desperate to make a positive impression on owners and crew alike those first few days, she made as many tasty dishes as she could and packed everything meticulously to be transported to the beach.

The boys went first and set up tables and the barbecue as Elle waited nervously for her turn to travel with the food. The first most obvious problem was the swell that was increasing and breaking as vast rollers on the beach. As they neared the shore, Ted shouted for her to jump over the side to steady the flat bottomed boat and prevent the food from being swamped, which of course she did, clean pressed white uniform, new shoes and all. By the time they finally achieved the dry, firm sand, she might as well have been a contestant in a wet T-shirt competition, and every once of her calm decorum was gone, borne away on the wind and spray. The two girls busied about laying out food and tableware and the barbecues were lit. The boats returned to wait for the guests to appear.

'Did you ever have a strong notion that someone might be spying on you,' Elle remarked to Lottie, scanning the low dunes behind their carefully chosen spot.

'Don't be silly, we are miles from anywhere and the natives are usually friendly, not man eating cannibals, with funny head-dresses. You've been reading too many books, told you it's not good for you, it fires your imagination.'

They carried on but unfortunately Elle's perception was correct, not a tribe of hostile islanders but six iguanas emerged cautiously at first, but then with more confidence emboldened by the odour of roasting kebabs. They were immense, not the sort of timid, little lizards that Elle was used to at all.

Ted spoke first, 'I think they are friendly enough, usually.'

'What do you mean usually, if there is any doubt in that area I think we should leg it, or swim for it,' said Lottie.

Elle had already started packing stuff away, 'No one will want to step ashore with them ready to pounce with their napkins tucked in, harmless or not.'

Back they went and Elle freshly soaked again, quickly dispensed with her sense of humour, the struggle of it all having strangled the last piece of the optimism with which she had started the day. The owner made some comment to Lottie about the food being "not up to the usual standard," driving her to retreat to her cabin as soon as she could.

The Atlantic crossing was dreadful with a violent head sea reducing the progress of the motor boat hourly. With all the storm boards in place, the interior was dark and depressing and although Lottie spurred them on by holding keep fit exercise sessions to music in the main saloon, morale fell and all were quarrelsome. The galley was clearly not designed for seas such as they encountered, and even opening the fridge was a dangerous operation as there were no fiddles to hold anything in place. Elle made the best of the situation but was not impressed by the skipper's lack of understanding of the difficulties below decks in such conditions.

Swallowing was painful and Elle felt ill. She asked Lottie to look down her throat.

'Tonsillitis, it looks like to me,' her friend announced, but Elle battled on, being chastised by the Captain one morning when she was late with his fry up. The temptation to chuck the food over him was enormous, although she was never one for exhibitions of temper.

At last they cruised through the Straits of Gibraltar and although in her experience this was not always the way, the sea calmed and the sky took on that wonderful Mediterranean hue. Elle sunbathed with Lottie on the top deck all the way to Via Reggio.

'I don't think this is the right position for you Elle,' the skipper told her soon after their arrival. On the one hand Elle felt snubbed and angry and on the other she felt undeniably relieved. He asked her to work her notice, which she agreed on condition she could catch the train back to France and collect her car, so that she could explore a portion of southern Italy, when she finished.

'I don't see why not,' he replied condescendingly, 'I am sure Lottie could cook for one weekend while you are gone,' and she could tell his bacon and eggs held prime importance over everything else.

During her brief weekend in France, Elle met up with the engineer from *Voyager* who told her about another job on a wooden sailing yacht, much more her style, destined for the Caribbean, so on her way back she called in to have an interview aboard the boat, that was berthed in San Remo. The skipper also asked her if she knew a suitable deck hand who could start work with her in a month or so and she immediately thought about Adam. She decided to contact him, if he was already employed at least she would have tried to make amends for their painful parting.

Her confidence restored on her arrival back in Via Reggio, she gleefully informed the others of her luck in finding a job on a sailing vessel where she would be far more at home. Having brought back her car she was able to take the them out and about and for her time left she became the star of the show, driving out at every possible opportunity to discover restaurants and picnic spots in the surrounding area. Italy was so different to France, the prostitutes lighting fires by the roadside to attract customers, was a feature so corrupt it belied the beautiful cities they visited.

Finally she made contact with Adam. 'I have a new job starting in a month and they need a deckhand too, if you want to come. I have missed you,' she added, because in fact she had.

'When will you start?' Adam asked, subdued, his voice full of doubt.

' In about three weeks, you could fly to Pisa if you like and we could have a holiday driving back through Italy, what do you think?'

'Call me again tomorrow when I have had time to sort a few things, okay, and yes I do miss you too.'

Elle replaced the receiver knowing he would come ... should she have let well alone and carried on with her own life, leaving him to his? She wasn't at all sure but she had given him the choice.

The date was fixed. She was to meet him at the airport. Lottie layered and permed her hair, the first time she had changed the long straight haired style of her childhood. New beginnings with Adam. She found herself, excited and overjoyed to see his familiar, boy-like face coming through the arrivals in Pisa. They booked into a small hotel far into the hills and lay in bed until late, rising for a champagne breakfast as if on honeymoon.

For two weeks they frolicked at Elle's expense for Adam had absolutely no money, but she didn't care. They had the promise of work ahead of them, and they were young and in love again, with never a cross word uttered between them.

Easter Sunday found them standing outside a restaurant near Florence. A sign on the door informed them it was "*CHIUSO*". Looking in they could see large table laid and people bustling about with plates of food. 'Must be a family do,' sighed Elle.

A cheeky looking face opened the door and instead of reinforcing the information on the sign, she beckoned them inside. '*Inglese?*'

'*Si,*' they said unanimously and she pulled both in, sat them firmly down at the table and continued busying about. Adam's mouth dropped open at the impressive spread before them, the centrepiece being the largest, chocolate egg either had ever seen. He gripped Elle's hand tightly under the table, and whispered, 'Well it would be rude to leave now wouldn't it?'

Elle smiled, lost in the magic of Italian hospitality.

A couple of hours later, she dragged Adam away, drugged by the food and Chianti.

They drove for just a few miles before she pulled off the road onto a track by an open field where the grass was already scorched by the heat of the spring sun. They fell out of the car into the shade of a hedge, and lay with their eyes closed.

'I know why we are so happy now, when we weren't before,' Elle remarked. 'Hey you need some sun cream or you will be a roast tomato, an Italian shaped one even,' so saying she placed her brown arm alongside the skin on his thigh, which was already turning pink.

'Why?' he asked.

'Why what?'

'Why are we so happy now?'

'Because the pressure has gone, Antoine is miles away, we have a new job together for once, the sun is shining, and we have had far too much wine at lunch time which we said we wouldn't do!'

'Doesn't matter does it,' and this was not a question for he pulled her closer raising her dress, bowing down to lose himself in the essence of her. Her mind flew as high as the wispy clouds above them, and they both fell into a deep dreamless sleep.

Elle woke first with a stinging pain somewhere in the region of her left buttock. 'Ouch, I've been bitten, feels like an ant, Adam come on, fancy seducing me on top of an ants nest!' Together they climbed back in the car and drove on to find their next hotel.

24

"In the midst of this spot stood a house, built with the bones of shipwrecked human beings. There sat the Sea Witch allowing a toad to eat from her mouth, just as people sometimes feed a canary with a piece of sugar."

Hans Christian Anderson, *The Little Mermaid*

Their first cruise working together took them to Venice. Yacht *Adriana* was a striking ninety-three foot example of Italian shipbuilding. Quite slim line compared to *Sea Princess*, the accommodation was less luxurious, but her speed through the water under sail was far more dramatic and often a little wet across the decks. Adam and Elle had two single bunks between them but chose to sleep together in the top one, much to the amusement of the other crew members.

Elle immediately liked the owners who joined them in Venice, and she delighted in preparing their favourite seafood dishes. Rising early she would walk to the market and come back laden with spider crabs. She had begun to notice Adam's annoyance with her dedication to her work, protesting that she refused to take the time in the early morning to breakfast with him, being already adsorbed in her preparations in the galley. 'This is just the way it is for a cook, and you must accept it,' she explained to him. 'We have time in the afternoons most days and after dinner.'

'What, when you want to sail one of the dinghies or fall asleep from exhaustion?' He was determined not to compromise and his sulks were insufferable, lasting for hours sometimes days.

They often quarreled to the annoyance of the rest of the crew, with no space or privacy in their cramped quarters. Their cruise took them down the Yugoslavian coast, familiar ground for Elle, back to Brindisi and on to Porto Santa Stephano, where *Adriana* was booked into a yard for major repairs to the teak deck. They were unable to stay on board during the work and moved into a bed and breakfast with an Italian family. Elle would make a picnic style lunch and in the early evening they would eat en famille with the Italians, wading their way through plate after plate of delicious pasta and risotto. Needless to say they all grew somewhat on the tubby side during their six week stay, through idleness and good food. The living arrangements afforded them more time for each other and their relationship improved. It really was hard living on top of the rest of the crew on the boat, leaving Elle wondering at times how much easier it would be to be single. An evening or two spent lying together on the bed drinking local wine and playing *Trivial Pursuit*, changed her mind again and she banished any thoughts of being without Adam beside her.

Elle took a few days off and returned briefly to France to move *Galuette* back to Antibes to entrust her care to her old friend Alain in the shipyard. Adam was forced to stay with *Adriana* to oversee the work as the skipper had taken leave during the refit. Antoine was nowhere to be seen, there was no reason for him to be aware of her return. She found out that *Sea Princess* had changed her flag and all the British crew had been forced to leave being unable to work legally under an American ensign. The tax loophole of sailing under a Panamanian flag had been closed forever.

Seeing Alain brought tears to the surface, she was not sure why, the emotions caused by a life of continuous change simmered under her cheerful grin. Sitting with him in the cockpit of *Galuette*, having travelled so many miles, made her heart and head swim and they embraced, gently as acquaintances, then closer as friends until they found themselves seeking a kiss with unreasonable fervency, as lovers might.

'*Non*,' she said softly, pushing him back with reluctance. '*Je suis avec quelqu'un et tu as ta femme*.'

'*Oui mais*,' his blue eyes held hers.

'There are no buts,' she replied in English and she knew he understood.

She carried the secret guilt of the kiss in her heart back to Adam, and in quiet moments she allowed herself to ponder upon the feel of Alain's lips on hers, hiding the memory away, in case Adam should detect her pleasure or the flush upon her skin.

Adriana set sail for Gibraltar in early October and the Gulf du Lyon was wickedly unkind forcing them to plough through a raging storm as the Mistral blew her worst. The deck leaked over the galley and Elle raised laughter at least by wedging herself under an open umbrella whilst preparing dinner.

No time for renewing old acquaintances in Gibraltar this time, they restocked and sailed straight on bound for Antigua. Elle was so busy watch keeping and cooking she was barely aware of the rising tensions between Adam and the skipper, but spiraling they were, ready to crash upon the Caribbean shores.

The journey seemed less arduous than previous crossings, they held an impromtu fancy dress party mid Atlantic, (Elle hated fancy dress) and then ten days later they were anchored in English Harbour. The skipper toasted her with champagne to thank her for sustaining meals prepared under difficult conditions. Elle began to notice the attention and praise he was bestowing on her, with little thanks directed towards the deck crew, Adam in particular.

She tried not to read anything into his behaviour and settled into enjoying showing Adam the delights of the island, one of her favourite places in all the world, she changed into a different girl in this tropical Eden, touched by the sun, the wind and island magic.

'I have booked a table for dinner Elle,' the skipper announced choosing his moment when she was alone in the galley.

'Good idea,' she said, 'Some crew bonding time?'

She did not warm towards this iron grey man, with his smoking and drinking habits, and the cloud of gruffness around him, nor was she comfortable with his running of the ship account where she saw receipts for taxis never taken and imaginary repairs, but his seamanship at least, was sound.

'No, just for you and me, I need to talk through the owners visit with you, fine tune some detail.'

Her steady world began to undulate, and the suspicion of his true intentions slithered back and forth through muddled thought. 'Okay then, if needs be, as long as you explain the reason to the others,' she said.

Adam, of course, rose into a rage as fearful as a thunderstorm, suspecting all forms of evil intention from the man he had already come to detest and mistrust in only a few short months.

'Can't you see what he's about Elle, forcing a wedge between us, to turn you against me so that you will stay and I shall have to leave. He's a worm, a calculating slug, he's been buttering you up for days, I'm not blind, but you seem to be,' he was talking in that loud cross whisper he had adopted of late, pushing his face close to hers in anger and panic. With the fear of losing her he shook with every breath.

'I will go and report every word back to you, so you must trust me or our relationship is worth nothing, a waste of every day we have spent together.'

At the table Elle's palms were damp, her mouth dry, nervousness bit deep into the pit of her stomach.

He was playing the perfect gentleman card but the truth did out. 'How is your relationship with Adam?' he asked.

'It's strong,' she said wondering if that was his business after all. 'We have been together when work has permitted for sometime now.'

'The others tell me a different story, that there is not much left between you except constant bickering and it's hard for you being stuck in a situation you can't escape from. I thought I could help.'

Gradually she began to grasp the situation. 'You mean by ousting Adam and keeping me, that's what you are suggesting isn't it? You are asking me to choose, I realise that now. What an awful position for me.'

So saying she rose from the table, 'If you will excuse me I suddenly have no appetite.'

'Fine Elle, but I need an answer by tomorrow night, for if you choose to go with Adam, which I hope you won't, I need to find another cook rather quickly. You should let him go, he's too much of a boy, you need a man.'

How could the whole course of her life be changed in one day? One moment she looked through a wide window at the full long season ahead in the West Indies, then with no warning the opening was slammed shut and all she could foresee was a cold, grey unemployed winter back in Europe. She would break Adam if she stayed. She needed to lay all of this before him that they might look at her choice together, because his decision had already been made.

They were given the day off the following day. Numbed from lack of sleep and anxiety they sat silently on the hot bus into St Johns. Once inside a small street bar, Adam began, the heat and smell of the town hung like heavy soiled curtains around them. 'You stay, please stay, I know you want to, you like the owners and will do well, like you always do.'

Was there a slight sneer in his tone or did she imagine it?

'This isn't just about me though is it? After all we have been through, why should he separate us, it's just not fair.'

'Maybe he's right and we have become a habit, only kept together by the situation.'

'Do you really believe that, or are you saying it just to convince yourself, and justify my reasoning if I should stay.'

All day they tossed the problem back and forth, hating and loving each other in equal measures, until they were spent, and all sense was gone. Suddenly Elle made up her mind and taking his hand across the dark stained table she said, 'I am coming with you.'

Afterwards, thinking about her final decision, she knew the reason she would go was loyalty rather than love, and also because she stubbornly did not want an outsider to have successfully spotted the flaws in their relationship. Relieved and tearful they went to sort out the first flights available, Christmas at home not seeming such a terrible idea, as the plan slowly became reality.

  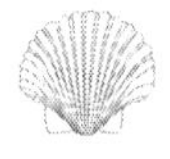

The weather was bitterly cold when they arrived and Elle, still in tropical mode, was lackadaisical concerning the amount of clothing she wore to protect her from the dramatic drop in temperature. She succumbed within a few days to a debilitating flu like cold which progressed to a full-blown chest infection. Adam was no nurse, and in his ignorance merely became impatient with her condition. As soon as Christmas was over she suggested they return to *Galuette*.

'Would you prefer I stayed here?' he suggested.

'For goodness sake,' she said ill and exasperated. 'Just do what you want okay, but I am going home.'

They were expecting an improvement in the weather conditions on their arrival but were shocked as they looked down from the aircraft, towards their destination. Thick snow lay along the beach, from Nice to Antibes. 'The first time in thirty years,' the taxi driver boasted. The cover over *Galuette* was laden with snow. Once inside with the heater on full blast, it was cosy, but the sides of the hull began to run with damp droplets of condensation, soaking bedding, clothes and spirits. Elle's cough worsened. Adam went in search of Alain who returned with antibiotics, as Elle was too ill to visit the doctor.

'*Au moins tu as ton cousin pour t'aider,*' he said, noticeably concerned.

Cousin? She remembered then that she had never corrected the story they had concocted so long ago. Alain was so kind and the sweetness of their kiss still lingered, so now, all things considered, was not the time to put him right. Slowly she improved. A friend who was guardian of a large luxurious motor yacht invited them to stay there (he lived ashore) at least until the weather improved, so gratefully if a little stubbornly on Elle's part, they moved aboard.

Their relationship deteriorated as Elle had foreseen. Adam dreamed of them having a yacht to run together but that had never been Elle's plan, she wanted to move on alone now, having become infuriated by his boyish fits of jealousy. She went back to work for Charles and Casja several days a week, helping to clean the large yacht they had taken over, and then luckily found a cooking position on a motor yacht in Cannes. This move defeated Adam, just as he believed he may have found a small sailing boat for them to crew as a team, but Elle was striving for bigger fish. They continued to live together but he began to frequent the bars at night alone.

'I may go out later,' she said matter-of-factly.

'I am going out now anyway,' he replied as he marched across the aft deck, defiant in tone and head held back but she could see the crushed slump of his shoulders. She had never foreseen that tensions between them could be as taut as this. A strand between them about to snap, release would bring relief and liberation from their complicated web of entanglement.

A white van dallied on the quay, masked by the commonplace appearance of such a vehicle. Elle ran, small steps, quickly, the first of many assignations. She was beginning to know who she was now, Mac the Smuggler had seen through her years ago and revealed the sea witch beneath, hard and salt encrusted, the battering of life had turned her young spirit as if in some grim fairy tale. She jumped in Alain's van and he drove off. No words passed between them, the brush of his hand as he reached for the gears made her shiver. They climbed on board *Galuette* refastening the cover behind them, no one could know they were there, undisturbed, concealed even from the gaze of the evening sun.

'I have wine,' she said, suddenly the hostess as she reached for glasses.

'*Non,*' he replied his voice both husky and soft in that moment.

'*Mais ta femme?*' she said, knowing they had already passed the turning point, the damage had been done.

'*S'est fini entre nous depuis longtemps,*' reassuring then and persuasive, his eyes wolfish and imploring, he lay her down and began to undress her slowly. Overcome and awkward for a moment she then threw her clothes aside, and he entered her hastily, forcefully, and she recaptured the sweetness as his mouth joined with hers. They slept a while, their desperate need of each other had calmed, but she knew this was just the beginning, and she would have to tell Adam to relieve her own guilt.

Elle took up the position in Cannes, a motorboat aptly named *Laissez Faire*. She slept aboard sometimes but moved her possessions back to *Galuette* leaving Adam on his own. 'Space for a while,' she declared, unable as yet to admit to the truth, hoping their relationship would dwindle to a friendship without the bitter harsh words of her betrayal.

Alain and she found a small hotel in Cannes to which they retreated for their love making, but Elle found this less than romantic after the first couple of occasions. She suggested they might go away for a few days before she became involved with the Monaco Grand Prix and the snowball of summer events planned for *Laissez Faire*. On the day of their departure he was to collect her from *Galuette*. He arrived with his skiing equipment and began to place the items in the small cockpit.

'*Je comprends pas Alain?*'

'*J'avais dit a ma femme que je pars pour le dernier weekend au ski.*'

'But you said you were not with your wife anymore, so why should you need all this charade?'

'*Je suis désolé, c'est pas facile.*'

She was cross already and they had not even left. She secured the skis and boots under the cover, took her bag and walked to the car without a word. As they approached, Antoine was walking towards them on the quay and there was no escape. She glanced at Alain but he seemed unperturbed. 'Might as well brave this one out then,' she muttered.

'*Bonjour Alain,*' said Antoine and nodding to Elle, '*Madamoiselle,*' he added.

'*Bonjour Antoine, ça va?*' said Alain and they shook hands as old friends do, Antoine buffing him on the arm with an exaggerated show of affection.

'*Bonne journée tous les deux …*' and he was gone.

Elle fearing her mouth might be slightly open in her surprise simply said, '*Voila, n'importe a quoi,*' a phrase she had learnt from Antoine himself which she believed to mean 'there you go, whatever next.'

They checked in at the hotel in St Raphael, made love, showered and had a glass of wine that left her feeling considerably better about the situation. Well almost, for she could not resist a dig at Alain.

'I can see your guilt in your eyes,' she said.

'*Je ne comprends pas,*' he said

'*Dans tes yeux,*' she translated, '*On peu voir ton culpabilité.*'

He walked to the mirror in the bathroom and stood looking at himself until she had to drag him away.

It had begun to dawn on Elle that despite his good looks, and gentlemanly manners, Alain was slow on the uptake and often looked completely bewildered in their new surroundings away from the familiarity of his own patch. He was not alone in this trait, as she had found that quite a few of her local French friends just simply, like the local wine, did not travel well. Of course this was a huge generalisation and one that made her secretly amused.

They arrived back at *Galuette* after a long lunch in the hot sunshine of a warm spring day, and immediately fell asleep in the forward bunk having pulled back the cover leaving the skis oddly protruding above the cockpit combing. Elle was awoken by the sound of someone climbing on board, the use of her name and the wriggle of the door latch, which she had luckily bolted from the inside.

'Elle? Are you there? I need to speak to you.'

It was Adam. Instantly she was gripped by the horror of his discovery of her, on *Galuette*, in a compromising situation with Alain.

'Wait I'm coming,' she said and hastily wrapping herself in her sheepskin coat less he should spot her state of undress, she peeped nervously through the wooden double doors, opening them just a crack so he might not see further.

'Can I come in?'

'Best not,' she said.

'What are you wearing?'

'My coat, I am sorry I never meant you to find out like this, I wanted to tell you, the moment just never came.'

In that instant he understood all, well nearly all, perhaps not the skis and he turned, jumped onto the quay and walked away without a backward glance.

'*Qui s'est.*' Alain was sleepy and uncomprehending.

'*Mon cousin,*' she said automatically.

'*Cette a dire ton copain realement.*'

'*Si tu veux.*' She knew she would cry now he had guessed the truth, and wanted him to go, to leave her alone.

Elle walked down the yard to Alain's office and told him their affair was over.

'*Comme ça? Tu me jette comme une veille chausette.*'

Old sock was not quite the terminology she would have used but since he had chosen the simile it would serve.

'*Si tu veux,*' she said and turned to survey the new additions to the yachts along the wall. Two wooden masts caught her eye and she strolled on to investigate.

Sea Witch, the name, the boat, she fell in love in an instant with her wide deck and varnished capping rail, the small chimney revealing the diesel stove that must lie below, and the proud bowsprit bringing her length overall to about thirty five feet. Perfect, she was just perfect.

'I have to have this boat,' she said.

A man below must have heard her for he looked out. 'She's not for sale I'm afraid but I'm off to the Caribbean and I need a crew.'

Kicking off her shoes Elle jumped neatly aboard.

For every story there must always be an end but a Sea Witch's tale will continue with no conclusion until the last time she steps on the shore, never to face the open sea not feel the salt spray on her cheeks again. In that moment her freedom to search for love beyond the horizon will be lost forever. Some, who she met along the way, will have been marked deeply with the lash that tortured her own soul, but some will still treasure her memory long after she has gone, licking their wound but finding no remedy to heal the pain of her embrace.

THE END